Books by Peter Dickinson

THE WEATHERMONGER

HEARTSEASE

THE DEVIL'S CHILDREN

EMMA TUPPER'S DIARY

THE IRON LION

THE DANCING BEAR

The DANCING BEAR

The DANCING BEAR

by
Peter Dickinson

Illustrated by David Smee

An Atlantic Monthly Press Book
Little, Brown and Company
BOSTON   TORONTO

SECOND PRINTING

T 03/73

Library of Congress Cataloging in Publication Data

Dickinson, Peter, 1927-
    The dancing bear.

    SUMMARY: A Greek slave, his dancing bear, and an
old holy man journey from Byzantium to rescue the
slave's young mistress from the Huns.
    "An Atlantic Monthly Press book."
    [1. Huns--Fiction. 2. Europe--History--392-814--
Fiction] I. Smee, David, illus. II. Title.
PZ7.D562Dan3   [Fic]   72-11530
ISBN 0-316-184268

ATLANTIC-LITTLE, BROWN BOOKS
ARE PUBLISHED BY
LITTLE, BROWN AND COMPANY
IN ASSOCIATION WITH
THE ATLANTIC MONTHLY PRESS

PRINTED IN THE UNITED STATES OF AMERICA

Contents

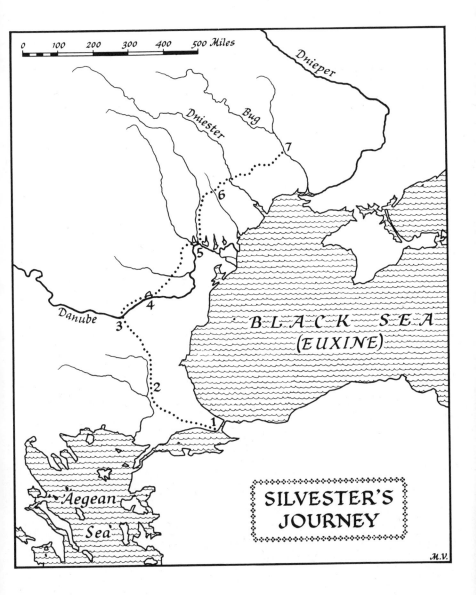

SILVESTER'S
JOURNEY

M.V.

history

THE YEAR is 558 A.D. (or according to some books 559). Rome has long fallen to the Goths; nation after nation of savage raiders has swept out of the east to batten on the remains of that rich empire. In the city built by Constantine (which I call Byzantium, to avoid muddles) another empire endures, ruled over by the great, strange Emperor Justinian, who has in his reign won back Rome for the Empire by his cunning and the brilliance of his generals, and then lost it again by his meanness. And still the tides of barbarians flood out of Asia, for gold and cattle and the glory of slaughter.

The main history is true — the Khan Zabergan, for instance, was a real man who led a raid on Byzantium and was bought off with a great tribute. But I've invented a lot of details, especially about how the savage tribes lived. As some of the real history books disagree with each other enough to put complete nations in different places; and as the Greeks who wrote about the tribes seemed to believe that everyone who wasn't a Byzantine was a complete savage, and so only wrote down things that supported that belief; and as it suited my story, I'm not ashamed of these inventions.

I haven't made anything up about Bubba. Bears are like that. They even like rolling down hills.

PART I · THE CITY

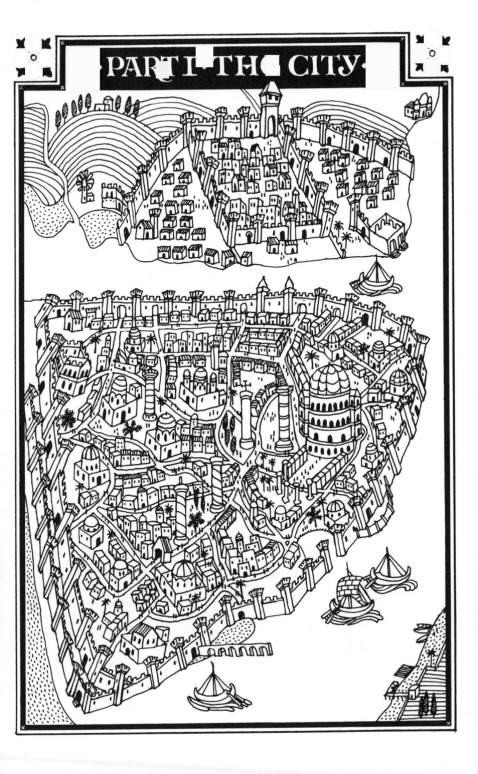

I

Yellow Crabs

SILVESTER first saw the new slaves down at the fish quay. They looked as wild as the wildest bear in the bear pits and as dirty as the City's dirtiest saint.

He didn't often get a chance to go down to the fish quay, but today was the Lady Ariadne's betrothal day, so Fat Luke the fish-cook had gone himself to buy the choicest of the night's catch for the betrothal feast, and Silvester had gone with him to steal a few crabs to amuse Bubba, the dancing bear he was supposed to look after. The regulations of the City forbade anybody but members of the fish guild to use the fish quay, which meant that Fat Luke had to show the quaymaster a pass sealed with the seal of the Lady Ariadne's father, the Count of the Outfields. The pass permitted him to set foot on the quay, but he then had to bribe the quaymaster before he could buy fish. While Luke haggled over the size of the bribe Silvester loafed and scratched and watched a large, untidy merchant ship getting ready to unload from the deep-water side of the quay. The ship was only interesting because it was unusual to see anything but fishing boats at the fish quay.

3

Half a dozen drunk-looking sailors staggered out of the deckhouse and picked up short pikes from a rack by the mast. One of them shouted down a hatchway, angrily, as though everybody below decks were deaf or stupid. At last the chained slaves came stumbling up into the strong May-morning light.

Five gangs, chained in gangs of twelve men each. A lot of slaves, Silvester thought, considering how unpromising they looked for training. Men so squat that they seemed almost square; yellow skins; dangling black moustaches but no beards; heads covered by turbans of different colors, but each with a fringe of blue clay beads hanging just above the savage eyes; legs absurdly bowed. The sailors with pikes shepherded them onto the quay, where they stood and gaped like tourists at the rattling wharves and the shining cliff of the Great Palace wall on the hill above the harbor.

(They had been landed at the fish quay because that was the rule and the City was run by ten thousand rules. Ages ago some official in the Great Palace had been asked at which quay slaves should be landed, and had decided on the fish quay because slaves were a catch, just like fish.)

A fish porter came up the quay trundling a tower of fish baskets on his rickety barrow, leaning his whole weight forward to keep it moving. He called to the slaves to stand clear, but they knew no Greek, so in high-spirited malice he drove the barrow straight into the nearest gang. Silvester heard a shout and a few animal grunts, and then with a yell two gangs of slaves brushed the sailors aside and closed around the porter like an anemone closing around its food. The porter vanished. The slaves began to chant in rhythm, finishing with another yell as a whirling shape shot through the air, arms and legs flailing, and fell with a splash below the bows of the merchant ship. The slave gangs separated, leaving the barrow on its side with its silver cargo spilled across the cobbles. Several of them had picked fish up and were tearing at the raw flesh with brilliant teeth. Their grins as the porter climbed dripping back to the quay made them look wilder than ever.

Silvester was disgusted. This was no way for slaves to behave, even raw, untrained ones. He felt strongly about such matters because he was a slave himself.

Haughtily he turned back to watch Luke finish his bargaining with the quaymaster; this had taken some time because there were two kinds of bribe, an official one fixed in the Palace because the fee for use of the quay was recognized to be too small, and an unofficial one which the quaymaster demanded for breaking the rules. Another man came up to watch, a tall Greek dressed in a rich orange robe embroidered with green; his curly dark hair had begun to grizzle and he would have been as handsome as an actor if some disease had not crumbled his face. Silvester moved sideways so he could study the ravaged skin without seeming to stare, for though like all educated slaves he was being trained as a clerk, he was also being taught the mysteries of medicine, and he wanted to be able to describe these symptoms to the Learned Solomon, his teacher. Not leprosy, none of the poxes, but the aftereffects of a curious flaking corruption. The Greek took no notice of him, but stood gazing in a lordly way at the harbor and the Palace, as though he owned it all.

Fat Luke counted three piles of coins onto the quaymaster's table—the fee and the two bribes—added a small tip, bowed and turned away. Silvester smiled as he followed the cook's waddling bulk—Luke must be pleased with himself because the Count's treasurer had allowed for a bigger bribe, so Luke had made a little for himself. But Silvester was mistaken, for the money he'd saved in bribes

Luke gave to the fish captains to let him pick over the fish which had been set aside for the Palace. He did it slowly, his pale, flabby hands caressing the rosy scales of mullet in a sort of ecstasy, his piggy eyes peering at lampreys still suckered to their dead hosts as if he were trying to guess what delicate juices lay in the ugly creatures. So Silvester had plenty of time to catch crabs.

The nets sometimes brought up little inedible yellow crabs mixed in with the fish, and as the baskets were tipped out for sorting these escaped and scuttled to the quayside where they stood in a baffled rank waving their claws above the appalling drop until another rank of crabs pushing from behind sent them showering down to the water. It was easy for Silvester to catch a dozen and drop them into the little pitcher he had brought.

Fat Luke paid well, so he got what he wanted surprisingly quickly by the standards of Byzantium. Another of the ten thousand rules said that no outside porters were allowed on the quays, so Luke had had to leave the Count's own porters at the gates. Now he held out a small coin to a group of dice players, one of whom got to his feet without a word, picked up the two heavy baskets, and staggered with them down the quay. As they passed the quaymaster's table Silvester saw that the tall Greek was now haggling with him, probably over the two big chests which had been brought out of the merchant ship and should by the rules have gone around to the cargo quays.

The Greek was adding a row of silver coins to the end of the quaymaster's measuring rod until rod and coins together reached the length of the chest—a process known in the City as "stretching the measure."

"But he'll never make that amount on raw slaves!" said Silvester.

"Depends what's in them chests," said Luke in his harsh

whisper. "Not a bad racket, bring them in with slaves to miss the Customs at the cargo quays."

"Silk?"

"Nerr. Black Sea ship, that. Furs. Hey! Where are those stinking heretics of porters?"

Silvester found the two porters in the Tavern of the Holy Toe, drunk but not so drunk that they couldn't point out the two beggars they'd hired to stay sober for them. One of these beggars was at least seventy, and the other had lost a leg and walked with a crutch. Luke snatched the crutch and started to beat all four men with it. The old man ran away but the drunks and the cripple skipped and yelled until one of the harbor policemen strolled across and told Luke to stop unless he had evidence that the men were heretics.

Luke glared at him, panting, and snatched out of his pocket the pass with the seal of the Count of the Outfields on it. The policeman gave the seal a lubberly salute, drew his baton and began to beat the porters, who reeled about laughing under the blows while the cripple lay on the ground and howled for his crutch. Another policeman came to help, until Luke lumbered forward and pushed the crutch like a barrier between the beaters and the beaten. The policeman saluted again and the porters clung to each other, giggling and moaning. At that moment the tall Greek stalked out of the gates, leading the uncouth gangs of slaves as though he were a general at the head of his army.

"Huns!" said one of the policemen. "Kutrigurs!"

Silvester's head jerked around. A little rivulet of chill ran down his spine. These were the creatures of nightmares that the Greek with the ruined face was bringing into the City. When he and the Lady Ariadne were tiny, Nonna—his mother—used to frighten them into good behavior by saying that the Huns would come and get them. At fourteen he was too old to be scared by bugaboos but Byzantines were always nervous about Huns, and always passing on rumors about fresh raids. There were two kinds of Hun; the Utrigurs were a sort of ally, and sometimes sent troops to fight in the Byzantine armies; but the Kutrigurs were like wolves. For the last month there had been a strong rumor that the Kutrigur Khan Zabergan was leading a vast horde of horsemen to attack the City itself; and perhaps it was more than a rumor, for the Count of the Outfields had advanced his daughter's betrothal day by a full fortnight, saying that *he* wasn't going to let such an important occasion be spoiled by the arrival of a crowd of raw-meat-eating barbarians. That sounded as though he knew something more than rumors.

"Your Greek might get his profit then," whispered Luke as he watched the Huns and their armed escort straggle up the slant road under the Palace wall. "They'll have a curiosity value."

That was true. Silvester could see the people in the street cease from their bustle as the slaves went by; he could almost hear the shock of amazement running through shops and stalls: "Huns! Huns! Huns!" The slaves goggled back at the citizens and the wonders of the City; their bow-legged waddle, especially the two gangs carrying the chests, was that of men more used to sitting on horses than walking paved streets.

"If he sells that lot all at once he'll bring down the price of slaves," said Silvester, who knew his own value almost to a coin and didn't like to think of it bucketing up and down according to the state of the slave market.

"Don't worry," said Luke. "None of them looked to me to have the makings of a doctor—might do you out of your job as a bear-ward, though."

"Nonsense," said one of the porters with the sudden aggressiveness of the drunk. "Bubba would never let one of those animals touch her. She's a civilized bear."

"The Lord Celsus might buy a new bear," said the other porter, melancholy drunk. He spoke as though that would be the end of the world, as unthinkable as the City falling.

But Silvester's world ended in another fashion.

II

Cure-Care

BUBBA WAS DELIGHTED with the crabs, which was just as well. Like a coach who is trying to bring an athlete into peak condition for a big race, Silvester had spent the past week—ever since the date of the betrothal had been changed—thinking about how to get Bubba into a perfect temper for the feast that night. The honor of his master's house demanded that she should neither sulk nor yawn in front of the long table of noble cousins who would be there to bless the happy child-groom and child-bride and who then would expect to be feasted and amused until the dawn rose bleak across the inner sea.

So now Bubba was feasted and amused with the yellow crabs, fed to her one at a time. She was fascinated, as a kitten would be, by their wayward and unlikely scuttlings across the floor of her cage. Her pleasure was doubled by the knowledge that as soon as she was bored with each crab she could pick it up, pop it into her mouth, and scrunch it up. She didn't think yellow crabs were inedible. The latest one tried to nip her paw as she patted at it, so she sat back, splay-legged, with her paw in front of her muzzle, and

peered with short-sighted little eyes at the yellow blob
which dangled by one pincer while its seven other legs
scrabbled at empty air. After studying it as though she'd
never seen anything of the sort before, though she'd already eaten three, she batted it tentatively with her other
paw and watched it swing to and fro. Then it dropped to
the floor, fell the right way up, and at once scuttled for the
darkness of Bubba's den. She allowed it almost to reach
safety before darting across and slapping it back to the
middle of the cage.

"Boy," said a strong, deep voice. Silvester turned.

The house of the Lord Celsus, Count of the Outfields,
lay on the northern arm of the Mese, the main street of
Byzantium, up beyond the Slave Ward. It had no outside
windows at all, only the arched gateway leading to the
street; otherwise every window and door and balcony for
four crowded stories looked out onto a large rectangular
courtyard in the center of the house. And in the center of
the courtyard, on the top of a twelve-foot pillar, lived Holy
John, the household saint. There he sat, or stood, or
mostly knelt, through all seasons and weathers, and had
done for the last twelve years. Only a rusty railing kept
him from falling off in his sleep or in one of his long
trances (which the Learned Solomon said were epileptic).
He had been in such a trance when Silvester had returned
from the fish quay, but now he had awakened and peered
with brilliant dark eyes around the courtyard for something
to exercise his holiness on.

"Your servant and God's," said Silvester calmly.

"But whose servants are those crabs?" said Holy John.
Faces showed at windows; servants began to gather in
small knots at ground-floor doors; they had heard the
reverberant voice and knew that there might be a religious
dispute brewing.

"I don't know," said Silvester. "No one's. Mine, I suppose. Or Bubba's."

"You suppose in error. You suppose in sin. Like all creatures they are God's servants, and yet you allow a soul-less bear to torment them."

Holy John's fingers raked in triumph through his filthy beard and found a louse. Unthinking, he split it with his yellow thumbnail.

"Wasn't that louse God's servant then?" called Alexius the pastry cook from the bakery window.

"All creation fell with the Fall of Adam," said Holy John, his big voice filling the courtyard. "Certain creatures are irrecoverably fallen, servants of the devil. Snakes, as is well known, but also lice and . . ."

"God plagued the Egyptians with lice in all their quarters," shouted Alexius. "Therefore the lice did God's work. Therefore they are God's servants. Do we read of a plague of crabs? Did not the Holy Daniel refrain from killing the lice in *his* beard, that they might serve as food for passing birds?"

Alexius fancied himself as a theologian and was jealous of Holy John. He was always bringing the Holy Daniel into arguments, because the Holy Daniel had spent fifty years on a taller and less comfortable pillar than Holy John's, and had never left it, whereas John quite often came down and rode about on a small portable pillar, so that he could carry his religious arguments to places where he thought they needed to be heard. John was about to blast him with counterarguments when the well-drawer, a servant new to the household, came up from the cistern with a dripping pitcher on his back and said, "Wasn't the Holy Theophant tended by crabs when pirates marooned him on a barren rock in Propontis?"

"The *Holy* Theophant?" said John. At the tone of scorn

the courtyard stilled. More heads craned from windows. There was a stirring of the curtains on the balconies of the women's wing.

"Er, yes," said the well-drawer. "I always thought . . ."

"The heresies of the abominable Theophant," began John, "were seventeen in number. First, in respect of the doctrine . . ."

Silvester returned to his bear. If crabs had tended the abominable Theophant, then they were probably servants of the devil, like snakes, and it was no sin to let Bubba torment them.

He was teasing her by witholding the last crab—not simply for the sake of teasing but to try and get it into her thick head that the supply of crabs must eventually run out—when the argument behind him rose into echoing screams. The eunuchs leaned from the balconies of the women's wing and shrilled their derision at the kitchen servants; the niched and crannied walls of the courtyard clanged with the argument, like cliffs where a hundred thousand seabirds nest. Bubba hated noise, as all bears do; she munched up her last crab in a hurry and lurched into the dark of her den.

Silvester turned and listened to the argument until a hand touched his bare arm. He bowed when he saw it was the Lady Ariadne; she must have come down the little private stair from the women's wing. She smiled and stood looking at him. He knew her so well that he understood. She was too nervous, because of the betrothal feast, to try to speak, even to him, in case her stammer came back that was so nearly cured.

"My lady?" he said. Her lips pouted with effort; at last words came.

"Mother sent me. She's got a headache, but, but . . ."

"The noise is too much for her?"

"Not if Holy John thinks the discussion is fruitful. I can't say that, can I?"

"I'll say it for you. Come on."

They walked together toward the pillar, not holding hands as they used to a few years back when they were too small for such things to matter, but with Silvester walking half a pace behind her shoulder as a slave should. He was pleased that she didn't turn to make sure he was following; that meant she trusted him, as a good slave is trusted. Holy John's face, almost black with dirt and weather, frowned down at them; with a gesture of his left hand he conjured a lull in the shouting.

"Father," said Silvester. "Yesterday you spoke of the efficacy of prayer."

"Yes, yes," said the saint, clearly impatient at being distracted by children from the beastliness of Theophant, but not quite prepared to snub the daughter of the Lord Celsus on her betrothal day.

"Then can you pray that the Lady Anna's headache be lifted from her?"

The frown fiercened. Compared with the day-long discomforts of life on a pillar, a headache among silk cushions was paradise.

"And," said Silvester quickly, "can you pray that the household remains silent while the Lady Anna recovers from her headache?"

Holy John threw his arms wide in a gesture of defeat and barked his sharp laugh. "To pray a headache away, that's nothing," he said. "But to pray the tongue of a Greek into silence is a task for a great saint."

Once more the courtyard rang, this time with laughter. Holy John was an Egyptian from the Thebaid, and liked to mock at the Greekness of Greeks; but he didn't join in the laughter. A slight movement of his widespread arms and the servants of the household stilled into attention. He had something important to say.

"Sinful people, tonight, in honor of the Lady Ariadne's betrothal, I will accomplish a mighty task. Before your serene master and his illustrious guests I will refute, finally and definitively, the Monotheletic Heresy."

A gasp ran round the courtyard. The Monotheletic Heresy had been refuted several times in the past twenty years by both Orthodox and Monophysite theologians, but never finally and definitively. It was a very unpopular heresy with both sides, because it was a compromise; the Emperor was still rumored to hope that it might somehow be used to reconcile the warring sects of his empire, which was the last thing the warring sects wanted. So to hear this attempt finally foiled in the Lord Celsus's own dining hall, as part of the betrothal festivities of his only child, would indeed be an honor.

"For this, sinful people, I need silence," cried Holy John. Now his arms fell at last to his sides as he sank forward on his knees; his eyes rolled up in their sockets until the pupils were hidden under the eyelids and bloodshot whites stared out unseeing; his breath began to come in slow heavings. It *was* very like epilepsy, Silvester thought. The servants withdrew, whispering, to the preparation of the feast; silence filled the courtyard like water filling a bucket; even Alexius, cursing the oven-stokers, cursed in a whisper.

"Thank you, Sillo," said the Lady Ariadne. He bowed again. She turned slowly away towards the private stair, as though she hoped he would think of a reason to detain her.

"My lady, if you were to visit the Learned Solomon, he could give you a drug for the Lady Anna's headache."

"But Holy John is going to pray it away."

"He may forget. He has the Monotheletic Heresy to refute."

"All right—if you'll come too."

The Learned Solomon was asleep and snoring. Silvester sniffed at the bottle on the desk and gave a priggish little click with his tongue.

"What is it, Sillo?"

"He calls it his cure-care—it's poppy juice and brandy and a few other things. He's been drinking a lot of it since My Lord changed the date of the feast."

"Why?"

"He'd chosen the first date with special care—he spent weeks calculating the positions of the stars and found what he thought was the exact moment. And then My Lord brought it all forward a fortnight so the moon's in her opposite phase and the stars are all unlucky."

"I know it's a sin to believe the astrologers, but it doesn't feel like a lucky day, does it?"

Now that they were alone, except for the snoring doctor, she could speak in her natural, slow, considering tones. Silvester and Nonna were the only people who ever heard that voice; for everyone else she used short, forced spurts of words. So suddenly Silvester was aware that as well as being nervous she was miserable.

"It's all right," he said. "My Lord would never choose a man for you who'd be a bad husband. He's rejected several. And everybody respects the Akritas family. And you won't have to go and live there for at least another two years, so the Learned Solomon can choose a really lucky day for your wedding."

Her smile was a lie.

"They've got a beautiful estate out beyond Adrianopolis," she said. "The Lady Helena Akritas, who'll be my mother-in-law, told me about it. It's by a bend in a big river, with a pear-shaped island beside it. There's a long marble house under huge old lime trees, and a deer park, and farms right up to the forest edge, and then above the forest there's a huge wild upland where they go hawking. So perhaps we can live there most of the year . . . only . . ."

Only the eldest son of the Akritas family would have to live ten months of the year in the City, working his way up the ladder of honor until he became a high official of the Empire, and his wife would live with him. For perhaps seven weeks of the year, the worst of the hot weather, they might go out to the house by the river, but they'd take with them the usual chaotic train of poor cousins and servants and slaves, yelling and feuding in the country dust, and the Lady Ariadne would be expected to cajole and control them.

"You can come too," she said, acknowledging the fantasy. "You can be part of my dowry. We'll need a doctor to help at the birth of foals and babies. Why don't *you* mix something for Mother now?"

"Well . . ."

"It's only a headache. You seem to spend all day here learning things."

"I can mix a drug, but I can't cast the horoscopes which will tell the Lady Anna which saints to pray to when she takes it."

"That doesn't matter. She never says the prayers—in fact she never prays to anyone except the Virgin—don't be shocked. Mix her something sweet. She loves an excuse to eat sweets, and all the Learned Solomon's medicines seem to be made with alum. She hasn't really got a headache— it's just that she's worried about this feast. She's supposed to be in charge, and everybody's so busy, and nothing she

can say will make them do it any other way than the way
they were going to, so she's got nothing to do herself except lie on her cushions and worry."

That was something Silvester had noticed before about
the Lady Ariadne. She watched the world carefully from
behind her mask of shyness, watched and thought and understood. He spooned honey into a mortar.

"The trouble is," she said, beginning to play with her
fantasy again, "that you're such a Byzantine that you
wouldn't be happy out there. You'd wake in the night
screaming at the silence."

"Probably. Will the Lady Anna put belladonna in her
eyes tonight?"

"Too much, I expect. She's hopeless at measuring, and
she wants to look extra beautiful to make up for me."

Silvester knew what she meant. The Lady Ariadne could
look as beautiful as her mother sometimes—when she was
playing with a cat or a tiny child and didn't know anyone
was watching. But she wouldn't tonight.

"Let's give her some of the cure-care," he said. "The
Learned Solomon won't know how much he's drunk, but
he might miss the other drugs."

He counted twenty drops from the bottle, added a little
arrowroot to stiffen the mixture, and began to work it into
a smooth paste. The Lady Ariadne dipped her little finger
into the mortar and tasted.

"It needs cinnamon."

"You're as bad as Bubba. The spices are on the shelf by
the books."

He added a pinch of the brown powder and worked it
in.

"Delicious," said the Lady Ariadne.

"If I'd known I could have made a calves-foot jelly and

let it set into little sweetmeats. I'll beg some biscuits from Alexius, to spread it on."

"Biscuits! Mother won't touch biscuits. I'll tell her it also whitens the skin and she can lick it off her fingers. She'll like that."

As they went down the stair she slipped her hand into his. He didn't withdraw it, but was glad when they reached the courtyard and he could drop the proper half pace behind her shoulder.

"After tomorrow," she said, "I'll have to wear a veil whenever I leave my rooms, and have a eunuch to attend me. It's funny to think you'll never see my nose again."

"When I'm your doctor I'll have to look after your teeth, and I daresay I shall catch a glimpse then."

Silvester had been uneasy about the fantasy, and was glad to be able to turn it into a joke. They stopped at the cage to pet Bubba, who had come out to enjoy the silence and to look round the cage in case any more crabs had appeared. She pressed herself against the bars and allowed the Lady Ariadne to tickle her under her armpit, the only place where her thick, insensitive skin let her feel a caress. Suddenly, with a movement too quick to see, her other arm shot between the bars and scooped the mortar out of Silvester's hands; she almost dropped it, but managed to clutch it to her chest with the bars running between it and her—it was too large to go between them, even if she had been less clumsy. The Lady Ariadne made a move as if to snatch it back, but Silvester pulled her away and stood watching the bear trying to get her snout down into her prize.

"Better let her have it," he said. "She'd savage us if we tried to take it back—bears will do anything for honey. I'll go and mix some more for your mother."

"It won't make Bubba too sleepy to dance?"

"I don't think so. Just make her happier, which is what we want."

But when they crossed the courtyard for the last time Bubba was weeping. She had managed to drop the mortar outside the bars and it had rolled beyond her reach, so she sat splay-legged with her muzzle raised to the sky and mourned her loss in high, whimpering sobs.

Silvester picked the mortar up, undid the complicated bolt of the cage, and rolled her treasure across the floor to her. She caught it up in her forepaws and raised it solemnly to her jaws, as though she were about to drink a toast. As she began to lick she tilted farther and farther back until at last she rolled over onto her spine with her hind legs paddling in the air and the mortar covering her whole snout; then she lay still, licking and crooning.

The Lady Ariadne laughed as she used to before the solemn problems of being a great lord's daughter had overcome her. Then she ran up the private stairs with the fresh mixture.

III

honey and Cider

THE LORD CELSUS, Count of the Outfields, was an eccentric. One of his eccentricities was to be a Monophysite, when almost every other nobleman of Roman origin was Orthodox.* Monophysitism was really an Eastern creed, born in the hot fanatic sands of Arabian deserts. The Lord Celsus redressed the balance by another eccentricity, wearing a Roman toga instead of the fashionable stiff brocades his friends and cousins wore. He also practiced fencing with the short Roman sword, and insisted that the

---

* It is easy enough to explain the meaning of these different beliefs. They were all attempts to describe quite what sort of person Jesus was, and how He could be both God and Man. The Orthodox belief was that He had two distinct natures combined into His one being. The Monophysites thought that that was a compromise—they were extremists—and that He had only the single nature of being God. The Monotheletists, whom the Emperor favored for a while, believed that Jesus did have two natures, but only a single will.

It is much harder to explain why these beliefs mattered so much that saintly men could bless the murder of people who believed differently from themselves. It was partly that the early Christians were an argumentative lot anyway, but mainly because they all, every one of them, sincerely thought that only those who believed exactly right would go to heaven, and all the rest would wriggle in hell for ever and ever. Finally, the Empire permitted no political freedom at all, so people's energies got channeled into theological disputes.

Lady Ariadne (and therefore Silvester) learn elegant clas-
sical Latin. This harking back to the days of old Rome
came out strongly at the betrothal feast, which he tried to
model on what he imagined a Lucullan banquet might
have been like in that other imperial city five hundred
years before, though even he had the sense to compromise
with certain Byzantine proprieties, such as the men and
women sitting at separate tables. Still, he was a genius in
his odd way, and his feasts were famously enjoyable, and
the first half of this betrothal feast was certainly up to stan-
dard, till well after midnight when the women went home.
Luke and Alexius and the other cooks had performed their
usual miracle and now wheeled a stream of delicate dishes
out of kitchens which, if you'd gone into them during the
cooking, you'd have found to be hells of chaos and rage.
The Lord Celsus had imported rare wines from the few
unsacked vineyards of Italy, so tongues were loosened and
stomachs satisfied. Between courses a choir of eunuchs
from the Diaconissa sang psalms, their voices lacing into
luxurious patterns of high sound as clear as well water.
Not many of the nobles present were rich enough to afford
such a choir, or important enough to persuade the bishop
to let it sing outside holy ground. The Lady Anna looked
elegant and quite, quite calm, despite a tendency to nod
off during the psalms. Silvester, watching for his entry
from a doorway, decided that ten drops of cure-care would
have been enough. He adored these occasions; they seemed
to him to sum up the whole purpose of the household, to
symbolize the way that intricate and humming hive all
worked together toward one end, from the Count of the
Outfields himself to the slave boy who looked after the
bear. The household was a creature composed of a host of
smaller creatures, and at moments like this the creature
sang. Only . . . He glanced along the women's table to

where the Lady Ariadne sat looking like a clever doll. Her makeup, as was the fashion, had been put on so thick that you couldn't see her clear, pale skin; her dark hair had been teased into a thousand cunning ringlets; her green frightened eyes were like clay beads; even her movements were stiff as a doll's with fright. Silvester sighed for her. She would see so few of her dream days, riding across bare uplands with a hawk on her wrist. He looked to the men's table, where the Akritas boy sat, flushed but handsome, talking with polite volubility into the Lord Celsus's deaf ear; he didn't look the type to put ambition aside and spend his days managing a country estate.

When the last of Alexius's astounding pastries was crumbs, the wine steward poured into the goblets a thick yellow wine, more than a century old, made in Etruria, and then Holy John was carried in on his portable pillar. He cleared his throat, glared at the company, raised one hand to make the Cross in the air, and spoke. For more than an hour his large, lush voice rolled out its perfect sentences, thrilling with glory as he praised his Creator, clanging with scorn as he rebuked his enemies, while he followed like a hound the twisting trail of truth through the jungle of error and sin. The guests listened, intent and eager, to every word, spellbound by the dirty old scarecrow; it was not just that they all loved a good intricate argument, nor just that they all hated and feared the Emperor. (Though they did—hated and feared him and whispered delicious scandals about his alliances with demons and about how he could detach his head from his own shoulders and send it floating through the maze of his palace to spy out the treacheries of his courtiers.) It was that Holy John had the power in him to seize men's souls and hold them, to still with a gesture the squabbling servants round the courtyard, to command total attention from the great Monophysite nobles of Byzantium.

But, as has been said, the Lord Celsus was a sort of genius. After Holy John had finished he allowed only two minutes for applause, and before any discussions could begin he made a sign to the flute players to start their tune. Silvester led Bubba into the center of the hall. The clamor dropped until the rhythm of the flutes and the little drum could be heard, and Bubba began to dance. Most of the guests had seen her before, but they were delighted to see her again though they were far too sophisticated to be amused for more than a minute by an ordinary dancing bear. Bubba wasn't that.

There was the story about her, for a start. When the Lady Ariadne was two years old, the Lord Celsus had taken her to look at his baiting bears one day and had propped her on the pit wall to see the big, furry creatures shambling about below. Then, being an absent-minded nobleman and unused to children, he had let go of her and she had fallen into the pit. Baiting bears are kept hungry, and one large male had rushed toward the tender meal so kindly tossed down to him, but before he reached it a young female bear had gathered the baby up and hugged it to her. The big bear became angry when the she-bear tried to cuff him away, but by then the bear keepers had the nets out and entangled him. They drove the other bears into their dens and nervously approached the she-bear, who sat against the wall, crooning over her catch; a wail told them that the child was alive, so they put honey cakes on the floor of the pit, and when the she-bear came to get them they snatched the Lady Ariadne to safety.

At this point the Lord Celsus's eccentricity had come strongly into play. Instead of merely thanking his God and the proper saints, he also tried to repay the she-bear. The bear warden had told him that this bear had been born on the very same day as his daughter, so he had given orders that it should be brought into his household and trained as a dancing bear, and that Silvester, also born on the same day, should have her in charge as soon as he was old enough. A boy, said the Lord Celsus, ought to have some task to do as well as the learning of the uses of drugs and the casting of accounts; it was fitting that the three, bear and boy and girl, should be linked together, though one was a soul-less beast and one a slave and one the only child of the best house in Byzantium.

It was a good story, and a good reason for the guests to like Bubba and to drink a toast to the Lady Ariadne, but there was another cause for Bubba's success. She was magnificent.

When the Lord Celsus had taken her from the bear pit he had given orders that though she was to be trained as a dancing bear she was not to be treated as was usual with dancing bears—that is to say, that the trainers were not to break her arms in order to force her to stand upright, nor were they to smash the bones of her chest to prevent her from crushing men in her huge hug. The trainers had clucked and shaken their heads and said that it was impossible, and the Lord Celsus had called them fools and sent for fresh trainers, until he found an old man with only one eye and one arm, who had lost his other eye and arm training bears but said he could do what My Lord commanded. And after her training Bubba had been cared for by somebody who loved her and understood her, as well as just exercising her and grooming her and feeding her good food.

So now she could dance, unmaimed, with her arms above her head and her neck straight and her mouth grinning. She was a brown bear, but so dark a brown that her fur, glossy as a fresh-peeled chestnut, seemed black but glinting with flecks of deep gold. She weighed as much as three big men, but shuffled lightly from foot to foot to the rhythm of the drum and flutes, turning in slow circles so that all the company could see for themselves how clever she was. The guests began to clap with the tune, and she turned faster, enjoying the furor. She was always a show-off and that special night, perhaps because of the cure-care, she was in a perfect temper. Each time the tune reached to its winding end Silvester tossed her an oatmeal biscuit glistening with honey, which she caught out of the air with a scything motion of her head. When she had eaten five biscuits Silvester made a sign to the flute players, who let their tune unwind to its end while the drum gathered to a rapid, pattering roll. Bubba stayed for a moment ridiculously poised on one leg, waiting for the next clear thump, then sat down in the middle of the hall with a thud that rattled the goblets. The guests laughed and cheered. The second steward carried a silver jug to the Lord Celsus, who poured into a huge brass goblet a mixture of cider sweetened with honey. Silvester took the goblet, kneeling on one knee, then carried it across to Bubba and placed it in her paws. She sniffed it, put it on the floor between her legs, dipped her claws into it as though she were hoping to catch a fish, licked them, then lifted the whole thing to her face and tried to drink from it like a man. Silvester had spent years teaching her this trick, and she was still very bad at it, pouring the drink all over her muzzle and getting barely a quarter of it down her throat and the rest of the sticky, reeking mixture all over her fur. When the goblet was empty she simply dropped it, looked slyly round at the laughing guests and began to lick what she could off her coat. Silvester bowed to the Lord Celsus and his guests and led her away.

So the first half of the feast went as well as any that the Lord Celsus could remember giving. In fact he said as much to his brother when he returned from bidding the women farewell. But the second half went otherwise because, in the darkest part of the night, the Huns broke out of the Slave Ward and went berserk. The house of the Lord Celsus was the first big lootable prize they came to. By dawn every man at the feast, besides almost all the servants and slaves in the rest of the house, was dead.

IV

Smoke

IT WAS only after the horror had struck and was over that
Silvester learned how it had begun. It had happened like
this:

The slave merchant with the ruined face had led his
slaves, carrying the two chests, up through the astonished
streets to the Slave Ward. This was a frowning prison of a
place near the northern arm of the Mese, where that great
street dipped and rose on its way to the Charisius Gate.
The warders were taken by surprise, being quite
unprepared for so large a haul; the price of unbroken
slaves had been dropping steadily for years as it became
cheaper to use serfs to farm one's land. Merchants no
longer brought large parcels of slaves to Byzantium; what
trade remained was in specialist slaves, who were already
trained and didn't need to be kept in the safety of the
Slave Ward. As a result the warders, who were paid a fee
for every slave in the Ward, had been losing money.

They had solved their problem in a typically Byzantine
way, by renting the cells of the Ward to anyone who would
hire them. The day the slave merchant arrived almost all

the Ward was occupied. Some of the underground cells, which had been built to house really dangerous captives like these Huns, were let to a dealer in wild animals, and now held several great apes from Africa. Others were let to a wine merchant, being as good cellars as you'd find anywhere in the City. The lower stories were used as offices by traders, or to store furs and high-class wools, and above that lived whole families of honest citizens. Certainly there was no room for sixty wild Huns arriving out of the blue.

The slave merchant, despite his arrogant air, seemed little put out by this discovery. The winter was over, he said, and he and his Huns could camp for a few days in the courtyard at the center of the Ward. Yes, several days—he didn't expect to find a market for them until the Khan Zabergan had been beaten back. Their shackles were strong, and he'd give the keys to the warders in case of accidents. Of course, in the circumstances, he could hardly be expected to pay the full fee. . . . Even so, he settled for a higher fee than he might have if he'd haggled hard. He seemed an easy man to deal with, and when the bargain was struck sent out for wine and drank with the warders.

About midnight, when all who used the Ward were asleep, he had a whispered argument with the leaders of the Huns. They began to suspect that he was betraying them, that he had really brought them here to sell them as slaves, and not for the Plan. They demanded, as proof of his trust, that he should release some of them from their chains. He fetched the spare keys and did so, explaining that it was too soon, but that there was no harm in their learning their way about the Slave Ward, so that when the breakout came it would be sudden and efficient. The chests, of course, contained their weapons, the small round shields, the jagged swords and the throwing spears. The Plan was simple. The night before their Khan reached the

Walls of Theodosius they would break out and rush the
Charisius Gate from the inside, and then hold it for the
Khan's attack.

But now one of the groups of Huns, creeping like stoats
among the shadows of the Ward, found their way down to
a wine cellar; they drank a pint or so each before dragging
a small barrel out to their comrades still in chains, and half
an hour later the slave merchant could no longer control
them. They were brave men and loyal to their Khan, but
by nature wild and free; to them the City was like one
enormous and mysterious trap; even the smells which the
night wind brought to their flared nostrils reeked with
strange dangers; yes, they were brave, but their nerve was
ready to break. The slave merchant cursed them in whis-
pers as they drank—so near to success, to his revenge and
his reward. When the chained men began to grumble loud
enough to wake the Ward, he unlocked their shackles with
steady hands, hoping that a couple of hours of freedom
would calm them; but they drank more, then moved in a
body toward their weapons. He backed against the chests
but they tore him off.

Drunk as they were, they were picked warriors and still
moved in silence, a dark cloud of men drifting out from the
Ward gate into the Mese. There they halted for a moment,
and he might have turned them back, but they looked up
at the stars and several arms pointed north. Without con-
sultation they knew what they were going to do, because it
was much more in the Hunnish style than the carefully
timed movements of the original Plan. Now they were just
another barbarian raiding party; they would loot what
they could and break free before they were cut off.

As they padded up the silent Mese they found what they
wanted—a great house, still lighted, from whose courtyard
came the noise of feasting, the smell of riches. Here the

slave merchant made his last stand. If he had been able to
keep them moving up the Mese they would have come to
the Charisius Gate, and stormed it, and perhaps even held
it long enough—the Khan's army was very near. For a
moment he stood between them and the Lord Celsus's
doorway, cursing them in their Khan's name with his
dagger in his hand; but he was between the wolves and
their prey. There was a grunt, and the thrust of a jagged
sword. No longer silent, they streamed yelling across his
body.

Silvester slept in the women's wing with the eunuchs, on
the floor below the women. He had a little cell of his own,
smaller than a closet. If he had been freeborn he would already have been sent to sleep on the opposite side of the
courtyard, in the men's wing; but slaves, even valued ones,
were treated as if they were almost women themselves, so
he expected to sleep in this cell until My Lord chose one of
the slave girls as a wife for him.

In his dream he rode a horse along a dreary and
endlessly winding river towards the Akritas estate where
the Lady Ariadne was waiting for him with toothache, but
the horse melted, and he was trudging with tired legs, and
the estate when he came to it was an empty hovel, and the
dentist's tools which he held in hand had become the Lord
Celsus's seal-brooch, and there was Holy John sitting at the
next bend on a juniper bush and shouting at him for the
sin of stealing it.

Shouts woke him and he lay sweating in the dark.

It took him some moments to be sure that the shouts
were real, and not part of the dream. Then he thought that
some quarrel had broken out between the Celsus and
Akritas families, and the betrothal would not take place—
Addie would like that. Slowly he realized that the shouts

consisted of sounds no Greek would ever utter; and then
the orange glare of burning began to stain the dark. He
threw his fur aside and stumbled to the window. Other
heads were already craning out on either side, and a shrill
screaming wail rose as the servants of the house saw the
armed savages below and the flames beginning to show
against the wall. The street front of the house was built of
imposing stone, but the wings and back of the courtyard
were mostly timber. Silvester withdrew from the window,
pulled his tunic on back to front, and ran up the private
stair to his mother's room. She had a candle lit and was sitting on the edge of her bed cradling the Lady Ariadne in
her arms.

"It's the Huns," he said. "I saw them in the harbor. Or
the Khan's come."

"Nasty vicious types," said Nonna. "I wouldn't trust
them."

"Why's Addie here?"

"She came to sleep with me after the feast. And *you* must
call her the Lady Ariadne."

"I know. Will they come up here?"

"If they do they'll get the rough edge of my tongue."

Silvester tried to pull himself together. Nonna was
talking like that—old servant's chatter—thinking the or-
dinariness of it would comfort the Lady Ariadne. Nonna
adored her, but had never understood her.

"We must hide," he said.

"They'll look under the beds," said Nonna. "I know the
type."

Her voice was shaking now. She was really frightened.

"Will Bubba let us into her den?" whispered the Lady
Ariadne.

Nonna cheered at once, and became her sturdy self.

"That's a notion," she said, easing the Lady Ariadne

upright. "You go with Sillo, darling. Sillo and Bubba will look after you."

Once he'd been given orders Silvester felt quite confident of carrying them out. It was acting on one's own that was hard for a boy brought up to be a slave. He took the Lady Ariadne's hand—she was still in her green nightgown—and led her out into the chaos of the corridor. Through the sharp stink of smoke, crowds of servants were jostling along, some of them screaming, and some trying to drag chests of their belongings away from the fire toward the back of the house, although there was no way out there. It took him several minutes to struggle the few yards to the private stair, and when he reached it he found why—the eunuchs were trying to climb up from below, and so jamming the corridor. He shouted the Lady Ariadne's name at Symmachus, who stared at him with unmeaning eyes but whose body somehow obeyed the habit of deference and squeezed to one side to let them pass. Nobody else was trying to go down; the panic of fire and sword swept through the house, each man's madness infecting the next. If the Lady Ariadne's hand had not been twined into Silvester's so tightly that it hurt, he too might have joined in the madness. But now he was obeying his orders.

The lowest flight of the stairs was a well of dark peace, with panic above and murder outside. They stood panting and listening behind the door, but heard only uninterpretable nosies. Carefully, Silvester eased the door open and stepped into the deep shadow of the fig tree that stood beside it. The far side of the courtyard was hidden by the stream of smoke from the burning wing, and above the smoke, lighted by flame, stood Holy John on his pillar with such a look of happiness on his face that he might have been drunk. The children slipped across the small gap to the cage. Silvester fumbled with the familiar catch and let them in, but only pulled the door to—in case the smoke became unbreathable and they had to leave in a hurry.

Bubba greeted them with a deep, nervous growl. Stupid though she was she knew that something unfamiliar was happening out in the courtyard. Silvester crouched by the stone arch of the den.

"It's all right, my beautiful," he whispered. "Nobody's going to hurt you. We'll look after you."

Bubba grunted when she heard his voice. Straw rustled as she lumbered toward him.

"Stay still, Addie," he whispered. "She'll want to smell who it is."

He crawled into the total blackness and let himself be sniffed at; then he called Addie in for similar treatment.

"It's fresh straw yesterday," he whispered. "Bubba sleeps in that corner, so we'll . . ."

He was interrupted by a prod on his chest with blunt claws.

"No," he whispered crossly, "not now. We haven't come to play games, just to borrow your straw."

Bubba growled.

"Oh, all right," he said. "Get into a corner, Addie, and keep out of the way."

Wrestling with an affectionate bear who weighs four times what you do is an art; the important thing is to go limp if you find yourself being rolled on. Silvester had never tried it in the dark and his head was singing with buffets against the stone walls of the den before Bubba tired of the game as suddenly as she had demanded it. He tickled her armpits briefly and then she sneezed, dug herself into her straw, sneezed several times more, and began to snore.

"Where are you?" he whispered.

"Here. I'm cold. There isn't any straw."

"She's probably taken it all into her own corner. She does that. But she's asleep now, so she won't mind us coming, too."

Carefully he eased enough straw away to make a nest for Addie against the warm bear hide, helped her to find her way in, then heaped the straw back on her. There wasn't enough straw for another nest, nor any reason why a slave shouldn't shiver provided his mistress was warm. He sat with his back against the wall and his knees drawn under his chin, and tried to guess what was happening by the noises outside and the changing light under the low rim of the arch. Now only a few of the guttural shouts of the attackers reached him, and the screams of the household seemed to be lessening, but the steady, coarse roaring of burning timber rose and rose. Twice, though, there were shouts that seemed to come from just outside the cage; then he heard the flap of bare feet running. Sometimes the entrance went almost black, and at other times was a strong orange with enough light reaching inside the den to pick out glitters from the straw. The racing of his heart and the gulping in his throat lessened. No one had found them yet. They would be all right.

The bright arch deadened and became dark. The air in the den, which had hitherto been sharp with burning but breathable, thickened. He gasped and lowered his head to the floor. Bubba coughed in her sleep, coughed again and woke, growling

"It's all right," he choked. "It'll go away. It's all right."

She growled again.

"Sillo. I can't breathe. Where . . . What's happening?"

"The house is on fire. I haven't heard any Huns for some time, but we'd better stay here."

"Where's Nonna? Mother?"

"Run away, I expect. They're all right."

"I can't breathe. What's happening?"

She was still half held by her shocked sleep, but Silvester could hear the beginnings of panic in her voice.

"I must look," she said.

"I'll go."

"No. Stay there."

He obeyed, as he had been trained to. He heard the sudden rattle of straw as she left her nest and groped for the entrance of the den. In any case, he thought, there was no danger in all this smoke—but the wind must have shifted, for suddenly he saw her shape sharp against the orange arch of the den. He was going to shout a warning, but then the arch blacked out completely; Bubba, moving with a bear's silence, had followed the Lady Ariadne and now squatted growling in the entrance of the den. Beyond her the Lady Ariadne screamed.

"Help! Sillo! Help! Help! Help!"

Silvester kicked and pummeled at Bubba's unfeeling back until with a harsh grunt she edged into the cage. Silvester rushed past her. A Hun clutched the Lady Ariadne by the arm and was backing away from the bear, not realizing that Bubba was just as alarmed as he was. Silvester flung himself at the man without thought, hitting at his body and kicking at his legs but from too close to do him any harm. It was like trying to fight a tree trunk. For a moment he saw a hairy arm in front of him, so he bit hard at it and tasted blood. The man bellowed, and then Silvester found himself hurtling across the cage and crashing into the wall of the den. He collapsed to his knees, sick with black pain, but managed to struggle up, shaking his head. As his vision cleared he saw the Hun stoop to pick something off the floor, a kind of satchel; the man had never let go of the Lady Ariadne, so he had no spare hand for his weapons. Silvester steadied himself against the wall for another useless attack, but at that moment Bubba gave a deep growl, rose on her hind legs, and lurched forward. Tethered to the rails of the cage, two of the Lord Celsus's town horses reared and plunged with terror. With a desperate, quick movement the Hun swung his satchel at the bear. Silvester heard a heavy thud and saw Bubba collapse backwards, put her paws to her snout and start weeping. Once again he rushed forward, hoping at least to give Bubba time to recover from that lucky blow on the only place where she could be hurt at all—after that she'd be really dangerous to the Hun. He saw, beneath the bead-fringed turban, the man's face grinning with the lust of an easy fight, but he never saw the satchel looping back to hit him on the return stroke. For an instant, in a pain-filled and tumbling world, he noticed the top of Holy John's pillar through a rift in the smoke, empty. "That's all wrong," he thought. Then the dark took him.

V

The Sard-Stone

HE WOKE to grayness. For some while he didn't know where he was, and thought that the chill light was something to do with the pain in his head. Then he knew it was dawn. Aching and shivering, he crawled to the side of the cage and pulled himself upright. His eyes kept crossing themselves, making everything blurred and double; his head hurt less when he shut them, but he kept them open long enough to see that the Hun and the horses were gone, and so was the Lady Ariadne.

While he stood clutching the grimy iron and swaying in the red dark of his pain, something nudged his side. He looked down and saw Bubba beside him with her nose all covered with dried blood, come to tell him that there were horrible men in the world who hit bears across the snout. Her piggy little eyes looked suspiciously round the courtyard in case there was another one waiting to leap out at her. Silvester thought the satchel must have held some heavy kind of loot, gold goblets or candlesticks; he put his hand up to the side of his face and found it very swollen, and there was a wincing lump on the back of his head.

Bubba nudged him again. Well, he was the bear-ward, and it was his duty to keep her looking respectable until someone (who? who?) gave him other orders. He let her out of the cage and led her across to the cistern.

There were several dead bodies lying about but he didn't look at them. When he had sponged the blood off her face, Bubba put her dripping muzzle on his chest and told him crooningly how much she loved him, and would he please not allow anything of the kind ever to happen again. He cuddled her for a bit, then took her back to her cage.

On his way he saw that Holy John was not dead. The corpse at the bottom of the pillar had been a Hun, and Holy John knelt on the paving deep in prayer. (In *The Life and Miracles of Holy John* you will find his survival explained as follows: he was standing on his pillar in the midst of the holocaust when a Hun came up with a throwing spear and took aim at the tempting target. Holy John cursed a mighty curse and a thunderbolt fell from heaven and struck the Hun dead. The less impressionable *Lives of the Small Saints* tells much the same story, except that the Almighty sent a goose flying over Byzantium at that moment and the bird, overcome by the smoke, fell out of the sky and broke the Hun's neck. Neither story is true.) Silvester felt comforted—if Holy John had survived, so might others. But the slackening of tension allowed him to be sick, and he vomited on the paving while his head rang with pain at each retching and Bubba watched with surprise. When he had staggered the rest of the way to her cage and shut her in, he sat for half an hour, sweating and shivering by turns.

Slowly the pain lessened and his weakness left him. He got up and started to maunder about the courtyard in an aimless way, like an ant that has drunk wine. The wing in

which he had slept was burnt from end to end, and here
and there among the smoking timbers and smashed tiles he
could see parts of people, but nothing moved; no one
groaned. In the corner between the burnt wing and the
still standing street-front he found the body of Lady Anna,
neither burnt nor wounded, but with her neck broken.
She must have thrown herself, or been thrown, from her
rooms. Silvester found a curtain which someone had tossed
into the yard, so he used it to cover her body; then he sat
beside it with his knees drawn under his chin, for the first
time weeping. She had been beautiful and vain, and so
vague and wayward as to seem a little mad, but she had
often been quite kind to him. With her, somehow, the soul
of the house —the creature that had sung at the feast—was
dead.

The crying eased him and allowed him to think. His
first duty was to his master, who would still have been
feasting when the Huns came. He rubbed his tears away
with the corner of his tunic and went to see what had happened in the banqueting hall.

The Lord Celsus's body lay halfway up the curving
marble stair, face down, with all his snowy toga blotched
with blood. A dead Hun lay at his feet, a short Roman
sword still in his hand. Silvester, weak as he was, had to use
the fall of the stairs to roll his master over. It had taken
three wounds to kill him, one in the thigh from which
most of the blood had come, and the others in his neck and
chest. On his left shoulder, ringed with gold, was pinned
the official seal-brooch of the Count of the Outfields,
which he used for authenticating all the documents that
came from his office. The dark red sard-stone was much
the color of drying blood. Guessing that looters might
come, like rats, to steal what they could from the dead
house, Silvester unpinned it with quivering fingers and

put it in the pouch of his tunic. Then he went on up the stairs.

The banqueting hall stank like a slaughterhouse with the thin reek of blood. The marble was slippery with the stuff. Though the flames had not reached here and all the stonework was unharmed, the room was a ruin, with the tables overturned and food and wine spilled across the floor, and the tapestries stripped from the walls, torn down by brute weight so that wisps of precious thread hung like gaudy spider webs from the fastenings. At first Silvester thought that everyone was dead, but as he picked his way between the pools of blood and wine he heard a groan from over where the women's table had been. What seemed to be three bodies lay in a pile together. Pulling the top one clear—it was the Lady Anna's drunken uncle —he found an arm that was still warm and flexible at the joint. The other dead man he didn't recognize, but beneath him lay the Akritas boy, with what looked like a broken arm and a long cut still bleeding slightly on his forehead. Silvester took a napkin, dipped it in white wine, and sponged the cut clean; he raised the boy's head and trickled a little wine between his lips. The boy groaned again.

Silvester cleared the space round him, folded a rug in four to make a sort of mattress and worked him gently onto it, taking care not to move the damaged arm more than he had to. Then he went to find help.

There was no help to be had. Though it was still early morning the shops and stalls should have been opening by now, but they were all locked and barred, as though the streets were still swarming with Huns. The few people he met were hurrying somewhere, their faces set with panic. The fire brigade had arrived soon after the flames were

seen from the City watchtower, but were not equipped to
fight Huns and so had contented themselves with wetting
the roofs and walls of the neighboring houses to prevent
the fire from spreading. From one of these men, a leather-
faced veteran now packing his pump and hoses into a
donkey-drawn cart, Silvester got what news he could.

The Huns seemed to have escaped through the
Charisius Gate. The gate captain, hearing the uproar in
the Mese, had sent scouts to investigate, and when they
brought news that Huns were sacking the Lord Celsus's
house he had taken all his troops out to deal with them.
But by the time he had got the off-duty watch awakened
and armed, and had given his orders, the looting was over
and the Huns were making for the gate. The two troops
had met in the place where the Mese widened just beyond
the Restaurant of Divine Abstinence. The Huns, still
drunk with wine and the glory of slaughter, had attacked
in a berserk charge, and the sleepy gate guard had broken.
Then they had got clean away through the undefended
gate, leaving a dozen Greek soldiers dead in the street and
only one dead Hun.

The man said that several Huns had found horses, but
he had seen or heard nothing of a captive girl.

He had other news, though, which accounted for the
hurry and fright in the street. The Khan Zabergan was
much nearer than anyone had known; the Walls of Anastasius, built twenty miles out along the peninsula against
just such an attack, could not be defended because they
had been broken by the great earthquake several years ago
and the Emperor had been too mean to repair them.
There were only three hundred soldiers in the City. The
Emperor himself was sending all the church treasures
across the straits to safety, as though the City were already

lost. But he had summoned the Lord Belisarius, Count of the Stables, and ordered him to do what he could to save Byzantium. The Count had ordered the standards of the army to be taken out of the churches and carried through the streets with trumpeters and a herald, summoning all veterans to gather in Bull Square. The fireman himself had fought for Belisarius round Rome, and was planning to go down to the square as soon as he'd stowed his cart.

"But there's not many of us in the City," he said. "Most of my mates were settled out on farms, and what there are haven't any weapons. Still, with the General in charge we've got a chance—he's never been beat yet."

The man stowed his last bucket, strapped the load together as though there were all the time in the world, slapped his donkey on the rump and clattered off. Silvester walked slowly back to the house of slaughter.

It was appalling to him how little difference the attack had made to the rest of the neighborhood. Apart from the frowning, hurrying people, everything looked much as it had done yesterday, as though this hideous wound meant nothing. A few cautious shops had begun to open. It wasn't until you stood under the arch and looked into the courtyard of Lord Celsus that you could see what horrors had struck.

As he stood there Silvester heard a long moan, like wind in a chimney, from the little cell where Peter the gatekeeper lived. But Peter was dead, half-naked by the gate, stripped of the gold-rich uniform he wore for feasts. Warily Silvester looked into the gate-room.

A man lay on the floor in his own blood. His eyelids moved, but the mask of death was on his face, making Silvester think he was a stranger, until a jerk of the head displayed the ruined profile. Silvester, quite ignorant of his part in the raid, knelt by his side and felt for his faint pulse. The slave merchant's lips moved, but he didn't ask for water.

"I die," he croaked. "Find a priest."

Silvester could see that even the Learned Solomon couldn't have saved the man. Some will in the body might keep the prisoned spirit there for another half hour, but that would be all. He rose and crossed the couryard to where Holy John still knelt by his pillar, praying.

"Father," he said.

"What is it? I am striving to talk with God."

"Father, there's a man dying. He asked for a priest."

"Help me up."

The saint's hand was as soft as a woman's and his deprived body as light. He put his arm round Silvester's shoulder to steady himself as they moved to the gate—of course he had hardly walked a step in the last ten years. Silvester showed him the dying man, then left. The thought of the Learned Solomon troubled him, so he crossed the courtyard again and climbed the stairs to the doctor's room, at the far end of the unburnt wing.

Solomon lay on the floor under a cairn of books which the enraged barbarian who had killed him had hurled out of the shelves, searching for treasure. Many of the bottles were smashed. The pungent odour of aqua vitae made Silvester's eyes water. So there was no help from his old teacher, either. He took the flask of poppy juice, poured a strong dose into a cup, added water and carried the cup back to the dying man.

He found the slave merchant whispering his life's history to Holy John, who knelt by his head frowning like the terrible face of the Christ in Judgment on the dome of the Diaconissa. Silvester slid his arm carefully under the limp shoulders and eased them up so that the slave merchant could drink a few sips from the cup. He only stopped speaking while he drank, as though what he had to say was of huge importance, a message that might save an empire. Silvester stayed, holding the man's shoulders and giving him a few more drops to drink when he wanted them.

He soon found out why Holy John was frowning. The man's life had been a chain of evil, link after link of cruelty, deceit, betrayal and greed. He had come of a noble family of Byzantium and had had a twin brother, but both had been disinherited in favor of a younger and better-loved son. The twins had then equipped a ship and taken to piracy, and after wild adventures been captured. One had been executed, broken on the wheel, but the other had escaped and devoted his life to vengeance. It was he who had made his way north to the Kutrigur Huns, earned the trust of their Khan, suggested the attack on Byzantium, and devised the ruse with the slaves. It was he who now lay dying in Silvester's arms.

"Men of the Khan's own tent I brought," he gasped, "wearing the blue beads. I tried to hold them but they were drunk. They cut me down in the gate."

"They have taken a girl," Silvester broke in. "What will they do with her?"

The man's lips twisted.

"Sell her. Give her to a favored wife as a servant. They take what they want, but Greek women they think ugly. Yes. They take what they want. They are free men. Hard and free. They take what they want."

He paused and drank.

"How old a girl?" he asked.

"Fourteen."

"Almost a child. I have never seen a Hun strike a child. Free . . ."

"How do they worship?" said Holy John.

"None of your Gods, old frowner. They praise the sun, and dread many demons."

"Not Christ in any kind?" cried Holy John, forgetting to frown in his astonishment.

"No more than wolves do."

In the silence that filled the small room Silvester fancied that he could hear this wicked man's life seeping away between the floorboards. He shivered.

"Son," boomed Holy John in a changed voice.

Silvester looked up, supposing that John must be talking to him, but it was to the dying man, and his frown had not come back.

"Son, take comfort. God works with crooked tools. Christ brings many sinners to His feast. You have sinned astoundingly, but by your crooked life God will work a mighty work, to be a glory for ages. Be happy. You have confessed. You have repented. You will find mercy at the Judgment."

It was impossible to tell whether the twist of the slave merchant's lips was a smile or a sneer as he died.

Silvester left Holy John in a fresh ecstasy of prayer and staggered into the open. Near the entrance to the courtyard he found a group of men staring at the horrors like sightseers. Most of them, he could see by their dress, were slaves or servants, but the two gray-haired men in the middle were clearly noblemen. A servant saw him and cried out. The noblemen turned and he recognized the stouter one at once as the Lord Brutus, who was the Lord Celsus's Orthodox cousin and head of the other branch of the family, but because of the religious difference had not come to the betrothal feast.

"And who are you?" this lord said, soft-voiced.

"I was the Lord Celsus's bear-ward, your noblest."

"Was? Is his Lordship dead, then?"

"Yes, sir, on the steps to the banqueting hall, and the Lady Anna is dead over there and the Lady Ariadne is carried away and . . ."

The Lord Brutus held up a pudgy hand to stop the babble.

"Perhaps it would be quicker if you were to tell us who is not dead."

"Everyone's dead, sir, except the young Lord Akritas, the bridegroom."

"Alive? Where?" said the other noble sharply.

"In the banquet hall, sir. I went to get help for him, but . . ."

"Show my servants. One moment, Lord Brutus . . ."

Silvester led five men away while the two nobles walked aside for a low-voiced discussion. The men chattered among themselves, clucking in astonishment at the sight of the Lord Celsus's body on the stairs, but raising real wails of desolation as they recognized some of the dead men in the banqueting hall. Silvester realized that they must be servants of some Akritas household.

The boy was awake now, pale and groaning. He recognized the servant who knelt by him and asked in a complaining voice for water. When he'd drunk, the servant said, "Come now, your noblest," and made as if to try to get him to his feet.

"No!" cried Silvester.

The servant—an important one because he wore a tunic of finest wool trimmed with silver—looked up with a snarl.

"Akritas keeps Akritas. Others stand clear."

It sounded like a family motto, but even a slave does not take orders from servants of another household.

"I've trained as a doctor," said Silvester. "The young lord must rest. If he is moved it must be very gently, on a litter."

"Yes, fetch a litter," muttered the boy.

The Akritas servants began arguing among themselves about whether to fetch a litter, and how to find one, and who should go and look. Greeks will always choose to argue about an action as a substitute for doing it. The noise of disagreement echoed over the tumbled bodies of dead lords. Suddenly it stilled, for live lords were among them.

The Lord Brutus was clearly distressed by the sight of so many dead men he had known, but the Akritas lord's dark, closed face was quite unchanged as he stood staring down at his young kin.

"Who put him on the rug?" he said suddenly.

"I did, sir," said Silvester. "It was the best I could manage. I was telling your servants that he should not be moved again without a litter."

"Quite right," snapped the Akritas lord. "Fetch a litter, Thomas. Break up a bed if you can't find anything better. How do you feel, Cousin Philip?"

The boy groaned but opened his eyes.

"They killed everyone," he moaned. "Father, everyone."

"Was the betrothal contract signed?"

"Signed?"

"The parchments, boy!" snapped the Akritas lord.

"I think so. Father and I . . ."

The Akritas lord turned as Philip Akritas fainted.

"It seems the contract was signed, my lord Brutus," he called.

The news shook the Lord Brutus out of his grief. His face at once became hard and careful.

"But if the girl is dead . . ." he began.

"Carried away, the slave says. Alive when last seen. Is that right, you?"

They both closed on Silvester and made him tell everything he had seen and done the night before, looking at

him all the time as though he were lying. He added what
he had heard from the fireman about the escape through
the Charisius Gate.

"Good servants my lord Celsus had," said the Akritas
lord drily. "Letting his daughter be carried off before their
eyes."

"The boy fought," said the Lord Brutus. "Look at the
side of his head."

The Akritas lord sniffed, but the Lord Brutus merely
smiled. Silvester saw that the Akritas lord was trying to
make the Lord Brutus angry, and the Lord Brutus wasn't
going to let him.

"We must find those contracts," said the Akritas lord.
"Where will they be, you?"

Silvester bowed and led the way.

The Lord Celsus's study was another ruin. He had been
a collector of fine knick-knacks, with a special delight in
jeweled clockwork toys. All these were gone. The silk curtains had been wrenched away, of course, and the table
turned on its side, and the chests emptied out, and the
mysterious singing crystals smashed, never to sing again.
Silvester watched the two lords poking among the chaos
with their staffs.

"Ha! What is that, you?" said the Akritas lord, not
deigning to bend.

Silvester knelt and worked a rolled parchment free from
the mess; two tasseled seals hung below it; the lords
unrolled it, put it on the window seat and read it together.

"The Cappadocian lands?" said the Lord Brutus suddenly, in a tone of amazement.

"A fair dowry," said the Akritas lord and read on. The
Lord Brutus clicked his tongue.

"Now here," said the Akritas lord. "Failure to complete.

Death—that looks the usual thing, dowry canceled, exchange of tokens and so on. Other than death—these lawyers! Fault of the party, whole dowry; negligence of the party, two thirds; no fault of the party, one third."

"He was mad!" exclaimed the Lord Brutus.

"Probably didn't read it," said the Akritas lord, smiling for the first time. "Celsus was always a careless fellow—you remember how he once dropped that girl into his bear pit. Those lawyers are going to get fat if it comes to court, my dear man. There won't be much of the dowry left by the time they've finished arguing whether it was negligence or not, and taken their fees. In my view we'd all be better off if we settled it between us that it was no fault. I think Akritas would be satisfied with a third."

"But . . ." began the Lord Brutus in horror, then pulled himself together. "I can't speak for the whole family, what's left of it, that is. There are a complicated set of trusts."

"Of course, of course," said the Akritas lord, now grinning like a fox. "Alternatively, you could always send and ransom the girl back."

Hope stirred and died at once. Silvester could tell, from the tone of one lord's voice and the look on the other lord's face, that this was a suggestion they both thought impractical, made simply as a bargaining point.

"Let's leave it for the moment," said the Akritas lord, rolling the parchment up. "There should be another of these somewhere, you. Look for it. Ah, that's right. I'll stick to this one, my lord, and you carry that home. Now, next I think the slave can show us round the place, see what assets are left, what can be done to save them, all that. Celsus had a superb cellar, I hear."

He sounded suddenly affable and easy, as if a very profitable morning had followed a good night's work. When

Silvester rose from kneeling among the papers something joggled against his thigh. The seal-brooch! But that was Addie's, the Lady Ariadne's now. He wasn't going to give it to either lord. The new Count of the Outfields would have a new one cut, quite different.

There were not many assets left. The Huns who had found the cellar had smashed what they could not drink, so that the floor was a foot deep in now valueless vintages, on whose surface the body of one of the cellarmen floated face down. The Akritas lord sighed. On their way across the courtyard they passed the cage where Bubba sat asking for comfort and assurance, which Silvester could not at the moment give. The Lord Brutus stopped and eyed her with interest.

"A very good bear," he said critically. "She'll have to have her arms and chest broken, of course, I told Celsus ages ago, but he wouldn't listen. She mightn't survive it now, but it's got to be done. She's not safe like that."

The Akritas lord was bored by bears. But his eye fell on Holy John, now kneeling again by the foot of his pillar.

"What's he, you?" he snapped.

Silvester explained.

"A damned Monophysite," added the Lord Brutus. "Old Celsus . . ."

But the Akritas lord was already striding off.

"That's luck," whispered the Lord Brutus. "Akritas can never leave a saint in peace. Turn and look at this bear, boy."

Silvester turned, but could not look. In his mind's eye he saw the glossy chest smashed with hammers, the strong arms crushed, while Bubba blubbered with pain and terror. But it wasn't Bubba that the Lord Brutus wanted to talk about.

"The Lady Ariadne died in the fire, boy," he hissed. "It was some slave girl you were cuddling in the den. Tell it any other way and you lose your nose and ears."

"My lord?" said Silvester, puzzled.

"What a bit of ill luck that Akritas brat surviving!" said the Lord Brutus. "But since he has, the Lady Ariadne must be dead. I'm not having the Cappadocian lands going to Akritas."

"Yes, my lord. But the other lord heard me . . ."

"And I heard you say that the Lady Ariadne was sent to her mother, and that was the last you saw of her. The only person you saw escape was the slave girl you took for a cuddle in the den, who was carried off by the Huns."

"Yes, my lord."

"Choose some girl who is known to have lived in the house. Stick to her. You will not have to tell the story long."

"Yes, my lord."

But Silvester, though he kept all tone out of his voice, was still puzzling about that last remark when the two lords left the courtyard in apparent friendship. He understood the rest well enough, from what he'd heard in the Lord Celsus's study. If the Lady Ariadne lived, the Akritas family could claim at least a third of her dowry, which would have been enormous as she was the Lord Celsus's only child. But if she were dead it would all go to various members of the Celsus clan, and the Lord Brutus would somehow find himself owner of the Cappadocian lands. And that meant Silvester lying steadily through law-court after law-court, which . . .

Suddenly he saw a further point. He was a slave. That meant . . .

Now when he gulped it was not tears but a sort of sickness. The sickness of terror.

VI

Wax

HE HAD TO ASK someone. When he had controlled his shaking he fetched food from the kitchens; there was always an enormous amount left from any feast, and the Huns had not managed to spoil it all. He took Bubba some choice tit-bits, as well as her usual raw roots, and carried the rest over to the pillar. From close up, he could see that Holy John was not praying, but thinking. The stillness of concentration was somehow different from the stillness of prayer.

"Father?" he said, tentatively.

"You are young to endure sights like this. Pray to God for strength."

"It is more than that, Father. The Lord Brutus . . ."

Holy John ate while he listened.

". . . but I am a slave," Silvester finished, "so if there's any doubt about whether I'm telling the truth they'll torture me. The Lord Brutus must know that, so he'll know the lies will be useless . . . and he said I wouldn't have to tell them long."

"The world is wicked," said Holy John with grisly enjoyment, "and a great lord can work greater wickedness than common people. No doubt he intends to have you killed before you can be tortured."

"And," cried Silvester, now unable to dam the flood of his fears and miseries, "he wanted the Lady Ariadne dead! And he's going to break Bubba's arms and chest. Bubba!"

At the sound of her name the bear wuffled distressfully from her cage. She was a conservative bear, and though she had liked the red mullet with her roots she would prefer the world to return to what it had been yesterday.

"The Lord works with strange tools, weak and crooked," said Holy John. "Without a doubt this is a sign from Him that you are to come with me—you and the bear."

Wild hope leaped, then faltered.

"Come? Where?"

"In the night, when the Huns came, I prayed for martyrdom. I readied myself for the stroke. But the Lord denied me. He cast me down. In the instant when the spear should have flown the smoke overcame me, the rail broke with my weight, and I fell from the pillar on my attacker, who, blinded by the same smoke, could not see me fall; so that it was not I but the Hun who died, and died in ignorance of Christ Jesus. Next He sent to our gates that man of sin, nor would He permit him to die until he had told me that these Huns have no knowledge of Christ. The Word of God is as clear to me as a cross of fire, lighting up the sky. I am to go to these Huns and carry Christ to them. And now He speaks again, that you and the bear are to come with me."

"Convert the Kutrigurs! But they are like wolves! The man said so."

"All men are like wolves. Homo homini vulpus. You have spoken with the Lord Brutus this morning."

"But . . . but what shall we live on? And you can't even walk across the courtyard without help. And even if we found a horse you couldn't ride—not if we've got Bubba. Bears hate horses and horses hate bears. And we can't travel along the roads without a permit. And . . ."

"God will give me strength. God will give us food. God will close the eyes of the officers of the roads. It is His work."

"But . . ."

With a snort Holy John struggled to his feet and tottered toward the gate, as though he were going to start his journey at once. But he turned to the right, along the wall, and then right again and came back past the burnt-out wing. At each stride his step became firmer and more certain. He straightened his neck. His arms began to swing rhythmically. Silvester ran and intercepted him.

"Father, your feet will become very sore. Let me wash them, and harden the skin with aqua vitae."

"The Lord will harden them."

"If the Lord's going to do everything, He might as well carry you up to the Kutrigurs on a whirlwind . . . perhaps it's part of His plan that there's someone left alive in the house who knows about aqua vitae . . . "

Holy John made a noise between a snarl and a laugh, but followed Silvester up to the Learned Solomon's room and allowed him to set about the disgusting task, as well as to dress two small sores where old dirt had worked into older cracks. When the job was over he looked at his legs in a discontented way.

"Twelve years no part of my skin has touched water, beyond the rain and snow sent by the Lord."

He spoke like an athlete who has tried to break a record and failed.

"But Christ allowed His feet to be washed, and washed the feet of His apostles," said Silvester consolingly.

"I am less worthy. What is that noise?"

It was voices, arguing, such as the courtyard had heard ten thousand times before. Silvester peered carefully out through the small window. A group of servants were pointing and gesticulating. Two of them carried weapons. He recognized the leader by the tunic with the silver trimmings.

"Akritas servants," he said. "They've brought soldiers. I think they may have come for me."

"No doubt. I will tell them that the Lord Brutus has already taken you. And if he sends, I will say that you are in the hands of Akritas. You must hide meanwhile."

"I'll go to Bubba's den as soon as the coast is clear."

From the window he watched Holy John limp across to the group and tell his credible lie. When they grumbled he cursed them into silence, until they moved off and started, with further argument and delay, to fetch the bodies of the slain Akritas lords down from the banqueting hall. Judging his chances, Silvester slipped from doorway to doorway, and at last into the cage and the darkness of the den. Bubba followed him in and immediately fell asleep. Given the chance a bear will sleep all day and three quarters of the night, but Bubba had been too worried and distressed to settle. Silvester lay and dozed by her side.

He was awakened by a loud voice. Holy John, speaking as reasonantly as if he had been preaching to a multitude, so that every word of the lie should carry to Silvester, was saying that Akritas had sent armed servants to carry the bear-ward away. There was no hubbub at the news, and that could only mean one thing—Lord Brutus had come himself. Silvester slithered farther into the straw, trying even in the dark to hide behind Bubba's bulk. This was a poor refuge, he suddenly thought—the Lord Brutus already knew he had hidden here against the Huns. Bubba, disturbed by his movement, woke and at once sensed his fear. She growled and moved to the door of the den.

"That's the bear, Damian," said the Lord Brutus's soft voice.

"A fine animal, my Lord. We could breed from her."

"Too old."

"Fourteen years, my Lord. She's been well cared for, and is still in her prime. Perhaps the first litter might be difficult."

At the sight of strangers so near her cage Bubba's hackles rose; Silvester could see the fur along her spine bristle against the daylight.

"Will you take her now?" said the Lord Brutus.

"Not in this mood, my Lord. If the bear-ward had been here she might have come. I'll return this evening and drug her water, and we can carry her home tonight."

"Break her bones while she's drugged?"

"In my opinion that would be a pity, my Lord. For breeding purposes the she-bear . . ."

The rest of the sentence was lost in the rising note of Bubba's snarl. Silvester sat very still as she came back to her corner—there was no telling how she might react in this mood—but she sank into her straw with a sigh and went to sleep again. Silvester crawled to the arch of the den in time to see the Lord Brutus and three servants disappearing through the gate. Other men were moving about, servants of both houses removing dead nobles, and the common undertakers piling the bodies of servants and slaves onto their carts. Silvester had to wait while the shadows of the fig branches crept across the cobbles, until the long noon lull stilled the bustle. Byzantium would be a sleeping city for the next two hours. He whistled, and Holy John limped across and sat in the shadow of the fig tree.

"I heard, boy. We must go now, you and I and the bear.

We cannot leave her behind, because the Almighty has shown me that she has some part still to play in His great work. The Lord Brutus has left a guard on the gate, a stupid heretic but not so stupid that he would fail to notice a bear beneath his nose. He can be drugged, if you can find the right herbs."

"I expect so."

"But God has not yet shown me how we are to pass the City Walls without a permit."

Silvester saw just such a permit in his mind's eye, an exact square of poor-quality parchment, with a few lines of writing on it and the big seal at the bottom. The Lord Celsus had had to seal many such, whenever he had sent messengers anywhere outside the City on the Emperor's business; mostly these documents were written by the clerks in the Office of the Outfields at the Great Palace, but sometimes an emergency meant that they had to be produced at home, and then, as part of his clerk-training, Silvester had helped to write them. Now his hand clutched at the stolen seal-brooch in his pocket.

"I can make a permit," he said.

"Good. First we must drug the guard. I will go to my pillar and call loudly to anyone who seems likely to enter the courtyard. You will have to hide."

"All right."

The servants who had removed the bodies from the banqueting hall had done the same for most of the wine, but Silvester found a round silver jug lying on its side in a corner, in whose curve there remained a good gobletful of the famous Etruscan vintage, a taste strong enough to hide most others. He carried it to the Learned Solomon's cell and added two measures of poppy juice. While he was there he packed a wallet with a few straightforward drugs whose uses he knew, then carried the jug and a drinking-

horn down to Holy John, who took them with a bitter grin
and limped off.

In the Lord Celsus's study Silvester added parchment,
pens, ink and wax to his wallet. Settling down at the
window seat he wrote out a careful travel permit for one
free man, one bear and a bear-ward; only when he was
about to stamp the red seal-brooch down into the hot wax
did his hand shake. But the impression was good enough.
He added yesterday's date in case the gate captain had
heard of the Lord Celsus's death, then left the parchment
to dry while he went to see if the Huns had found the
drawer in the Lord Celsus's table.

There was no need for the Lord Celsus to have a secret
drawer, but it pleased the same part of him as the clockwork toys had. In fact it pleased him so much that you
could hardly call it secret, as he had shown it to most people who came to his office, especially children. With the
table on its side Silvester had to look all along the parade
of ebony saints on its rim until he found Saint Andrew;
with one hand he twisted the ivory halo and with the other
pressed the center of the tilted cross, and the ebony flap
popped smoothly open. Silvester slid his hand in.

Disappointment shook him. There was only one leather
bag in the drawer, and from its feel he knew at once that it
didn't contain coins. He pulled it out, opened it and shook
its contents into his left palm.

The huge ruby glowed with inner light. His first
thought was that it was astonishing that it wasn't warm to
the touch; his second that of course this was going to be
the Lord Celsus's gift to his daughter, a real secret, which
was why he'd never seen it; his third to wonder what it was
worth. He'd helped sometimes to write out inventories of
the household valuables, including the Lady Anna's
jewels, so he had some knowledge of the sums of money in-

volved. But he couldn't guess at the value of this. A king's ransom? A ransom.

Quite calmly he slid it back into its soft pouch and hid it at the bottom of his wallet.

On his way out something rattled beneath his foot. The chest in which the Lord Celsus had kept money for ordinary household outgoings had been rifled, but in such a hurry that some coins had fallen on the floor and simply been left lying. Even by daylight it was always difficult to spot a small object which had fallen onto a mosaic floor, because it at once seemed to be part of the pattern of little tiles. Silvester knelt by the door and put the good side of his face flat on the marble so that he could look with his left eye along the plane of the floor. At once he spotted several more coins, all silver. He picked them up, rolled and tied the permit, and left.

Holy John was waiting by the gateway.

"The fool sleeps," he said, rubbing his hands together with pleasure at his own cleverness. "We must go."

"One moment," said Silvester over his shoulder as he ran toward the kitchen. There was not much room in his satchel, and he didn't feel strong enough to carry more than one load, but he found a small pitcher of honey and some rough oatcakes, and filled the remaining spaces with dried fish, which he knew would last several days and had real sustenance in it. But the honey was what really mattered.

He needed it almost at once. Bubba came out of her cage with a little coaxing, and fidgeted while Silvester fitted her collar and chain round her neck, but she started growling as she padded beside him toward the gate. She seemed to have grown much more suspicious of the world since yesterday. And when she actually reached the archway the snores of the drugged guard so alarmed her that she refused to pass him until Silvester smeared honey on a cake and coaxed her through with it.

Out in the Mese Silvester turned left, toward the center of the City. He was in a panic lest either Lord's men should return and catch them; the noon lull was almost over and already the pavements were beginning to fill with people. He could have gone north, straight to the Charisius Gate, but that was on the main road to Adrianopolis, and likely to be well watched by edgy sentries after last night's fracas. But the gate of the Fifth only led out to an area of market gardens, and was notoriously slack in its discipline. That was the next gate along, and worth the extra mile.

The morning's panic had subsided, but knots of gossipers stood about exchanging rumors. From overheard snatches Silvester learned that a vast horde of Huns was already pouring through the breaches in the Wall of Anastasius, and also that there were only a handful of them and they were in full retreat. Ahead of him a middle-aged man, armored, and carrying weapons, marched towards Bull Square while the bystanders cheered with a mocking note.

"Fools, all fools," snarled Holy John. "Yet God will not allow His City of fools to fall."

"How do you know?"

"Because my work is to be done in the north. That is His word, and how can it be fulfilled if the Huns come to me, here? Why are we not going north?"

Silvester explained about the Fifth Gate, and turned, with a sigh of relief, down a twisting lane that wound west, with houses on either side older than any of the building regulations, so closely built that the projecting upper stories almost met above their heads. Out in the Mese Bubba had been scared of the strangers and the noise, but in this dim tunnel she was full of the inquisitiveness of bears, straining at the chain to see what new smell or sight would be found round the next corner. Silvester had to bully her into slowness, for Holy John's sake. The old man was already limping badly: if he took half an hour to cover the mile to the Gate of the Fifth, and was then exhausted, how many days, how many years would it take to trek the unknown distance to the land of the Kutrigurs, up beyond the Black Sea? And what were they going to live on? And . . .

A child, seeing the bear padding towards it out of the shadows, yelled and ran into a house. Otherwise they saw no one until they came out into the vegetable market, which was really the wide street that ran north to the Gate of the Fifth. To Silvester's surprise the market people were still about, with their stalls well-stocked. Normally they'd sold everything and gone home by noon. There were shops on either side of the stalls, many of them selling the sort of things that farmers whittle or stitch by firelight on winter evenings, wooden spoons and bowls, pretty patterned leatherwork, straightforward working harness, spinning wheels. Silvester handed Bubba's chain to Holy John and turned into a dark little shop that sold simple musical instruments, but before his eyes were used to the dimness he heard a curse and a scuffle outside, and then Bubba dragged Holy John in behind her.

The shopkeeper, old and fat and smelling of the cloves he chewed, bowed politely to all three of them, while Bubba sniffled at Silvester to make sure he wasn't some sort of changeling.

"Can you sell me a cheap flute?" said Silvester.

"Take your pick. They'll all be burnt by the Huns before morning, so I'm selling them half-price."

He named a sum a little over twice the proper one.

"The City cannot fall," said Holy John. "God has sent me word."

"That is good news," said the shopkeeper politely. "What are the bear's opinions?"

Bubba, pleased with the attention and the smell of cloves, sat back on her haunches and clapped her paws above her head.

"Ah," said the shopkeeper, "you want a flute for healing."

"Healing?"

"I remember when I was your age, up in our village in Dalmatia, there was a beggar who came once a year with a bear. We brought out those who were sick and the beggar played his pipe and the bear walked to and fro on the sick people where they lay in the street, and their sicknesses left them and went into the bear. He played a black flute, like this one."

He reached a dusty flute down from the back of a shelf. Silvester put it to his mouth and found that it was longer than he was used to and that the fingering was slightly different. When he blew the notes were lower and richer, but he managed to pick out a snatch of the familiar tune. At once Bubba rose to her hind legs and started to thump out her dance, so that every instrument in the place rattled and clacked against its neighbor. Silvester stopped; Bubba thudded down, baffled.

"How much?" he said, ready to haggle, but not for long.

"It's a gift—a thanks for God's word that the City will not fall. You see those fools out in the market; they have picked all their vegetables unripe and are going to stay here selling them until the Huns go away. And already they're trying to charge famine prices. I shan't get any sleep to-night, with their country babble."

Silvester thanked him as politely as he could in his im-

patience. Holy John blessed him. Bubba sneezed. He
smiled and bowed to each of them.

The captain of the gate gave a slovenly salute to the seal
but didn't even bother to read the wording.

"Going out, then?" he said. "Traffic's all been the other
way, so far."

"What's happening?" said Silvester.

"Don't ask me. The General hasn't, so why should you?
But if he *did* send, I could tell him where I've seen smoke
from my tower, out beyond Phocis way. That's well inside
the broke walls."

"Are you going to have to fight?"

"Not me. I was sent for, but I paid my cousin to go instead in my second-best armor. He's never held a spear in
his life, but nor have most of the others. Three hundred
veterans, the General's got, and those softies from the Palace Guard, and behind them a mob—and he's arming
them with stage weapons from the theaters, and pots and
pans and mother-knows-what. He'll need his famous luck,
won't he?"

"The City cannot fall," said Holy John. "God has
spoken to me."

"Glad to hear it," said the captain, moving towards the
barred gate. "I've got a plague of black-fly on my melons—
ask Him what He's going to do about that."

He opened a wicket in the main gate, but held his thigh
to the door as if ready to slam it at once should a Hun
show his nose. Silvester led Bubba through, stepping over
the heavy bottom beam, out of the lackadaisical bustle of
the City he knew and into the dangerous, slurred muttering of a sullen crowd.

PART II · THE TRAIL ·

VII

Flint

THE LAW was perfectly clear: no permanent building of
any kind was permitted within two hundred yards outside
the Walls of Theodosius. But the buildings were there
despite that, a ramshackle hotch-potch of shacks and
stables and trading depots and storage sheds huddled right
up to the dry moat, and often with their rubbish dumps
half filling it. None of the buildings was, or looked, permanent, but for thirty years the strength of the Empire had
seemed to grow under the conquests of its great generals,
Belisarius and Narses, until nobody really believed that
any attack could reach right to its heart, which was the
City. Though of late years many barbarian raids had
ravaged the provinces to the north, this shantytown had
grown, not marked on any maps, shifting a little whenever
some energetic officer decided to make a start on clearing
it; free of the strict rules about planning and sanitation
which held inside the City. An ungovernable slum. Its
people were mostly there because they had failed to get a
permit to work in the City itself—indeed many of them
had no proper documents at all and were serfs who had

run from the hard life of being bound, father and son, to the same patch of land forever. No documents meant no entry to the City, even under the threat of a Hun attack. It was against these people that the gate captain held the door.

The note of the muttering changed. These people knew a portent when they saw one, and the appearance through the gate of a pale, handsome boy with a bruised face, leading a bear and followed by an obvious Holy man, was a portent to these people, though they couldn't tell of what. The shanty dwellers, like all deprived and hopeless communities, were superstitious, even more than the Byzantines themselves. The wildest and least respectable sects and heresies were rife among them, and it was said too that here the old religions lived on, that once a year the sentries on a certain part of the wall heard the horrible animal bellowing and then the more horrible human cries which meant that somewhere below the Bull was being ripped apart, all living, by bare hands and eaten while the flesh still steamed. These people had often listened to the promise of perfect worlds for those who endure the miseries of this one, and would listen often again. They were ready for a message.

"I carry Christ to the Huns," trumpeted Holy John. "Nor will God permit the City to fall."

Neither piece of information was of much interest to his audience. The murmur began to swell to its old note.

"What about us? What about us, big-beard?" shouted a little old man who wore nothing but a torn sack.

"He has not shown me," said Holy John.

They were disappointed, but too used to disappointment to be angry. A way opened to let the travelers through.

"Those Huns eat boys," shouted the old man.

"Raw," added a fat woman with one eye, as though she would prefer to be eaten well roasted, with gravy.

Silvester grinned as far as his bruises would let him. This was the sort of talk he was used to.

"There's only one lazy man on the gate, mother," he said.

She winked her single eye.

"Carrying Christ to the Huns, is it?" said a man at the back of the crowd in a meditative way, as though he were thinking of joining them.

"By way of Adrianapolis," said Silvester, though of course they'd have used the Charisius Gate if that had been true. But any sort of lie, however thin, might help to confuse their trail. The horror of the torturer's tools washed suddenly through him so that he stood shivering in the dirty road. Holy John took him by the shoulder and led him on.

They had gone a hundred yards when the noise of the crowd behind them rose to an excited roar. Silvester looked back and saw the people jostling over the bridge and round the gate; slowly, like sand going through the neck of an hourglass, the crowd became smaller as it pushed through the little wicket, each man too anxious to make his escape inside to stop and open the main gate for the others. The enormous walls stood solid on either side, looking as though they could hold the City alone, without the help of soldiers; but the ease with which the rabble had broken through made Silvester see how thin they really were—like the shell of a crab, a little brittle bone guarding all the rich meat within.

That night they camped in an apricot orchard, just beyond where the last real suburbs thinned out and the market gardens began to be more like proper farms. All the houses were totally deserted, though a few dogs had been left to bark thieves away, and the less valuable cattle simply loosed to roam and forage. Holy John had been able to manage only another two miles beyond the walls, and Silvester was sick with the ache and singing in his head.

Beside the orchard was a vegetable patch in which Silvester found a line of the big sweet radishes Bubba was so fond of. She knew the smell of them at once, but it obviously puzzled her that some idiot had buried them in the ground and let green leaves grow out of their tops. Silvester had to dig a couple out for her before she tried herself, and even when she had them free she patted them a couple of times to make sure they weren't alive and about to scuttle away. He fetched her water from the well which was used to irrigate the patch, then settled in the orchard to chew smoked fish.

Much later, when he was wearily rubbing Holy John's thighs and calves with a little of the olive oil he had brought, he heard a noise that did not belong to the night, extremely faint and far.

"What's that?" he said. "The sea's not that way, and there's no real wind."

But it was quite like the sea, if you could imagine a small, fierce storm troubling one place only. A long, wavering roar, which might also have been a crowd at the chariot races, or a big riot (both of which noises Silvester knew quite well). Only there was no city or arena in that direction. There was a curious metallic tone about it, if you listened carefully.

"A battle," said Holy John. "They have met . . . no, that is too steady a sound—a battle rises and falls."

"How do you know?"

"I have fought in battles. I have gloried in the strength

of my horse and the gleam of my armor, and laughed with
the lust of killing when I saw my lance skewer home between the plates of my enemy's cuirass. I was not born on a
pillar, alas. There would have been fewer opportunities to
sin."

With one of his sudden changes of mood he snatched his
legs away, and by clutching at a tree trunk hauled himself
into a praying position. Silvester wiped his hands on the
grass, and stretched himself for warmth alongside Bubba's
furry back. The strange noise went on and on.

It troubled his dreams. If he had not been so exhausted
he might not have slept at all, blanketless on the chilly
earth. As it was he slept and woke and listened to the noise
and tried to get comfortable and slept again. When he was
awake his head hurt more than it had all day. When he was
asleep he was bothered by buzzing dreams, which developed into nightmares where the real terrors of last night's
slaughter were muddled with the imagined terrors of torture. Once, when he could have sworn he was awake, the
orchard was filled with smoke through which the servants
of Akritas came creeping. He cried a warning and his own
voice woke him.

It was dawn, soft with dew and full of country smells.
Bubba was snoring and Holy John was asleep on his knees
—the posture to which his pillar had accustomed him.
The only stranger in the orchard was a donkey, which at
Silvester's cry looked up from grazing and stared at him
with violet eyes. His cry also woke Bubba, who sneezed,
grunted plaintively like a child who has been awakened
before it is ready, reared her head out of the grass and
gazed around at the astonishing green world. Silvester
could see that she had forgotten all the events of the last
two days and was quite baffled by the disappearance of her
den, her cage and the Lord Celsus's courtyard. Suddenly

she spotted the donkey; she put her head on one side, as though looking at it like that might make it go away; when it didn't she sat right up and bellowed at it in horror and disgust. The donkey rushed a few yards farther off, turned and brayed back at her—a louder and more raucous noise than any Bubba could make, so she bolted to the end of her chain and lay there, growling. With a sigh Silvester picked up a stick and drove the donkey away—it would have been useful if Holy John could have ridden it, but he saw no way of coping with two animals that reacted to each other in such a fashion.

He pulled the last of the radishes for Bubba, then picked up the well-bucket and went to fetch water. Coming back through the pearly silence he realized that the noise that had puzzled them the night before had now ceased.

They were four miles farther along their road before they heard anything like it again. The country had grown steadily more countrified, the estates grander, the crops less specialist. There were even wildish patches of woodland and scrub, and rocky outcrops where gorse bloomed and only goats could graze. Holy John was sitting on a milestone for his third rest of the morning when he held up his hand.

"Now, *that* is a battle," he said.

Silvester had heard nothing, but now he thought he could just distinguish a similar sort of noise to that of the night before, but fainter and more erratic. The unmistakable far note of trumpets pierced it.

"A charge," said Holy John. ". . . they have met . . . they have broken."

"Who? Who? Which side?"

"No telling."

That was all they learned that day, as they moved slowly

through the empty fields. But in the evening Bubba discovered something worthwhile, at least to her. Silvester had caught a stray chicken on the road and wrung its neck, and now Holy John was crouched at the bottom of a steep little dell, clicking away with an old bit of iron and a flint he'd picked up, trying to start a fire to cook the bird on. Silvester took Bubba up the bank and showed her a patch of cow parsley and other rank herbs, and she started to dig away, though evidently displeased at the meager results compared with the rich roots in the vegetable patch. Suddenly, at the steepest place, she lost her footing and went rolling to the bottom of the dell, almost squashing out the tiny tent of flame that Holy John had at last brought into being. Silvester was alarmed for her until she picked herself up, grinning and panting in a way which showed him that she was thoroughly pleased with herself. She climbed the slope again, sat down, pushed herself off and descended like an avalanche, again almost obliterating the fire. The third time she did it Holy John moved his dry kindling to a less threatened area and lit it with a flaming twig.

"I could chain her up," Silvester said.

"Let her roll. Bears have no soul, and therefore can expect none of the glories of the life hereafter. It is charitable to allow soul-less creatures such pleasures as they can achieve in this world."

"Bubba's got a soul, or almost."

"You must try not to think so, boy. It is a damnable heresy. I myself have sometimes considered that perhaps the All-maker so ordered His creation that all creatures of one kind, for instance all bears, have a single soul which they share, so that in the Eternal City there will be one perfect bear, an Idea of bear, such as Plato describes. And yet the whole creation fell with Adam, and flesh is undoubtedly sinful, and the bear is undoubtedly flesh . . ."

He paused to watch four hundredweight of sinful flesh

tumble deliriously into the camp. Silvester was astonished
to hear Holy John thinking aloud like this. On his pillar
he had been always full of certainties, always laying down
the everlasting law. Now it was as though he were trying to
decide what the law might be. He guessed Silvester's
thought.

"I am born again, child," he said. "I am younger than
you, two days old. The Merciful slew the John who dwelt
on the pillar and brought into being a new John, who
must now discover the world, groping as a baby does in its
cradle."

"The Huns looked a lot wilder than Bubba. Are you
sure *they* have souls?"

"They are Man, as you are. Don't be too proud that you
are a clever Byzantine. You said they were wolves. If so, the
Byzantines are monkeys. I will show these wolves their
souls, and make them Man. I will find them a treasure
richer than all the gold of Byzantium."

The dell rang with the bronze of his voice. Then he shud-
dered, his lips frothed, and he was lost in one of his long
talks with Christ.

Next day the roads were full of people streaming out
from the City, hurrying back to their property to see what
had been burnt or pillaged or stolen by neighbors, and to
steal from neighbors who had not come so fast. Holy John,
though his legs were strengthening, could only make
twelve miles in the whole day, so they were often
overtaken, and when at dusk they reached a village near
the Walls of Anastasius it was almost back to its full population, all feasting over the defeat of the Huns. Silvester
brought out his black flute and made Bubba dance as part
of the feast, and collected a cupful of small coins which
allowed him to buy three days' food at monstrous prices.
Then he fed Bubba and chained her clear of the village

dogs and sat with his back against a stable wall listening to Holy John gossiping with an old man who had also once been a soldier.

". . . though I didn't do any fighting this time," said the old man. "But I was out there, banging a brass lid the night before till my arms felt like falling off."

"We heard the noise."

"I bet you did. And hoarse! Make a noise like a big army, the Count said, so we lit fires and banged and shouted—*I* never heard an army making that sort of racket but we kept it up most of the night. On the top of Ribbon Ridge, so they could see us a long way off, moving about in front of the fires. Then, next morning, we moved forward, Forward! Us! A rabble of cits with a bit of stage armor to shake . . ."

"How many?" said Holy John.

"Oh, six thousand. Seven thousand. Something like that. Three hundred regulars from the Palace Guard, and three hundred veterans in junk armor, but riding good horses— the Palace Guard remounts. About forty archers, some of them just with hunting bows. But we went forward—that's the Count for you! He sent the archers and all the trumpeters he could spare on ahead before dawn to hide in those couple of woods out beyond Pege—you've been there? Oh, two longish bits of wood running side by side with a good strip of open ground between them. Don't ask me how he knew the Huns would be coming through that way, but they did, and he timed our march—march, hear that?—you'd have laughed—he timed it so we met the Huns in that strip between the woods. And the minute he saw them he put his regulars and veterans into the charge, and there they went, whooping to the Virgin like the old days, and nothing behind them but a lot of soft cits kicking up all the dust we could to make as if he had a hundred squadrons in reserve. Don't ask me how he *got* men to charge, all out, with nothing but that to back them up, but there you are, that's the Count. They wouldn't have done it for anyone else, would they? He threw it all into that one charge, and they hit the Huns like a house falling, though they were only two deep, and the trumpeters bust their guts blowing in the woods, and the archers shot all the arrows they had, and the Huns . . . you fought with Huns?"

"Neither with nor against. I fought Persians."

"Ah, well, Persians, they're civilized. But Huns are wild animals, especially these Kutrigurs. So they're always afraid of a trap. They might have stood that charge—after all there were several thousand of them—but when the trumpets started to blow and the arrows came in from the flank, they thought they'd been caught, and all they wanted was to get out again, and the only way out was back. Break? Why I've never seen anything like it. They were racing back where they came from like a cat that's met a dog on the street corner. Only a couple of hundred dead, and they broke. That's the Count for you!"

"No pursuit?"

"Well, I ask you, how could we? Get out in the open and give them a chance to see what we really were? They'd have turned and cut us to bits, and *then* took Byzantium. But that charge! Did I tell you . . ."

He had, but that didn't stop him telling again. Holy John listened and asked a few questions, always about Huns—how many, which direction their retreat had taken, what were their fighting habits, anything else the old man knew. Most of his answers were not about the Kutrigurs but the Utrigurs, whose territory lay east of the Black Sea and stretched down to the Asian corner of the Empire. The Utrigurs were Christians of a sort and allies of a sort

—indeed Belisarius had won many of his victories by his ability to control and use the almost unmanageable squadrons of Utrigur cavalry. Silvester was surprised by how practical Holy John could be, how he could systematically tease out of the old man all the knowledge that was in him. When it was all gathered Holy John blessed his informant and moved off to search among the roistering villagers for anyone who could tell him a few scraps more.

Silvester shifted away from the crowd to where Bubba lay sleeping like a soft blob of shadow in a patch of moonlight. Hidden by her bulk from the crowd he wrote out a permit to pass them through the walls of Anastasius. He had to wait till very late at night before he could get to the embers of the fire to soften his wax for the seal; he did not want any inquisitive villager watching him then, because the laws of the Empire decreed a slow death for forging official documents.

VIII

Pine Tree

AN ARMY in retreat leaves a trail like that of some vast snail; not glinting silver slime though, but smashed crops patched with black where the farms have been burnt. And their hunger is worse than the green lust of a snail, for they drive away with them the cattle they cannot eat. Anything else they kill. The stolen cattle graze the young spring wheat.

Silvester turned sadly away from the black beams which were all that were still standing of what must once have been a smallholder's home, and now was only a letter in the horrible alphabet of war.

"Why do they burn everything?" he said. "It must be easier to loot a house which isn't on fire."

"Easier but slower," said Holy John. "When the flames catch, the householder runs out with his most valuable possessions in his arms, which you take and move on. It is rough harvesting."

The trail ran west-northwest, choosing the best passage for horses, distrustful of roads. The stolen cattle slowed the Huns down, but Holy John moved even more slowly. The roads were all busy with merchants and messengers and the gleaming escorts of senior officials. Anybody might ask questions, and though Silvester had one more permit written, in the vaguest terms possible, it would soon be dangerous to use it. There would be a new Count of the Outfields now, and samples of his seal would have been displayed at all provincial centers. So it was safer to follow the rough trail of the Huns.

But inevitably the trail crossed a few roads. On the second day they came to a busy one, where Holy John insisted on waiting to try and pick up gossip about the movements of the Huns. Silvester was too scared to risk being seen with his bear, so he hid in a little wood and watched. Holy John got into talk with half a dozen passersby, and spoke for some time with a sallow young man who was dressed like some very junior official. Silvester was surprised when Holy John rejoined him looking rather disgruntled.

"Nothing," he said. "Each fool contradicts the next fool."

"What about the young man with the yellow face?" said Silvester.

"He was a fool too."

"But he talked to you for ages!"

"Ah, yes. He had news, but not for me. For you, boy. Lord Brutus is the new Count of the Outfields."

"No!"

"Yes. Furthermore there has been an affray between the servants of Celsus and Akritas, and Lord Akritas has been banished to a country estate that he has just inherited. So there is one of your enemies disposed of."

"But the other one's got much more power."

"He will be too busy in his new office to think of you, boy. And he will have many opportunities to make himself rich."

But Silvester, as they moved slowly on through the desolation left by the Huns, felt depressed and worried.

On the third day Holy John developed a sore place on
his left heel, and though he cared little about pain his
rebellious foot insisted on limping. Food was scarce. There
was little to eat after the locustlike passage of the Huns,
and for what there was the peasants asked high prices.
Luckily the Huns had not understood the value of root
vegetables, and sometimes there were clumps of last year's
parsnips still unfinished, and winter leeks. So Bubba at
least throve, though every now and then she would nudge
at Silvester's satchel to remind him that he had a pot of
perfectly good honey in there, which it was a waste to carry
any farther.

She grew glossier and stronger with the exercise she had
never known; where their path led beside woods she
tugged at her chain and tried to go and explore; any steep
slope was an excuse for a slide. But Silvester wearied of his
harsh diet, and the slow change of the landscape, and the
loneliness. His mouth lusted for meat, and fish, and bread
with a crackling crust and tender warm innards. All his life
he had lived in a torrent of talk, like a fish accustomed to a
rapid river. Now he was more and more oppressed by the
silence and loneliness, and his own emptiness, as Holy
John limped ahead, waiting in patient silence for another
message from his Maker, and Bubba padded four-footed
beside him.

The emptiness was not just in his stomach, it was in his
heart and soul. As a slave in the house of a great Byzantine
noble he had known use and purpose; his whole life had
lain clear and planned before him, and he had accepted it,
shaping himself to become a trusted slave, to marry a slave
girl chosen for him by his master, and to become the father

of more slaves. There were far worse lives in the Empire, and he had thought himself lucky.

But now all that was abolished. The wine, long before it was ready to drink, had been poured out of the bottle, wasted, and the bottle tossed into a river to float with the current. At times like these he felt in his satchel for the little leather purse and took it out and clutched it hard for mile after mile, feeling the sharp edges of the jewel under the leather. This was his purpose. He was going north to ransom the Lady Ariadne and bring her home to be mistress of a great household, as she was born to be, with himself a slave in it.

Otherwise he tried not to think about her. He was slightly comforted by the dying Greek's saying that he had never seen a Hun strike a child, because Addie looked younger than she was. But the darker corners of his mind were full of imaginings which he tried to keep invisible in their darkness—not so much death, but misery and maiming, servitude and grime. It was stupid to pretend that the wolves who had made this trail could be treating her well.

"What are you thinking about, boy?" said Holy John in an aggressive tone.

"Nothing."

"The Lady Thingummy? Suffering is a mystery, and the suffering of the innocent a greater mystery still."

"Is she part of God's purpose too?"

"Everything that happens is part of God's purpose, but I have not been shown whether she is part of *this* purpose. But pray, child, and she will find mercy. Or if not mercy, strength. I have been thinking further of the matter of the souls of animals. . . ."

Silvester was glad to be led into this obvious diversion, partly as a refuge from his own thoughts, partly because he was Byzantine enough to be deeply interested in the niceties of religious thoughts, but mainly because Holy John, sensing his need, chose to give his argument the full force of his own soul, as if he had been preaching to a gathering of great lords. The question of whether the gluttony of a bear is sinful in the same way that the gluttony of a man is sinful, may sound dry, but he filled it with sap and intellectual pleasure. Silvester became completely absorbed, and only noticed with the gathering dusk how far the trail had funneled into a valley with woods on the hills and a broad river running between fields at the bottom, and how badly Holy John was limping. He realized that Holy John had done this, on purpose, like a magician's spell, to drive his nightmares from him; but when he tried to thank him the old man became surly.

They had an interesting lesson in the gluttony of bears later that evening, when they camped in the pines above the trail. The steady, patient chink of Holy John's steel and flint filled the wood. Silvester was gathering dry branches when he stopped to watch Bubba, who was behaving in a manner he had never seen before, first sniffing like a dog all round the base of a big tree, then rearing on her hind legs to sniff among the branches, then moving back to peer with short-sighted little eyes between the pine needles. He could tell from her panting and manic grin that she was very excited about something, and he was trying to see what it was when she started to climb.

She had never climbed a tree in her life, but she was remarkably good at it, testing each branch for rottenness and keeping her paws close to the trunk all the time, where her weight imposed least strain. Where she couldn't find a branch she dug her claws into the bark and scrabbled up. Her shape became unrecognizable, a blob of shadow in the many-shadowed tree, only to be traced by her excited panting and the shower of twigs and bark that rattled down.

Suddenly a new noise was added to the crunching of her climb and the chink of the flint—a steady, humming whine, growing in volume, becoming harsh and rasping, filling the underwoods until it seemed to be all round them. Holy John slapped himself.

"Ouch!" cried Silvester. "She's found a bees' nest!"

He snatched up the precious satchel and set off up the hill, stumbling between the tree trunks and waving his arms as he ran, but he was stung several more times before the bees left him alone. Then he lay panting on dry pine needles, deep in the wood. As the tenseness of flight left him the pain of his stings began to burn until he was weeping with it. With shaking fingers he dug in the satchel for salves, though he didn't remember bringing anything that would help much.

"Boy!" called a deep voice to his left.

"Here."

He had to call twice more before Holy John came limping between the trees.

"Are you much bitten?" he said.

"Seven times," sobbed Silvester.

"I am more bitten but less hurt. Living on a pillar may weaken the muscles but it thickens the skin. What about the bear?"

"They can't hurt Bubba. With luck she'll follow my trail by smell when she's finished with the bees. Oh, they hurt!"

"We can't camp here." said Holy John. "—if wolves were to scent us . . ."

"Wolves!"

At least this new fear helped to dim the pain of the bee stings. They picked their way down through the darkening

wood with difficulty. Where they had camped some forester must have trimmed the lower branches of the pines,
but here they grew bristly right down to the ground. Silvester thought of calling for Bubba, but the wood was now so
still that he was afraid to intrude on the stifling quiet. He
had become so used to thinking that all his enemies were
part of the City, and that the uncivilized wild was an area
of safety, that he had forgotten that here too were terrors.
In places the dark under the trees was impenetrable, and
could have held any number of beasts in ambush, but then
at last they broke out at the edge of the forest.

The bees had evidently driven them over a shoulder of
hill and now they had come down on the other side,
because they saw below them a quite different landscape.
The same river glimmered in the valley bottom, but here
it took a slow curve to the east and in the middle of the
curve lay a pear-shaped island. Though it was now almost
night Silvester's eyes were still accustomed to the thicker
darkness of the wood, so he could just make out, on the
near bank of the river, a straggling group of buildings—
farm sheds and cottages, and over to one side a long house
standing by a grove of tall trees, all very black against the
dark gray fields and vineyards. The land was farmed right
up to the meadow at their feet. A few sparks shone among
the blackness of the buildings, and one or two of them
moved about.

"We are less conspicuous without the bear, at least," said
Holy John. "We can beg for food there."

Silvester stared at the scene. He felt he had looked at it
all before, the river, and the tall-treed park, and the island,
and the big house under the limes. How did he know they
were limes? It was too dark to see.

"It is the Akritas estate," he said. "Look, there are lights
in the main house. He is here himself—exiled, the Greek
on the road told you."

"It could be any noble's country place."

"The Lady Ariadne described it to me."

Holy John grunted, and was answered by a grunt from the darkness behind them. Silvester leaped for the nearest tree but Holy John said calmly, "It is the bear."

Bubba shambled out of the dark, sloppy with love and the excitement of finding Silvester again. She couldn't imagine why he hadn't stayed to share the delicious honey she'd so cleverly found, and had deserted her. She nudged him reproachfully with her nose, trying to persuade him that it was a good time for a wrestling match. Her coat was sticky with honey and covered with dead bees, and when Silvester managed to convince her that he was in no mood for wrestling she licked herself all over and immediately fell asleep.

"I will watch," said Holy John. "I need little sleep. With four-footed wolves above and two-footed ones below it would be foolish not to be vigilant."

Silvester was awakened by rain. He had chosen to sleep where he could at least see a few stars, but this meant that he was unprotected by the thick umbrellas of pine branches on either side. He moved into the dry, but could not settle to sleep again; so he sat with his back against Bubba's warm hide and watched the slow dawn come. The rain stopped, and a thin and bitter light drew the valley into shape, stretching its distances, making the objects in it stand solid from their background where all night they had simply lain like shadows. Now he could see that the tall trees were indeed limes, that several of the sheds and cottages were roofless, and that black streaks smeared the marble of all one wing of the great house, where smoke and flame had left their mark. It was a beautiful place even so, as though the hills had cupped their hands and held peace here brimming between them. It was very easy to believe that Addie could have been happy here.

Holy John had been asleep on his knees, as usual, which meant that he woke straight into prayer. Silvester only knew that he was awake by the movement of his lips. There was very little food in the satchel, the last of what they'd raided from a deserted farmstead down the valley— three raw onions and a few elderly carrots, bungy from their winter storage. Silvester ate a carrot, nibble by nibble, trying to stomach its mustiness, until Bubba woke. He watched her sniffing herself all over, relishing the memory of wild honey, and then go nosing excitedly along the area of rough weed between the grassland and the trees, as though there were bees' nests all over the place. Silvester was getting ready to run again when a large brown bird exploded out of the grass under Bubba's nose and she started back in fright and astonishment. Then she gave a little wuffle of interest and plunged her muzzle into an extra-thick clump of weeds; she emerged licking her lips and with her whole jowl dripping with yellow goo— eggs! Silvester darted forward to look for the nest, but she had eaten all its contents except for a few blue chips of shell. Biting his lip with disappointment, he went back and fetched her chain, fastened it to her collar, and let her lead him on along the rough ground. Twenty yards farther another bird took flight and he managed to lash her chain round a thorn tree before she could reach the nest; he found it himself and in it four beautiful eggs, half as large as a hen's, blue mottled with purple. He gave Bubba one of the eggs, petted her and told her how clever she was, and let her lead him on. They found two more nests, and after Bubba had had her share he had eight eggs for himself and Holy John. On his way back he recognized, from having seen the stuff for sale on market stalls, the bright serrated leaves of what the Greeks call "horta," a whole range of wild plants which can be cooked like spinach; some of it is sweet and some bitter, but it is all edible. He picked as much as he could hold and went cheerfully back to where they had slept.

Holy John had stopped praying and was staring at the estate below.

"Look," he said, "they are busy so early, reroofing that barn. Certainly their lord must be here, to stir them to work."

"Even so it's probably not the Akritas lord I met. Philip Akritas would have inherited this estate, and he's only a cousin."

"A child, wounded and protectorless. Your Akritas probably had himself made guardian."

"Yes, but . . ."

"Boy, God sent those bees," interrupted Holy John.

"But they were there already. He couldn't have sent them."

"Time is nothing to Him. He placed them there, ready for us, to drive us over the hill to a point where you would recognize this place. Why should He have done that unless your enemies were down there? Otherwise we would have stumbled in on them in the dusk."

"We've found eight eggs and quite a lot of horta."

"Good." Holy John's thin arm pointed north, up the line of the valley. "Look, all that must be Akritas—you can see that it must be one estate. With their lord here, the servants will be busy in the fields and the huntsmen out in the woods beside his land. We must go up through the woods—you see how the river bends—we can cut that corner and come down to the river beyond his land."

"I expect you're right," said Silvester. In fact he hardly thought about it. Holy John had given orders, and he was trained in obedience.

They ate by a small stream, coddling the eggs in the

ashes of their fire in a pot which Silvester had taken from a house on the second evening of their journey. The birds in the eggs were half grown, but they ate them without disgust. The horta was sweet and delicious. It must have been midmorning before they moved on, making very slow going through the steep woods, less than a mile an hour.

Silvester was hungry again by the time the woods ended, though the slope still went upward. This new country was rocky scrub, but soon it leveled out and became an open, bare upland where it was possible to see for miles across tufty grasses and long screes of shale. Three small deer galloped away to their right as they emerged over the crest.

"If we could catch one of those!" said Silvester.

"Small chance," snarled Holy John. "We must fast, unless your bear can find us eggs again."

Silvester let Bubba off her chain—she would be too afraid of losing him to stray far. He knew by now that every word the old man said had a meaning. "Your bear," instead of "the bear," was a sign of bad temper. Obviously there would be no eggs on a barren upland like this, and now it was going to be Silvester's fault for not finding them —and no use arguing that God had not put them there, for His own reasons. They trudged on, peering without hope into tussocks, oppressed by the vast, drear, hawk-ruled plateau. After two hours Silvester began to believe that Holy John had lost his way, and that they would stagger round in this barrenness until they starved. As usual the old man guessed his thought.

"I have fought in deserts," he said, "and fasted in deserts. Compared with the big sands this is a compact paradise. And beyond that next rise we will dip to a stream which will lead us back to the river."

And so it was, but they did not take that path for three more days.

IX

Willow Leaves

THEY HALTED on the crest and hissed at each other for silence. Somebody was camping by the stream, a strange and lonely bivouac. A very rough pony, saddled with a weirdly patterned saddle, was tethered where it could reach the water. It had eaten a circle on the bank from which every scrap of green had vanished. To judge by its droppings it had been there several days. Nearer the watchers was a long, flat boulder, from which a piece of cloth had been stretched down to the ground and weighted top and bottom with stones to form a curious thin tent. The cloth was ornate Byzantine work, stitched with gold, never intended for so wild a purpose. Nothing but the stream and the miserable rough horse moved in the hollow.

"Hun," whispered Holy John.

"How do you know?"

"The saddle, and that hanging—looted."

They stood wondering what it meant and what to do. Bubba made up their minds for them. Though Silvester had let her rove free she had been bored with the upland after the excitements of the forest, but here in front of her was a nice steep slope. She trundled forward and rolled happily into the camp. The horse turned, saw her and reared to the end of its tether with lashing hooves. Bubba sat up from her spree to look at the commotion, noticed the horse for the first time, and came charging back up the hill to the safety of Silvester's side. Gradually the horse quieted. Still nothing stirred under the looted hanging.

"Dead," said Holy John, and picked his way calmly down the slope. Silvester took Bubba round the rim of the hollow to where the stream slithered into it down a slant of black rocks. This cataract had made a small pool with a willow by it, to which he chained Bubba so that she could reach the water but was too far from the horse for either animal to worry the other. Then he went back to the bivouac.

Holy John was crouched peering into the funnel between the rock and the hanging. Over his shoulder Silvester could see a pair of good quality leather boots, such as a lord might wear for riding round his estates. Between the crude tent and the stream, sticks had been gathered for a fire, but never lit. By them lay the backbone of a small fish, with pieces of raw flesh still sticking to it and a little dance of flies buzzing round it.

The same buzz rose as Holy John picked up the stones that weighted the hanging and twitched the cloth aside.

Yes, it was a Hun, just like the ones Silvester had seen on the quay, with same yellow face and lank moustache and the same fringe of pale blue pottery beads running below the dark red turban. The man's clothes were hidden by a leather-sleeved cloak, worn with the fur side inwards, and all mottled with dark patches of crusted stuff which Silvester knew at once for dried blood. Looking more closely Silvester could see that his skin was a grayer yellow than that of the false slaves had been, and that the grayness was not dirt, for at the center of each cheek was a small circle of flushed flesh. So he wasn't dead yet.

Silvester knelt to feel for the pulse, but took some time to find it, so feeble was it. And just as he had it for certain the Hun's other arm slid over and gripped him by the wrist.

He leaped to his feet with a cry, and the grip was too frail to hold him. As he stood waiting for the unnecessary pounding of his heart to lessen, Holy John picked a shallow silver cup from the folds of cloth and studied it with an odd expression.

"Churches provide good loot too," he said drily, then limped to the stream and filled the vessel with clear water. When he knelt where Silvester had been the Hun's arm rose as if to strike him away but he did not flinch, raising the head gently and holding the cup to the dry lips. As the Hun sucked painfully Silvester heard the quiet mutter of a prayer. Then the head fell back and Holy John stood up.

"Will he live?" he asked.

"I don't know. Did you feel how hot he was—that's fever. And if he got his wound in the battle and it hasn't been treated at all . . ."

"It is nine days since the battle," said Holy John as if he were making up his mind about something. "He cannot live."

"We can't leave him!" cried Silvester. "He's wearing the blue beads."

"There is vanity even among wolves."

"No, don't you remember what the Greek said when he was dying—he'd brought men of the Khan's own tent, wearing the blue beads? If we can get him back, that's a way of reaching straight to the king. And the man who took Lady Ariadne was . . ."

"God does not ask the impossible," explained Holy John. "You have seen the trail his comrades left. How are we to carry one wounded Hun through country that has been ravaged like that? Every peasant we pass will try to slit his throat, and the officers of the Empire . . ."

"Look," interrupted Silvester. "If God put the bees there to drive us past Akritas, how do you know he didn't put Akritas there to drive us to this place?"

Holy John grunted dismissively. He did not appreciate suggestions from anyone else about what God's motives might or might not have been. But he had no answer.

"Anyway," said Silvester, "let me look at his wound."

That proved difficult. The few sips of water had revived the Hun a little, and now he lay glaring at them with the too-bright eyes of fever. As Silvester knelt again the Hun hissed like a cat and his farther arm struck over in a short arc; but his fever spoiled his stroke, so that the squat dagger he was holding missed Silvester's thigh by an inch. Silvester backed off and considered.

"The horse first, then," said Holy John.

This animal too was wild and vicious, but with careful approaches they calmed it enough to remove its saddle and shift it to a patch of fresh grass. Holy John carried the saddle over to the Hun and put it on the ground by him to show that they had no intention of robbing him. The Hun's tongue was licking dry lips again, so Silvester picked up the silver cup and carried it to the stream, moving out of sight behind the rock so that he could add poppy juice to the water. It was difficult to guess the right amount for a wounded man with fever, but he decided on a large dose, intending to snatch the cup away if the Hun tried to drink it all. When he knelt again by the wounded man he saw that the dagger was out and clutched on the chest, but he pretended not to notice it as he lifted the foul head and tilted the cup to the shivering lips. The Hun drank half the mixture, apparently too ill to notice the altered taste, then sank back with a gasped syllable that might have been thanks. Silvester straightened with a sigh of relief.

"The bear has found something in the water," said Holy John.

It would take some time for the poppy juice to work, so Silvester went to see what Bubba was doing. He found her straining at the end of her chain toward the little cataract, watching the water intently and grinning with excitement. As Silvester approached she lunged at the water with her farther paw in a scooping motion which sent a bright spray hurtling toward him. Drenched, he cursed with the vivid obscenities of Byzantine back streets, but she came rushing over as though she'd done something extremely clever. He braced himself for her greeting but she ran past him, again to the limit of her chain, and stood there straining. Just out of reach a brown fish flopped on the grass. Then he saw a smaller one a little beyond it, already dead. He picked them up, stunned the live one and gave the dead one to Bubba. From the smell of her breath he could tell that she hadn't scooped all her catch beyond her reach.

"You are the cleverest and most beautiful bear God ever created," he told her as he took her chain off. "Now show me how you do this marvelous trick."

She knew the note of his pleasure well, and went eagerly back to the cataract where she crouched in stillness beside the hurtling water. Several minutes passed, but she didn't move a muscle. Silvester began to think her earlier catches had been nothing but wild luck. Suddenly her right foreleg darted out in a scooping arc and water was spraying across the bank with something dark in the middle of it. Silvester just won the race to the fish.

Now he knew what to look for, he learned how to see them as they threshed their way up through the shallow foam. They were dark brown above but mottled with olive blobs below, and they seemed all to be fighting their way up to the headwaters of the stream, drawn by the mysterious impulse of the seasons. They climbed the cataract four or five at a time, with longish intervals between each fresh attempt, so he waded across at the top of the hollow and tried to help Bubba with her work. It looked easy, but he caught nothing. He had nothing like the bear's speed of strike, and though she was usually much more shortsighted than he was her eyes had apparently no difficulty in adjusting to the refraction of water. So all that happened was that she was able to eat all she caught while he fished in vain. In the end he chained her out of reach of the stream, not wanting to spoil her appetite for fishing next time the humans were hungry, and took five good-sized fish down to Holy John.

The saint stared at the catch so long that Silvester thought he was about to go into one of his epileptic seizures.

"What's the matter?" he said at last.

"A sign," muttered Holy John. "I have been praying for guidance whether we should stay or move on, and heard no answer. But now God has sent these fish, the Christ-sign, to tell me that we must stay. Blessed is He. I will make a fire."

The opium held the Hun now. He was breathing slow and shallow, but Silvester thought his temperature was a little less. In sleep the wild man looked wilder still, proud and dangerous and—even now, on the borders of death—not at all pitiful.

With steady care Silvester opened the fastenings of the

cloak and worked the arms out of the sleeves; the fur, where it wasn't matted with blood, was fine and soft and beneath it the man was wearing clothes far richer than Silvester expected to find on such a barbarian, including a silk shift pinned with a brooch made from one large amethyst. The clothes were made either to be laced down the front or to be put on over the head; the laces he could undo, but he had to use the man's sharp dagger to cut the others loose. Soon the position of the blood-stains told him that the would must be at the back, so he undid all the lacings he could reach and called Holy John. Together they carefully rolled the man over onto the strip of looted cloth. Glued together by the blood, all the clothes insisted on coming too.

"I could cook the fish now, if you're ready," said Holy John.

"I'd rather finish. But if you could warm some water . . . there's an iron pot tied to the saddle . . . and put a lot of willow leaves in it—several handfuls?"

"A magical charm?" said Holy John with surly suspicion.

"I don't think so. Learned Solomon said the infusion of willow leaves was an aid against the putrefaction of wounds."

Holy John grunted and moved off while Silvester went back to the slow, difficult and disgusting business of trying to detach fur and silk and linen from each other and the torn and suppurating flesh below. He could smell the putrefaction at once, so different from the acid goatish odor of the man's unwashed skin; but it was nearly an hour before he could look at the actual wound.

It was deep and had originally been about three inches long, running from near the base of the spine towards the right hip. It might have been made by one clean cut, such

as a spear thrust, but since then it had been worsened by
travel and its own decay to a patch of flesh as large as a
plate, all bruised and inflamed, centering on two gaping
lips of pus and blood. It stank. Silvester poured some of
the steaming infusion of willow leaves into the silver cup
and added cold water until he achieved the temperature of
blood. With this, using the cleaner strips of the man's own
clothing, he set to work to wash the wound. The parts that
didn't matter were easy, all the bruised and inflamed skin;
but on the horrible central hole he could make very little
impression. With a sigh of worry he went to look at the
droppings of the horse, poking among them with a stick
until he found what he wanted—a nest of wriggling white
maggots. He picked these out with his fingers and dropped
them in warm water, to clean them as best he could; he
squashed a couple by mistake as he fished them out, but
then he learned how to handle them. He placed the rest
into the wound and covered it with a cloth damped in the
willow leaf infusion. Holy John watched the whole of the
last operation in silence.

"What are the worms for, boy?" he said when it was
finished.

"They clean the pus out. I've never seen it done, but it's
in the books. Only I don't know if they're the right sort of
maggots. I hope it's all right—it seems strange and horrible."

"God made each of His creatures for a purpose. Shall I
cook the fish?"

"Yes, I'm nearly finished, only I'd like to keep him
warm."

"There are two good blankets rolled at the back of the
saddle," said Holy John.

Silvester stood up and looked round the dell, shaking
with exhaustion. He had been conscious for some time of

having to peer at what he was doing, but had thought this
was just tiredness. Now he saw that night had almost come,
and the banks of the hollow were glowing with the orange
of the firelight. He covered his patient with blankets and
made him as comfortable as he could, staggered up to apol-
ogize to Bubba for having neglected her, and at last settled
to a meal of tepid fish, burned in some places and raw in
others. Holy John was no cook.

When he had finished he tried to pick the maggots out
of the wound but found that he couldn't see them, even
with Holy John holding a flaming branch as near as was
safe. With another sigh of worry he covered the place up
and drew the blankets over his patient. All the while the
Hun lay as still as a man slain in battle.

Next morning he was delirious, shouting and struggling,
and had to be drugged again. To his relief Silvester found
all his maggots, who had indeed cleared much of the pus
from the wound; and the poultice had reduced some of the
inflammation. He made a fresh one of a pad of leaves and
left the Hun to sleep. Bubba fished and slid. Holy John
prayed. The day dribbled away. The Hun was still
delirious when he woke, but less feverish and fierce. He
even ate a little cooked fish.

On the second morning, before dawn, Holy John
walked down out of the hollow to get what food and news
he could from the little town in the valley which Silvester
had spotted from the hillside. He had plenty of money as
the Hun's saddlebags contained, among strange loot some
of which no Byzantine would have bothered to pick up if
he'd found it lying in the road, twenty-eight gold coins and
a lot of silver.

The Hun woke about half an hour after he had gone.

He stirred and tried to turn onto his back, but didn't struggle when Silvester restrained him; he allowed himself to be persuaded into his face-down position and then lay perfectly still as Silvester bathed and dressed the wound. The second batch of maggots had cleared almost all the pus away and Silvester was able to ease out two splinters of bone; he could see some threadlike scraps of tissue, finer than veins, shriveled into the soft scab near the spine. He ought to have tried to find their broken ends and somehow join them, but he knew this was beyond him, and probably too late anyway. He was appalled by the smallness of his knowledge after all those years of teaching by the Learned Solomon. Last night he had looked at a clear sky, full of stars, whose powers and influences a real doctor would have known so that he could cast an exact horoscope for the illness and tell the sick man's friends precisely which saints to pray to. (Holy John had laughed when Silvester had asked for suggestions, and told him to pray to the All-creator. Silvester would have expected a near-saint to have more respect for the company he would one day join.)

When the dressing was done, Silvester tied it into place with a strip of linen torn from the Hun's clothes and worked carefully under his belly so that it would hold the bandage firm. This meant that he could be rolled slowly onto his side and allowed to look about him. He nodded with an odd sort of satisfaction as he looked round the hollow, as though he was confirming to himself that he had returned to honest earth after the sick wanderings of his delirium. Then he looked at Silvester and spoke.

"I don't understand," said Silvester. "Can you speak Greek?"

The man frowned, then smiled and tapped himself on the chest.

"Urr-guk," he said.

"Silvester," said Silvester, tapping his.

"Sil—Sill-ges-turr," tried the Hun, pointing.

"Ur-gook," replied Silvester politely.

They practiced each other's names for a bit, though the Hun was quite unable to say the "v" sound and Silvester never got the rolled "r" before the "g" right. Tired of that, the Hun called out a word which Silvester couldn't have tried to pronounce, but the horse understood it and whinnied and strained toward them on the end of its tether. Silvester undid the rope and led the animal over. It nuzzled gently at its master, who spoke to it in a strange, metallic language all of whose words seemed to have one hard emphasis on the first syllable and then to trail away. Silvester took the horse back and tethered it well down the stream before he went to fetch Bubba. He was anxious that she should make a good impression, because he felt it was desperately important, for Addie's sake, that they should get on well with this Hun—though, as Holy John had said, it was difficult to see how they were to smuggle a badly wounded man for two hundred miles though country that had been taught a cruel lesson in hating Huns.

When Bubba ambled into his line of vision Urrguk cried out in astonishment and smiled like a happy child.

"Kutt-ri," he said several times. "Kutt-ri. Kutt-ri."

Then he prodded himself on the chest with his short thumb and said, "Kutt-rigur," and glanced at Silvester to see whether he had understood. Silvester smiled politely at the mild pun, wondering whether the Hun thought it a lucky omen that the Hun's word for "bear" was much the same as his word for his own race. But Bubba watched Urrguk with growing suspicion; the hackles on her spine rose and she turned her head half away—a gesture that looked like shyness but that Silvester knew for a sign of distrust and danger. He guessed what was troubling her.

"Stupid bear," he said in his gentlest voice. "This isn't the man who hit you. This is a quite different Hun, altogether more refined and polite. Besides, he's got a great hole in his back, and if you ask my opinion as a medical man I doubt if he'll ever walk again—he's broken a lot of nerves. In fact it's a miracle he's alive. He must be as tough as a charioteer. . . . Ah, come on, you fat female, he *likes* you. And you're going to have to keep company with him all up to the Danube; and if you make that amount of fuss about a barbarian man, what are you going to say to a barbarian *horse?*"

Bubba liked to be joked with, though she never understood any of the jokes. As Silvester cajoled her the hair on her back sank smooth, but she still clearly felt suspicious of the Hun and wheeled away from him before Silvester had finished speaking. This brought her round so that she was face to face with the horse when he referred to it; she'd become quite used to its presence in the camp, but had not come as near to it as this before. Her snarl rumbled and rose, and she tugged Silvester off balance in her determination to get away from the obscene creature. He released the chain and let her go, but looked to see how Urrguk was taking her reaction to all things Hunnish. Urrguk was laughing, but the movement of his diaphragm must have twitched some tattered nerve, because a squall of pain blew across his face and he sank sweating to his rug. Silvester persuaded him to lie on his front and rest, and then took Bubba fishing.

When she was bored with that they had a wrestling match, in the course of which he found that her breath was beginning to smell horribly fishy, so he took her down the hollow and chained her to a thorn tree in the middle of a patch of coarse weeds, hoping that she would dig for roots and restore her breath to its proper warm, sweet vegetable odor. She promptly went to sleep, so he picked some "horta" for the humans. While he was doing so he recognized by its unmistakable aniseedy smell a feathery plant of young fennel—the herb God made for fish, as Fat Luke used to say. He picked it in memory of that gross artist, built up the fire, and cleaned the fish that Bubba had caught.

Before he started cooking he went to see whether Urrguk was awake, because he didn't want to break into healing sleep in order to feed him. He found that the Hun had worked himself up the rug until his head was clear of it and now was carefully twitching out all the grass and weeds from the patch of earth he could reach. At first Silvester thought this must be a symptom of returning delirium, but then he saw that the work was too methodical, that there was some purpose in it. He mimed that he was angry, that rest was important, that it was vital not to strain the wound, but Urrguk clicked at him and grinned and went on.

Silvester wrapped two of the fish in wet dock leaves and left them in shadow. The other two he stuffed with fennel and then threaded nose to tail onto a long stick of peeled willow. He set a little water to boil for the horta, then placed the willow stick into the forks of two branches stuck upright in the ground on either side of the fire. It was tricky work, not only seeing that the stick didn't burn through and the fish cooked properly, but that none of their scarce wood was wasted—they had found a dead tree half a mile down the stream, but it was a slow business breaking logs off it and carrying them up to the camp. The juices of the fish fell into the ashes and hissed into little sputters of yellow flame. At last the skin began to puff itself into bubbles where the steam from the hot flesh below couldn't escape, and he decided they were done. He slid them onto two silver dishes which he'd found in Urrguk's loot, drained the horta, and carried the food over to the

Hun, who made greedy noises and stopped his strange task of smoothing the earth in front of him.

He reached out for his plate, but Silvester wouldn't give it to him. Instead he teased the pinkish flesh away from the bones with his own knife and Urrguk's dagger, then held out a morsel on the point of the dagger and popped it into Urrguk's mouth. Urrguk allowed himself to be fed in this effortless way—like a baby bird—until Silvester tried a mouthful of horta on him. He immediately spat it out. Silvester clucked at him like a nursemaid and ate some horta himself, smiling despite the acid taste as he chewed —he hadn't realized he'd picked bitter horta.

"Purifies the blood," he explained, putting on a bedside manner, and tried again. This time Urrguk eyed the green mess with suspicion but ate it. But when he'd finished only half his fish and three mouthfuls of horta he shook his head, muttered what might be thanks and returned to his strange task. Silvester brought him water to drink, ruthlessly doped. If the man wouldn't rest of his own will he must be made to.

Bubba slept all afternoon and when she woke Silvester let her off her chain. She drank at the stream and then decided on an enlivening tumble. Sleep, or something, made her careless, so that her usual slithering roll turned into a somersault which finished with her sitting bolt upright in the shallowest part of the stream, looking round her in bewilderment and outrage at the world that had pranced about so. She shook the water out of her fur and climbed the slope, sniffing at it as she went to see whether it had been booby-trapped. Silvester was lying with his chin on his hands watching her let herself down her slide a couple of inches at a time, and between each small move-ment peering round at the landscape as if to dare it to stand on its head again, when a deep voice spoke above him.

"I have news and bread, boy. Which will you take first?"

"I could listen and eat at the same time, but Bubba's caught some more fish. Shall I cook them?"

"Do that, while I pray."

By the time the fish were ready the sun was out of the hollow, leaving it a pool of shadows in which the stream burbled, the horse stood patient and inscrutable, twitching at flies, and Urrguk and Bubba snored on different notes. Holy John rose wearily and opened the sack he had carried from the valley. It contained a slab of heavy, blackish bread, a bag of oatmeal, a cheese, a small flask of oil and a parsnip.

"How is the Hun?" he said.

"Better—he wasn't delirious today, but I had to drug him again because he wouldn't rest. His name's Urrguk. Thank you for the parsnip."

Silvester thought it oddly kind of the old man to carry all the way up from the valley this heavy vegetable, almost valueless to anyone but a bear. But Holy John was frowning at his plate.

"What have you done to the fish?" he asked.

"I stuffed it with fennel."

"Gluttony is among the greater sins."

"Fat Luke used to say that God made fennel for fish."

"Luke was the slave of men who were themselves the slaves of gluttony. Now . . ."

"Then what did God make fennel for?"

"To be itself. To stand feathery in the wind. Who knows?"

"But its flavor—it goes so well with fish. He must have had a reason for that."

"It is in its pure essence, boy, that each thing rejoices in

its Creator. To compound those essences in order to titil-
late the curious palate of fallen man . . ."

We will not follow Holy John through the many-
winding paths that connect theology with cooking. Even
Silvester was sighing with impatience before Holy John
had had his say out and was eating now-cold fish.

"You said you had news," he said at last.

"Rumors only, but all with the same hard center. The
people in the market were almost rioting with rage
because they have heard that the Emperor has made a
truce with the Khan Zabergan, and offered him a vast sum
of gold if he will take a safe conduct across the Danube and
ravage the provinces no more."

"But that can't be true! Belisarius beat them!"

"Only one battle. Each day without defeat their courage
grows, and their greed grows with it. The Emperor's offer
may not be honorable, but it's sensible."

"Why were the people in the town angry?"

"The Huns came fast and took little plunder, but on
their return they have pillaged all they could. This town
has already suffered, and they think it unjust that their
neighbors to the north should not suffer equally. Furthermore a proclamation has been made that Hun stragglers
are not to be harmed, but helped on their way."

"So at least we can use the roads."

"We are still very near Akritas. I asked in the town, and
your enemy is indeed there. So we will have to go carefully,
and you be ready to hide. But Lord Akritas is in disgrace,
so his influence will not reach far."

A new thought struck Silvester—a new hope.

"Do you think the treaty will include the Huns returning their captives?"

"Not without ransom. A beaten army is difficult to hold.
If the Khan tries to separate them from their loot, there

might be a new Khan. How soon can your Hun move?"

"I don't know. I think his legs are paralyzed. However tough he is it'll be at least a week before he can sit on a horse."

But Urrguk had other ideas.

Silvester woke later than usual, to find the fire lit and Holy John praying. He went to see how his patient was.

Urrguk had evidently been awake a long time, because the smooth patch he had made was smooth no more. It contained a picture, scratched in the earth with the point of a dagger in simple, coarse lines, but very vigorous and unmistakable in its meaning. There was the horse, walking, riderless. From its saddle two long poles stretched back to trail on the ground—Urrguk had drawn this part of the picture tilted sideways, so that Silvester could see the crosspieces between the poles forming a braced rectangle. On the rectangle lay the body of a man. Urrguk pointed at the body, said his own name and prodded his chest. Then he pointed north.

Silvester knelt beside him and took the dagger. In another part of the cleared patch he drew a line, and pointed east; then he drew a second line and pointed west. Those were the two horizons. On the eastern horizon he drew the rising sun, then drew it again high between the lines, then setting in the west. That was a day. Slowly, counting in Greek as he did so, he extended three fingers below his picture. Three days. Then he pointed at Urrguk's picture and then toward the north. They would go in three days, trailing the Hun on an improvised stretcher. Perhaps, he thought, if he could find a tree downstream with branches long enough, their springiness might ease the dangerous jolting.

The Hun frowned, furious. He pointed at his own picture and began to jabber. He erased the setting sun from Silvester's picture and stabbed his finger down on the noon one. He wanted to leave that very day.

Silvester spoke to him gently, and pointed at the wound in his back; then he started to draw a picture of a man digging a grave, but before he had finished the spade Urrguk snarled like a trapped beast, snatched his dagger, and rubbed the grave scene out. He pointed several times at the noon sun, himself and the north. Silvester could only keep smiling and shaking his head like an idiot. At last Urrguk sank back, rested for a few seconds, then cried out five syllables like a war cry.

A commotion rose at the bottom of the dell. The inscrutable horse was heaving towards them, tugging and jerking at its halter, which Silvester hadn't bothered to fasten at all securely as the animal seemed so unlikely to stray from its master; a branch snapped and it shook its mane and trotted over. At another command from Urrguk it moved up until it stood close beside him, trembling from the sudden urgency of action. He looked under its belly to where his saddle lay on the ground, frowned and muttered, then reached his hand up to the horse's foreleg and used that to pull himself slowly into a sitting position, talking all the time through gritted teeth to steady the horse. The pain in his face was awful to see.

"No! No!" cried Silvester, trying to loosen his grip, but Urrguk simply struck him away, a blow like iron, and reached for the long mane. Urgently Silvester pointed at the pictures.

Urrguk ceased from his fierce effort and stayed where he was, looking sideways over his shoulder. Quickly Silvester knelt and drew in the setting sun, laid one finger on the picture, and pointed at the rising sun. They would leave tomorrow morning. Smiling through the sweat of pain, Urrguk allowed himself to be lowered to his rug.

Silvester looked round to see why Holy John hadn't come to help him. The saint was still on his knees, but shaking with what might be some huge spiritual effort or might be simply an epileptic fit. In either case his mind was far out of reach. So Silvester knelt and dressed the wound, finding it oozing or bleeding in several places and freshly inflamed all around. Urrguk stood his ministrations with total patience, but sniffed the water Silvester brought him to drink and tasted it with suspicious care. No more poppy juice.

Even so he was asleep by the time Silvester left the dell to look for poles to make a litter from. He was carrying Urrguk's sword with a curious feeling of embarrassment, though there was no one but hawks to watch him on the wide moor. It turned out that a tool designed and perfected for taking life is extraordinarily ill-adapted for lopping branches.

X

hare

THE OFFICER gleamed on his horse, the steel and brass of his armor made brighter by the poppy-red cloth of his tunic. His horse fidgeted; the file of soldiers slouched on the paved road. Holy John, proud and dirty, stood firm and answered the questions. Urrguk lay like a corpse on the litter. *His* horse didn't fidget.

The road here ran across a marshy flatness through which the river doubled and twisted; the road had been built by the old Romans to take their legions north for Trajan's wars, so it had been engineered to last for a thousand years, running straight across the marsh on a high causeway. When Holy John had flung up an arm as a sign of possible danger, Silvester, walking a hundred yards behind, had plunged with Bubba down the bank and worked forward, looking for a culvert to hide in. There had been no culvert, but the grass was long on the bank, so now he crouched with Bubba directly below the group on the road and listened to the talk.

"I carry Christ to the Huns," said Holy John.

"It doesn't look like Christ," shouted one of the soldiers.

"It looks like a bloody Hun."

The other soldiers laughed and repeated the jeer to each other.

"Silence, there!" squealed the officer. "The next man to open his mouth without my permission will be flogged. Flogged, d'you hear me?"

The soldiers burst into song:

Flogged for the Emperor,
Flogged for the Lord,
Why was the sentry flogged?
WHY? Because he snored.
Flogged when we come and
Flogged when we go.
Why are we standing here?
Flogged if I know.

"Silence!" yelled the officer, as soon as they *were* silent. "You'll have to hurry, my man—we're herding the Huns north as fast as we can drive them. Have you got a pass?"

"God wrote my pass," said Holy John.

"Who took the bribe?" shouted the soldiers. The officer didn't even trouble to scream at them.

"You'd better have a proper pass," he said in a fretful voice. "Go to the magistrate in Lycopolis—that's ten miles on—and tell him you're accompanying a Hun straggler north. You're entitled to sustenance allowance, of course."

"The Lord will sustain me."

"Yes, yes, I daresay. You haven't come straight up from Adrianopolis?"

"My feet were led through byways."

"Uh-huh. Byways. You didn't come across a boy leading a bear, by any chance."

"Not by any chance," said Holy John quietly and with perfect truth.

"Well, keep your eyes skinned and if you do spot them report to the nearest official. There's a reward . . ."

"For the official," called a soldier.

"And they were last seen heading . . ." continued the officer, but not for long. Silvester heard a brisk scuffle, and suddenly there was the officer, towering over him at the top of the bank, all foreshortened by the slope and the added height of his horse. It was a terrifying manifestation of the authority of the Empire. He threw himself into the grass and lay cowering, not having given himself time to see that the officer was not looking down the bank but shouting curses over his shoulder.

Holy John said afterwards that the scuffle had been the officer's horse trying to bite Urrguk's horse, and that Urrguk's horse had been experienced enough to bite first. But Silvester didn't know that, and could only lie cowering, locked in fright. Bubba, however, reacted with violence, rearing on her hind legs and bellowing at the horse. The horse bolted down the road.

The soldiers shouted as the hoofbeats died away. Bubba's bellow had been muffled by the officer's curses and the bank, and they were not aware that anything had happened to cause the bolting other than the bite from Urrguk's horse.

"Wonder if the old scarecrow's got any cash on him," said one of them.

"Loot in those saddlebags, more likely," said another. "Grab hold of that bridle."

Silvester heard another shout, not in Greek, and then the rapid rattle of Urrguk's horse making off down the paving with the stretcher bouncing behind it. Silvester

winced for the wound. The soldiers swore at each other for
their slowness.

"We've still got the scarecrow, anyway," suggested one of
them.

"Sons of Belial," said Holy John in a slow, heavy voice.
"I hereby curse you. May the Blessed Thomas withdraw
his ward from your eyes, that you become blind. May the
Blessed Luke cease his vigilance over your intestines, that
they be afflicted with cramps and vile parasites. For your
skin may the Blessed . . ."

Against those eight sullen infantrymen he paraded the
armies of heaven, armed with incalculable potencies and
summoned in the voice of true authority, not the ranting
of a chinless stripling who hadn't yet learned to control his
horse. The soldiers shuffled.

"Now then, now then," broke in one of them. "It was
only a bit of fun, Father. You don't know what life's like in
the army. If . . ."

His voice trailed away. Holy John allowed the silence to
thicken.

"I withdraw my curses," he said at last with a strange
mildness. "And seeing that I am ignorant of life in the
army, I will give you a blessing."

The soldiers grumbled uneasy thanks.

"I bless your weapons," said Holy John, "that the ser-
geant does not notice the dirt on them. I bless your sentry
boxes, that the officer does not see you asleep in them.
I bless your packs, that the loot finds its way into them. I
bless your noses, that they lead you to the wine barrels. I
bless your bodies, that the enemy attacks the other end of
the line."

"Holy Christopher!" cried a soldier. "Who taught you
that?"

"I had nine years on the Persian frontier," said Holy John. "What is this about a bear and a boy?"

"I dunno," said a soldier. "It seems they're on the Lists —the boy, anyway. I've never heard of a bear being on the Lists."

"Poor child," said Holy John. "March on, my children, but listen to me first. I have seen a lot of officers, and that one of yours is near breaking. Next time, or perhaps the time after, someone *will* be flogged."

The soldiers discussed the notion almost soberly, lapsed into ribaldry, and shambled off to look for their officer. From time to time they shouted back at Holy John as though he were an old comrade-in-arms instead of a traveler they'd intended to beat and rob. Flat on his belly Silvester crawled up the bank and watched them go from the weeds at the edge of the road.

"How much did you hear, boy?" said Holy John.

"I'm on the Lists," croaked Silvester.

"If they have the story right," said Holy John. "Can the Hun travel, except by road?"

"I think it would kill him," said Silvester. "You know what the jolting was like coming down the stream."

"And you cannot use the roads—at least until we find whether this story is true. Very well, we will follow the road across the marsh, you and the bear walking at the bottom of the bank. If I see any danger I will start to sing a hymn. At those hills, you will have to leave the road and work round the outskirts of this town, Lycopolis. I will go to the magistrates for this permit, and that will take me all day tomorrow. While I am there I will try to confirm this story about the Lists. We will meet at the fifth milepost beyond Lycopolis the day after tomorrow. You must take the food—we can buy more in the town."

But the road became very busy by the time they reached the low range of hills at which the marsh ended. It proved impossible to exchange food from the saddlebag to Silvester's satchel without acting in a way that might look odd to passersby, though they waited for twenty minutes.

"It's all right," called Silvester at last, hoping that the noise of a cart rumbling away would muffle his voice from other hearers. "Bubba can find me food. Goodbye."

"May the merciful Christ guide your footsteps. And may the bear behave herself."

Crouching for cover behind the terrace of what had once been a vineyard, Silvester led Bubba away. Despair was rooted in his heart. He was on the Lists!

Lycopolis was a small town, lying in a bowl of the hills, deriving what importance it had from being at the point where two paved roads from the south joined to run north. The bowl was farmed for some way round the town, and the heights of the hills were wooded, but between the fields and the woods ran an erratic strip of more open ground, which was usually almost a mile wide and kept from going wild by large flocks of sheep. These parts made easy going, with the air fresh and sweet and the close-nibbled turf pleasant to walk on, though he had to make several detours through the fringes of the woods where there was a danger of Bubba's appearance alarming the sheep. And at times a stream from the hilltops cut deep into the contours, making a narrow but steep gully which it might take him half an hour to find a way through.

But even across the springiest turf he trudged with leaden steps. The Lists, the Lists, the long Lists of the names of men and women wanted for questioning by the shambling, slow-witted but implacable monster which was the government of the Empire. Not names of criminals wanted by provincial courts, but the prey of the Great Palace itself. Once a man's name was on the Lists, nothing would ever remove it, not even death. There were frequent tales of men who had lived a life of disguise and hiding and at last died in peace; and then their widows, fearful for their husbands' immortal souls if they buried them under a false name, had told the truth to their priest, and the Palace at last had come to hear of it, and the bodies had been dug up and beheaded, or tortured even, according to sentence. The Lists were arranged in categories of importance, and when those in the first category were caught they disappeared into the dark cells beneath the Palace and the light never saw them again, nor they the light.

Silvester could not imagine how his name was on the Lists in any category at all; but the man who had asked for news of him had not been a bored and busy minor official, but an officer in command of a file of soldiers. So he trudged on, without pleasure, without hope, and Bubba slid beside him as silent as cloud-shadow.

In that total stillness of midafternoon when all sane animals are lying in the shade, he struggled through crackling brushwood out of a difficult shrubby gully and stumbled, careless with weariness, onto the grassland of the other side to find a flock of sheep. The sheep bolted, bleating, at the sight of Bubba. A lean dog yelped at the scattering fringes of the flock, trying to herd it together. A dark boy of Silvester's age stood stolidly in front of him, with a leather strap drawn back between both hands over his left shoulder.

"No!" shouted Silvester, jumping in front of Bubba. A stone from a shepherd's sling was unlikely to kill a bear—

though it might a wolf or a man—but it could hurt her enough to make her dangerous.

"She's quite tame," he said. "I'm sorry we frightened your sheep."

The boy answered in a dialect of the hills which Silvester didn't understand except for the negative tone. With a sigh he pulled his black flute from his satchel and played a few notes. When Bubba started to dance the boy smiled. Silvester smiled back and put his flute away.

Far down the meadow the dog had rounded the sheep into a tight knot and now had turned, watching up the hill to see whether his master had coped with the enemies. The boy shouted. The dog lay down on the grass. The bunch of sheep broadened as they began to graze again.

Laughing, the boy sat down on a hummock of short grass and picked up a pipe, on which he played, note-perfect, the tune Silvester had played. Bubba reared on her hind legs at the sound, but when she saw it wasn't Silvester playing she sat down, baffled. Silvester teased and petted her, then led her back to the gully to rootle for food. When he returned to the hummock the boy offered him a hunk of flat, gray bread and a piece of reeking goat cheese. He ate them with relish.

Neither he nor the boy knew one word of the other's language, but they were happy together for an hour, trying each other's tunes on their pipes and watching the sheep move through the heat-haze. Bubba badgered her way up to the dark woods. Suddenly the boy stiffened, laid his hand for stillness on Silvester's arm, and with slow movements picked up his sling. Silvester could see nothing different about the meadow anywhere. The sling whipped forward with a fizz and a crack. A brown blob bounced into the air thirty yards down the hill. The boy crowed a

triumphant cry and ran forward, stooped and carried his
prey back to show to Silvester—a dead hare with no
wound, only a dribble of blood from its nostrils.

Silvester was astonished, and also filled with envy that
this ignorant shepherd who could speak no Greek and had
probably never seen a proper city could yet do a trick like
that. The boy led him up to a place where a jutting rock
cast a small shadow of coolness and showed him his larder,
which contained another dead hare, the rest of the bread
and cheese, and a curious flat brown object, leathery above
and spongy below. Silvester pointed at it and made questioning noises.

The boy took him into the edge of the wood. There lay
a huge old sweet-chestnut tree, uprooted in some gale, but
still with a few bright leaves at the tips of its wizening
boughs. From its bole forty or fifty of these brown objects
grew, jutting like balconies from a wall. The boy broke
one off with some effort and handed it to Silvester, who
put it to his lips to taste. But the boy restrained him and
went into an elaborate mime to show it must be boiled before it was eaten. At that moment Bubba came grum-
bling between the trees, sulky with the meagerness of the
menu of roots in the gully. On an impulse Silvester offered
her the brown fungus. She sniffed at it, took it in her
jaws, dropped it to the ground, patted it with her paw and
when it didn't offer her any sport by trying to run away
chewed it up raw. The shepherd boy laughed with delight and helped Silvester break off a couple more to put
in his satchel, and when Silvester mimed that he must go,
he insisted on giving him one of the hares.

There was nothing to give in return, but when Silvester
shrugged his apologies the boy drew a wickedly sharp little
knife and pointed at Bubba. He laughed at Silvester's
alarm and snicked off a little lock of his own hair to show

what he wanted, so Silvester held Bubba still while the boy
cut a few dark hairs from her tail. There was no telling
what he wanted them for—a symbol of manhood, perhaps,
or some country magic or medicine. So on this odd bargain
they parted.

Silvester was lucky with his fire that evening. He had
picked up a couple of flints on his way, and the hollow he
chose to camp in was full of wood so dry that it gave no
smoke at all. He roasted the hare slowly, thinking about
the shepherd boy—a serf, presumably, the son of a serf and
father of serfs to be. Less lucky even than a slave, who
could be freed by a satisfied master, whereas the laws of the
Empire allowed no escape from the linked generations of
serfdom. But the boy was free, too, happy in the world he
knew and his own position in its order; able to kill hares
with a stone and a leather strap and to defend his flock
from bears also. He was not on the Lists.

Suppose . . . suppose all the unlikely luck in the world
worked for Silvester and he found Addie and ransomed
her and brought her home to be the Lady Ariadne, even
then all her enormous wealth couldn't buy him off the
Lists. That was almost the only thing in the Empire
beyond the reach of a bribe—oh, you could bribe the
officer who came to take you, if you were rich enough and
he prepared to take the risk, but all he could do for the
money was to report that you had fled, or perhaps died.
Your name would still be on the Lists.

But even so the meeting with the shepherd boy had
whittled away something of his despair. He was now no
less lonely, but felt a little less exposed. He was so far from
the City that he met inhabitants who knew no Greek; he
would have starved in that wood without ever recognizing
that the big tree-fungus was edible; he had lost Holy John
and Urrguk. And yet it was possible to meet people who

were not enemies, who treated him with kindness, who gave him food without payment. It was even possible that Addie, too, had met someone like the shepherd boy.

The roasted hare was unspeakably tough, so he chewed the juices out of it and spat away the fibers. At last he slept, curled up against Bubba for warmth, hoping too that nothing else in the woods would care to attack so large an animal.

By noon next day he could see the northern road from the hillside, running so straight across a plain of fresh green growth that it was easy to think that giants hiding in the hills at either end were pulling it taut. This road was even busier than the old one, and seemed totally exposed all around where he guessed the fifth milestone must be. So he ate the last of the hare and dozed the afternoon away. Bubba appreciated the rest so much that she was difficult to wake when he started down the hill in the dusk. His intention was to search for a hiding place somewhere along the road, and if he didn't find one to chalk a message on the milestone with a soft white stone he had found on the edge of the wood. This was common practice among travelers, though against the law, so Holy John would be sure to look.

It was almost night when he reached the plain, and found it nothing like so flat as it had seemed from the hills, but a series of rounded hillocks and rises, and all covered with a uniform growth of knee-high grass. Being a city boy it took him time to realize that the earth itself was softer than was natural, and then more time to decide that this was because it had been cultivated, which in turn meant that the grass was not grass, but wheat. And no landlord, however rich, could possibly own a single stretch like this, all down to one crop. He halted on a rise in the middle of that desert of fresh growth and laughed aloud. Bubba was startled out of her sulks by the sudden noise.

"We're trespassing on the Emperor's wheat," he said. "If we aren't on the Lists already, we will be now."

Absurdly cheered he wallowed on, up and down the wavelike rises, until suddenly there was the road.

He came to a milestone only a hundred yards along it, but so old that the writing on it was illegible, even under the rising moon; but patiently running his fingertips over the surface he discovered a shallow groove, slanting, and another slanting away from it. That was the V. Now that he knew where to feel he quickly found a vertical groove beside it, but only one. VI is six. He woke Bubba again and plodded back to the fifth milestone.

XI

White Wand

THE ROAD was busy by midmorning. An ox wagon was moving south along it carrying a load of timber. The oxen hauled with a slowness that seemed drowsy until you reckoned the weight of the clumsy trunks behind them, and the load itself was almost as wide as the road, so that there was a lot of shouting and argument when anything on wheels wanted to pass them, either from in front or behind. Even pedestrians didn't seem able to get by without a few curses.

Lying in the young wheat, Silvester watched an imperial messenger come clattering up from the south. For him, at least, the sullen ox drivers had to haul in to the side of the road. The charioteer forced his horses at the narrow gap, and Silvester could hear his sudden shout of anger when the near-side wheel teetered above the embankment; but the messenger, a fat bald man, didn't even look up from where he sat hunched in the back of the chariot, nursing the white wand of his office. The ox whips cracked and the slow beasts leaned into their yokes to start the big cart

creaking south again. Silvester watched the chariot hurry
north; half a mile farther on it slowed again for the bald
messenger to stand and exchange the necessary salutes with
an inferior messenger on horseback, coming in the other
direction. Both messengers halted to talk. Silvester's nape
prickled with the notion that they must be talking about
him, that every road in the Empire was scurrying with
spies looking for a boy leading a bear. He was relieved
when they exchanged salutes again and parted.

Farther south the timber cart was again in trouble, but
not with any officials this time, for it had refused to budge
an inch from the center of the causeway, and the traveler
coming the other way had chosen to struggle through on
the far side. Silvester heard the drivers' raucous curses
stilled as suddenly as if a charm had locked their tongues; a
deep and unmistakable resonance took over, seeming almost to reverberate to the far hills. Out of the dust of the
ox cart's passage emerged a gaunt pedestrian leading a
horse. Behind the horse trailed a litter. Silvester watched
the horseback messenger hurtle past them and through the
moving dust-cloud of the ox cart. He looked north and
south along the road. The chariot was now almost a mile
away. For the moment no other travelers showed.

He jumped to his feet, put his hands to his mouth and
let out the long and whooping call with which the Greens,
the Monophysite faction, cheered on their charioteers in
the arena. It was a chant intended for ten thousand
frenzied spectators; here, now, in this green desert, coming
from a single throat, it sounded wild and strange.

It was also unmistakable. Every Byzantine would know
it, even one who had spent his years in the City perched on
a pillar. Holy John shaded his eyes and peered against the
morning sun. Silvester waved. Holy John saw him and at
once made an urgent gesture for him to drop back into

cover. The grimy arm pointed north, then at the sun, then traced the long arc to the western horizon. They would meet again that evening.

And the story was true. Silvester was on the Lists.

"In the first category, and starred for urgency," said Holy John. "Offences against the Emperor's person."

Silvester found himself unable to speak. He opened his mouth in silence a couple of times, but no words would come. In any case he had nothing to say, so he turned back to the mundane business of removing the bandages from Urrguk's back; the wound had bled and oozed again, and not being tended for three days had stuck the rags to itself. Holy John spoke again in a musing tone.

"If I did not know it was the Lord's doing," he said, "I would think it strange that all the muscles and nerves of the Empire are bent on finding one boy. It is as though the Empire were a monstrous beast, plagued by many mortal sicknesses, which ignores them all but cannot rest until it has contrived to scratch a little itch on its back where its hoof does not reach."

"But I've never seen the Emperor!" cried Silvester, so loud that the cliffs of the ravine echoed.

"You a Byzantine," scoffed Holy John, "and unable to grasp a metaphysical concept! My guess is that Count Brutus, new in his office, thought that he could safely use the imperial agents to find you. Then some other official, anxious to put this newcomer in his place, demanded justification, which Count Brutus gave by saying that you were a spy who had helped the Greek slave master in his treachery. So now he will never have you as his witness. He has overreached."

"But how do you know? Are you sure?"

"The lists give no reasons. Even to see your name on

them cost a gold piece. But there is an imperial messenger on the roads with no task but to organize the search for you."

"A fat man in a chariot carrying the white wand?"

"That is him." Holy John was quite unsurprised by Silvester's guess. "He is a second-grade official in the Department of the Outfields."

Silvester had been neglecting his work, and now Urrguk spoke suddenly.

"He is asking how long you will be," said Holy John.

"Some time. Oh! How did you understand him?"

"He has been teaching me the language. I carry Christ to the Huns, and the All-creator aids me; but it is asking Him for too easy a path that He should by a miracle, as at Pentecost, make the Huns understand my language. Therefore I must speak theirs."

"Well, you can tell him that his wound hasn't healed much because it hasn't been looked after, and the journey is a strain on it, but I'll do what I can."

"I bought fresh cloths in the town. But I haven't learned all the words in the medicine book yet."

In fact, as Silvester could hear, Holy John knew only a very little Hunnish so far. His tongue had trouble with the clatter of syllables that came after the heavy opening stress of each word. But he talked with Urrguk all the time he was making up the fire and stirring the lentil soup (for the saddlebags were full of real food, bought off stalls and not simply culled from the wild). He tried each new word several times over, shaping his tongue to it, and allowed Urrguk to correct him with a meekness that the servants in the household of the Lord Celsus would never have thought him capable of. Urrguk was amused. The notion that anybody should attempt to learn anybody else's language was clearly strange to him, so he treated the lessons as a sort of game, a way of passing the time, and probably of distracting his attention from the steady ache of his wound, now increased by Silvester's unavoidable nagging little tugs as he tried to loosen the dressing.

Before he had finished Bubba came whining up from the meager stream, to complain that somebody had forgotten to put any fish in it.

Silvester had kept in touch with Holy John by occasional glimpses of the road. He had seen that Holy John was traveling very slowly, and had imagined that this was deliberate, so that Bubba and Silvester should be able to keep up despite the rougher country they were forced to travel. In fact Silvester had come first to this convenient camp, a stony but wooded ravine which was crossed by the road on a bridge built by the old Romans.

Now, though, Silvester noticed that Holy John was limping much more heavily than before as he moved about the little clearing, and when they at last settled to eat he saw a jagged cut running slantwise across the old man's instep. So perhaps he'd been forced to travel slowly.

"You've hurt your foot," he said.

Holy John was angry at his even noticing it, and refused to let him look at the wound or to tell him how it had happened. His vehemence became agitation, which changed suddenly into one of his strange trances, or seizures—a violent vibration of the whole body, followed by long gasping sighs and then rigid stillness. Bubba stirred from her doze, growled, and moved farther away from him.

"Foolish bear," said Silvester, though he in his heart was also frightened by the gaunt old man who knelt, shadowed by the firelight, while his spirit roamed the gray marches between the living and the dead. But after he had licked the last of the lentils out of the pot and drunk a little of the dark wine which Holy John had bought in Lycopolis,

Silvester became inquisitive. First he lit a fresh fire of small, bright burning twigs behind the saint and used its brief light to inspect the sore instep, which was exposed by the attitude of prayer. He cleaned it out as best he could and still Holy John did not stir, no more than he would have if he'd been drugged. So with trembling fingers he took the saint's pulse. It was as slow as a funeral march, and the flesh was as cold as that of a two-hour corpse. With renewed shudders Silvester crept away to the other side of the clearing and lay down beside Bubba.

He was fetching water from the stream for breakfast when he was startled by a strange, half-mad cackle from the camp; he went back with a chilly prickle of alarm on the nape of his neck, though it was now almost sunrise and far too light for ghosts or ghouls. Holy John had been praying when Silvester woke up, but when he carried the water into the clearing the saint was obviously back in the waking world and smiling with a strange ruefulness.

"What was that noise?" said Silvester.

"That was I. You may look at my foot, boy, and do what you can for it."

So Silvester settled to the task, which was of course less gruesome than tending Urrguk's wound but still not very enjoyable before breakfast. Suddenly Holy John spoke again.

"I have been rebuked for my pride," he said. "I gloried in my conquest of pain, not for my God's sake but for pride in the power of my will. But in the night I spoke with God, and He rebuked me. Pride is a great sin, and this morning I sought how to do penance for my sinfulness, and suddenly I saw that to scourge myself, or to fast, punishing my body for my will having chosen to punish my body, would be ridiculous. That is why I laughed."

"I thought it was always good to mortify the flesh," said Silvester.

"The flesh is nothing, either mortified or pampered. I have sometimes been tempted by the Gnostic heresy that flesh is in fact illusion, created by the devil to lure man to neglect his everlasting soul. But it is the creation of the All-creator, and is given us to do His work. If that work can best be done by suffering, then the flesh must suffer. The man who carved the holes in your flute paid no heed to the suffering of the tree, from which it had come. When he buffed it to that fine black sheen, he paid no heed to its pleasure. I am God's flute, and His breath blows through me. So in Byzantium it was good that my flesh should suffer, for by great severities of life I could draw men to listen to His word. But now my task is to carry Christ to the Huns. Therefore to delay my feeble flesh by willfully inflicting suffering on it is sinful. I have even meditated during the night on the question of my appearance before these Huns. For they too are indifferent to suffering, and will not be impressed by my indifference. Furthermore it does not appear that they set any great store by cleanliness . . ."

It did not seem strange to Silvester, for he was a Byzantine, that an old man crouched in a riverbed gnawing black bread should spend twenty minutes debating the question whether he had a moral duty to wash off his twelve-year dirt and comb out the tangles of his beard— which was indeed so tangled that combing it out would have been a greater mortification than leaving it as it was.

The hundred and fifty miles to the border took them fourteen days. Perhaps it was lucky that Holy John had hurt his foot, otherwise he might have become impatient with Silvester's slow progress through the outlands where the imperial couriers never came. Sometimes the boy and the bear could travel for a whole day without going more than three miles from the road, and made a good march; but at other times, for instance, they would come to a fertile valley branching off the road, and here a great landowner had laid down a vast estate with its own hierarchy of servants, and probably its own private army to keep the oppressed serfs from revolt—and of course to arrest and question passing vagabonds. One such area took Silvester nearly two days to work round.

He and Bubba must have traveled twice as far—perhaps three times as far—as the road party. His whole body ached with weariness each night, and most mornings Bubba was difficult to wake and still more difficult to get moving, though once under way she plodded on steadily enough. He kept in touch with Holy John by a simple code of marks chalked on milestones. Each time they managed to camp all four together he was astounded by the progress the saint was making with his Hunnish lessons.

"Isn't Urrguk getting impatient?" said Silvester one morning after a night whose first three hours he'd spent hurrying along the road to catch up, boy and bear padding silent as shadows under a half moon.

"No," said Holy John. "He is eager to return to his country, but does not want to do so without the bear. I do not know why. At first I understood him to say that the Kutrigurs worship a bear-god, but this is not so. They worship the sun."

"Yes, that's what the slave merchant said."

"Urrguk speaks of the bear unwillingly, in words we do not have in Greek. The bear is something holy or magical to his people. They do a bear dance. He believes that it is she, and not you, who is really healing his wound. So he is patient. But I am having trouble with the officials on the road, who ask why I am taking him home so slowly. I say it is for his wound's sake. The bald man who is hunting you . . ."

"Still?"

"Yes. A shepherd spoke with you on the hills, apparently, and some slaves pulling thistles from the Emperor's wheat found bear tracks by the road. I have seen the man several times. He says you are journeying to the Huns to claim your reward."

Silvester shivered. The bald man had begun to haunt his dreams. Before he slept his fear was all of natural things; he would lie close to Bubba for warmth, smelling the sweet wild smells that seem to well out of the ground as darkness comes, with all his muscles tense and his hearing trying to reach into the dark and interpret any rustle or whisper in the stillness. But when at last he slept he met, again and again, a different enemy. In some dreams he was doing some vague task and looked up to see, waddling down a far path, the bald man with the white wand. There seemed to be plenty of time, but suddenly he was running with leaden feet along a forest path and finding the perfect hiding place and lurking there, panting, only to see the bald man turn without hesitation toward his lair. Or else he was creeping from pillar to pillar though the Khan's palace, easily eluding servants and guards, but then stumbling clumsily into a room where two people sat side by side on thrones, watching him with mocking eyes—the bald man and the Lady Ariadne, she is her betrothal costume. And then he would wake and find himself clutching for comfort at Bubba's warm, bear-smelling hide while she grunted through her own dreams—she never seemed to have nightmares. And he would lie awake and wonder whether there was any escape, any bribe the bald man would take. The ruby? But that was for Addie's ransom.

For eight days they had slowly approached a range of hills higher than any of the mild ups and downs in the cultivated areas north of Lycopolis. At last they camped, all four together, close enough to see that they were almost mountains, a long escarpment running east and west, rising direct from the lower ground, all forested with oak and sweet chestnut.

"Now we must travel by night," said Holy John.

"Why?"

"I have been asking travelers about the road. Henceforth it is wild land, almost all the way to the Danube. You have no hope of finding your way except on the road, so we must travel when no one else does, and pray to God in His mercy to spare us the attentions of robbers and wolves."

So now, though the way was much steeper and the road itself, though marvelously engineered, in very poor repair, they moved faster. On their third night's journey they changed worlds. One day they had camped among pale, deciduous trees, and the next they were in a dark pine forest—they were over the summit of the range and moving down the northern slopes. And where the south had been that clean, magnificent escarpment, this was a muddle of broken valleys through which the road felt its way northeast for a two days' march and then northwest for another two. There were no farms up here—just one mean village walled for defense by the old Romans and the shaggy hamlets of foresters and hunters, from every one of which a dozen dogs barked at the clop of hooves in the dark.

The hills lessened. One chill dawn they picked their way up a forester's track and came to a clearing where a number of big pines had been felled. Silvester was very tired, and solely concerned with leading Bubba clear of any soft earth where the marks of a bear's pads might show. It had rained in the night, so this was almost impossible, and several times he had to go back to scuff her trail out. And then there was the problem of settling in so that if a stranger came to the camp he would see only Holy John and Urrguk, who could produce impressive travel documents. And then there was the wound to be dressed. So it was after sunrise that Silvester, with his mouth full of salted mutton, at last raised his eyes and looked north, expecting to see over the trees at the bottom of the clearing only another pine-swathed slope.

But there was space, and space beyond space. The plain lay flat and green with summer and apparently endless, though right at the limit of vision there seemed to be a misty something that could be hills. Silvester gasped at the vast, unnatural flatness. He could not conceive that anything in wild nature should be so smooth—only Man irons out the hummocked earth for his use or his pleasure, but men could not have done that to so huge a plain, not even the Old Romans. The pagans would have said that this was the work of some God.

"What is it?" he said.

"The Danube plain," replied Holy John.

Yes, there, a full ten miles away, but compared with those stretching distances almost at his feet, lay the creature that had ironed out the hills. In places it gleamed and in places it was only a dull streak, a vein of water, two thousand miles long, draining the dark inner lands of Europe.

"That is the frontier," said Holy John. "Beyond that the laws change. Even the Emperor has no authority out there, only alliances with wild tribes."

"The Lists mean nothing there? The white wand?"

"Just another stick."

PART III · THE CAMP

XII

Bear-Magic

IN THE SULTRY, MUD-SMELLING NOON Silvester lay by the Danube bank and watched a hideous creature, two inches long, crawl to the top of a reed; once there it rested before beginning to palpitate with a strange, jerking movement that pumped dark blood along the veins of filmy tissue on its back; the tissue became long wings; the creature became a dragonfly; in a green blur it was gone.

From the flats behind, he heard a raucous noise which it took him some while to recognize as a deep voice chanting a psalm, badly off the note. As he crawled out of hiding he thought how strange it was that Holy John could summon such golden tones into his speaking voice and yet should sing so abominably. The saint saw him and strode across the pastures. A mile up the river the wooden town lay silent in the noon haze.

Silvester was surprised to see Holy John on land at all; he had expected to hear that psalm coming from the water. More disturbing still, the old man was leading Urrguk's horse with the empty litter trailing behind it.

"No boats," said Holy John.

Silvester's heart sank. He looked across the shimmering width of the river. It must be almost a mile to the far bank.

"The trade is strictly licensed," said Holy John. "I could not ask direct, but my guess is that no boatman would risk his ears and his boat to take a fugitive from the Lists across."

"What shall we do?"

"Moreover, the magistrates took my pass from me, and had Urrguk taken straight onto a raft, which leaves tomorrow. Do not despair, boy—God's hand is here also."

"I don't understand."

"They cut timber in the forests of middle Europe, and lash the tree trunks into a raft, and then traders pay to be taken on that raft down the river, some of them right out to the Black Sea. This town is sited at this point only because the river current bears in here toward the south bank. Now, the army of the Huns crossed the river a fortnight ago and are far ahead; but the magistrates say that if we take the raft and go with it down the river, the river bends for sixty miles north before it empties into the Sea, and at a place called Great Bend we will be only two days' march from the Khan's country."

"But what about me? And Bubba? We can't get into the town. And the gate will be guarded. The man with the white wand is bound to have told all the border garrisons to watch out for me."

"That is so. There is a gate guard of twelve men. They could be drugged."

"Twelve men! I haven't got nearly enough for that! And how . . ."

"If we cannot close their eyes we must close their minds. Have you enough drugs to keep the bear still?"

"I think so."

"Good. I have brought the horse out so that I can cut forage. Now . . ."

Bubba was sulky at being waked up, but accepted a slice of honey-smeared bread and never noticed the poppy juice. It took a long time to act but at last she flopped from sentimental drowsiness into an unwakable lump. They rolled her onto the litter where it lay flat on the bank and lashed her firm, then Holy John led the inscrutable horse over and spoke to it in Hunnish. It gazed at him as if it didn't understand his accent, and refused to lie down, though Urrguk had taught him the words. In despair Silvester heaved the pole upward, and found to his surprise that despite Bubba's weight he could just lift it—with the bear lying more than halfway towards the back, the pole itself became a lever. Holy John prayed quietly for his God to strengthen his old sinews, then lifted the other pole. Mercifully the horse stood still while they dragged the pole ends into the harness.

"Will the wood stand the weight?" said Silvester. "It's sagging so she's almost touching the ground."

This was in fact the third litter they'd made during the journey, and a great improvement on the earlier versions. Holy John tested it with his bony hand, prayed again, said, "Give me twenty minutes—if you do not hear my voice do not try to enter," and strode away. Silvester covered Bubba with the piles of grass they'd cut while they were waiting for her to fall asleep, lashed the whole bundle firm and led the horse toward the town.

There was a crowd at the gate, listening in silence to a new prophet. He stood on a bale which had been packed with half-threshed straw and then left to stand in the rain, so that the fresh young blades were sprouting through the sacking. He spoke to them of the sins of the City—astounding scandals and luxuries, the perfect bait for country ears. He had altered his style completely from the elaborate arguments which had entranced the nobility of

Byzantium; here he spoke to peasants, in short sentences, full of homely ideas and images and good old peasant jokes. The crowd sighed or gasped or laughed all together, including the sentries. Silvester had to push his way through, and the people moved out of his path like men in a dream, noticing him no more than they did the dogs that sniffed round their legs. One of the dogs sniffed at Bubba and began to growl, but a man in the crowd kicked it for preventing him from hearing the preaching and it ran yelping. Silvester led the horse down a street of dirty wooden shacks to the river, where he found the raft moored at a jetty.

"Who you?" said a ginger-haired man with gold bracelets on his enormous forearm.

"Holy John sent me. The old man who is looking after the Hun."

"Am knowing him. One crazy old man. Are coming on my raft, no?"

"Yes, down to Great Bend, please."

"One big silver is cost. Ho! What carrying in that grass?"

"Nothing, only . . ."

The man pounced to the back of the litter. He moved like an ape, and looked like an ape, barely three inches taller than Silvester, but hulking with muscle. His red hands parted the grass.

"Ho! One bear! Why bringing one bear so?"

"She's quite tame, but . . . but they want to break her arms and chest bones, or use her for baiting, so I'm taking her away."

"Ho! Stealing one bear. So two big silvers is cost. Have got?"

"Yes. Yes."

"Is good. Putting bear not near horses—I show you."

Shaking with relief, Silvester took the horse along a

gangway of rough planking and rolled Bubba into the lee
of one of the tiny huts which dotted the raft. By the time
Holy John limped down from the town he was beginning
to wonder whether he'd given her too much poppy juice—
whether she would ever wake.

She had awakened all right. Perhaps, in fact, she had
been sleeping normally for some time when the grunting
chant of the polemen stopped and the current took the raft
and the trumpets of the town rang farewell. Probably it
was the trumpets that woke her, or else the sucking noises
of the river between the tree trunks, but whatever it was
she woke in alarm, rearing from the deck and bellowing.
Everyone on the raft turned to look where she stood on her
hind legs, swaying groggily. The farewell crowd on the
shore shouted and pointed. Silvester saw a man running
up the street, a soldier.

It took Silvester some minutes to calm her and get her
out of sight again and settle her to chewing a turnip, and
by then the people on the jetty were so far away that he
could hardly distinguish them individually. But one man
stood a little apart from the others, waving both arms desperately; he was stout, and the morning light gleamed on
his scalp. Of course at that distance it was impossible to see
the white wand.

"You are beyond the Empire now," said Holy John. "He
cannot touch you."

The raft twirled on the current, a movement slower and
more massive than even Bubba's most ponderous dancing.
The Empire slid away and was replaced by the mile-wide
river, which was in turn replaced by the northern bank.
All of it was one vast, unvarying flatness, but south—now
coming into view again, was home and prison, civilization
and the torture chamber. Then the neutral river, then the

barbarian lands where Silvester would be free but lost, safe
from the white wand but open to unimaginable dangers.

"Wouldn't it be safer if we asked the raft captain to land
us over there?" he said next time the north bank swung
into view.

Holy John spoke to Urrguk, who shook his head.

"Slabini," he said, drawing his finger across his wind-
pipe and grinning as though he thought that to have his
throat slit by his fellow barbarians, the Slavs, would be a
fine comical end to his adventures.

"Man is man," said Holy John. "Whether he is a luxurious dweller in cities or the wildest horseman of the plains
he reserves his fiercest hate for his nearest neighbors. But
the enmity between Kutrigur and Slav is nothing, Urrguk
tells me, compared with the enmity between Kutrigur and
Utrigur. For the Utrigurs are not only neighbors but kin."

"Are they pagans, too?" said Silvester.

Holy John stiffened.

"They call themselves Christians," he snarled, "but they
were converted by damned Orthodox heretics. I shall carry
the true Christ to the Kutrigurs."

"I do not bring peace, but a sword," said a mild voice
above their heads. Silvester looked up from where he was
sitting on the round of one of the big logs and saw a
middle-aged man, dark and small and richly dressed, but
not in the fashion of Byzantium. His Greek was good, but
nasal.

"There will be peace enough in heaven," said Holy
John. "But it will be given only to those who have fought
for the truth on earth."

"A good doctrine for one who carries Christ to the Kutrigurs. And you are well advised to trade in a different
brand from that consumed by the Utrigurs. With war
brewing between them, they will not follow cheerfully
along the path taken by their cousins."

"War?" said Holy John.

"We hear good gossip on the river. The messengers wait for a crossing in the frontier towns, and while they wait they drink. The word is that your Emperor has sent an embassy to the Utrigurs. As you know, he pays them an annual tribute of gold to keep the Asian frontier safe from invaders in the north. This year he has sent no gold, only a message that the Kutrigurs have taken it, and that if the Utrigurs want it they must fetch it from them. The Khan of the Kutrigurs—this Zabergan—is already troubled with the Avars . . ."

"Avars?" said Holy John. "I have not heard speak of them."

"Oh, a new horde of savages from the East, more barbarous even than the Huns, they say. The Khan accepted the Emperor's tribute without haggling because he was anxious to return and defend his territory from these Avars, and now if the Empire succeeds in stirring up the Utrigurs against him . . . well, I do not deal much with the Huns, my trade is with the Alans, up West, but I doubt whether the Empire will be troubled with Huns for some time."

"If the story is true," said Holy John.

"If it is true," agreed the merchant affably. He paused and gave a little cough which told Silvester, who was used to the nuances of the market, that he had finished the preliminary gossip which had allowed the three of them to become acquainted and was now about to embark on the real subject of his visit.

"The bear . . ." he began.

"She is not for sale," said Silvester quickly.

"You are too sharp for me, you Byzantines," said the merchant, laughing. "No, I only came to ask a favor. One of my Alan bearers is sick with a marsh fever, and his companions have sent me to ask whether your bear will walk on the man."

"I have heard of that," said Silvester, remembering the old shopkeeper who had sold him the flute, "but Bubba's never tried it. She's a dancing bear. And I've got some horehound powder which is a febrifuge . . ."

"These Alans," sighed the merchant. "They'd die rather than take medicine from anyone except their own witches. Why, each man cooks his own food—sometimes I think they believe the whole universe is hell-bent to poison them. Let your bear dance on the man."

"I suppose we could try."

"Good. Tonight, then, for they say that by dark the fever spirit will slide more easily from body to body. Remember to strike a hard bargain, my lad, or they will not believe that the bear has worthwhile powers."

Night came soft and cloudless over the unvarying plain. The river moved all with one movement, without wave or ripple, black as the pupil of an eye but streaked with reflected stars. They were too far from either bank to hear it fidgeting with the reeds.

The raft people lit lanterns and turned themselves inwards, walling off the indifferent dark with their backs. The rectangle became a village square, noisy with disputes and reeking with the cookery of eight nations. The journey down the river had begun as soon as the ice melted and had passed the known dangers, the wild robbers of the hinterland and the roaring waters of the Iron Gates. Now it was floating peacefully to its end and the raft people were in high spirits. Silvester felt at home among them, loving the shouting and the bustle and the sheer crowdedness after those lonely hillsides.

The Alans—tall, skinny men who never looked straight at you when they spoke—brought out their sick friend and laid him on one of the planked areas, naked except for a loincloth and shuddering with his fever. Silvester led Bubba over and showed her the man; she sniffed at him and slumped down with her back to him. The Alans began to shout at Silvester.

"They are asking how much money she wants to take the fever from the man," said the merchant. The joy of a hard bargain, and nothing to lose, rose strong in Silvester.

"Half a solid," he said.

The merchant translated, grinning. The Alans threw up their hands and yelled in dismay. The sick man sat up and croaked that his life wasn't worth half a solid.

"He is the interested party," explained the merchant. "He will have to repay the others whatever they agree to. They suggest the forequarters of a sucking-pig which they bought in the town."

"Well," said Silvester as loftily as if he'd been freeborn, "you had better tell them to cover their friend up. This is going to take time."

In the end the bargain was struck at the whole sucking-pig, plus a tiny piece of amber and an iron Alan dagger almost half the size of a real sword, but the last two only to be given if the man's fever improved. This struck Silvester as fair, as he had no notion whether Bubba could be persuaded to walk on the man, and his little honeypot was almost down to its last scrapings.

Bubba took some time to get the idea. Silvester played the tune and she danced, grinning, while the raft people shouted their appreciation. He rewarded her with half the honey, spread thin on a crust, then led her to the man, but when the Alans twitched his furs off him she sniffed at him, as though she thought he didn't appreciate good dancing. Silvester heaved her front paw off the ground and put it on the man's chest. The Alans grunted encouragement; but Bubba just stood there, looking round the ring of raft people with one foot on the body, as though she were a mighty hunter and the Alan some creature she had just killed.

When Silvester tried to lift her other forepaw onto the man she nudged him with her muzzle and sent him sprawling. Silvester spread the last of the honey on another crust and gave it to Holy John, who stationed himself at the sick man's head. He himself took Bubba round to the feet, positioned her as best he could and then started to play the old tune on the black flute. Bubba rose and started her dance, hesitant and baffled, knowing that she was expected to perform some trick but not knowing what. But at least there was the honey, and she might as well dance toward it, so she began to edge up outside the man's left leg. Holy John moved the bait the other way, so that she had to cross the torso to reach it. For five whole steps she teetered on the insecure footing of belly and chest while the patient bellowed with her weight and the other Alans shouted. Then she reached her reward and sat down, looking round the audience with the old, sly look while she licked her chops and the Alans wrapped their friend up and hurried him into the darkness of their reed-thatched wigwam.

Silvester was beginning to relax, and his saliva to stream at the thought of roast sucking-pig, when a hand touched him on the shoulder. It was the raft captain.

"Bear is healing my mother," he said in his awful pidgin Greek, all smattered with the gutturals of the forest. Silvester made an astonished noise, but the raft captain stood nodding in the lantern light, square and humorless, then swung away like a bullock and ducked into the dark space under the little platform from which he controlled the raft. A minute later he came crawling out with what looked like a bundle of expensive furs in his arms.

A new noise pierced the dark, the unmistakable shrill rattle of an old woman cursing. When the raft captain laid his bundle on the deck Silvester saw that she was indeed very old, bent double with arthritis, but with brilliant eyes. The curses emerged through a thick veil over her nose and mouth.

"Is bended," explained the raft captain, poking her with his toe. "All crooked, see? Stuck. Not showing our women to strangers, my people, but for bear to walk on, showing. Yes?"

"But Bubba's so heavy! She'll kill her!"

"Is good. My mother is old. Time for dying."

Silvester's dismay must have shown on his face, and then been disbelieved.

"Not paying you enough, huh?" shouted the raft captain. "Listening to me, bear thief! Bear is walking on my mother, or I am landing you on bank. South bank."

Silvester wanted to explain, but the raft captain was too angry to listen. He snatched the flute and thrust it at Silvester's face. Bubba had already been growling to hear her master so spoken to, and now she came lurching towards the raft captain, heavy and dangerous; all Silvester could think of was to take the flute and blow. Bubba snorted with surprise, stopped her attack, remembered the taste of honey and rose to her feet.

Perhaps she didn't see the old woman. Perhaps she thought it was only a few furs lying on the deck. At any rate she danced to and fro across her, stepping on her several times, while the old woman shrieked and hooted and the raft captain yelled to his friends to come and watch his mother being killed, or cured, as the case might be. The raft people jeered at the old woman's shrieks. Silvester stopped playing as soon as he dared, and when Bubba sat down all he had to give her for reward was the honey pot, at which she licked contentedly enough. Meanwhile the raft captain stood in the middle of the lantern light, grinning so that all his huge teeth gleamed, and holding in his arms the inert body of his mother. There was no telling whether she was alive or dead, but the raft captain seemed satisfied with either result, because her tongue was still and he could waggle her fragile limbs to and fro to show everyone how easily the joints now moved.

Not everyone slept well that night. Bubba had got it into her head that her new trick was supposed to be walking on inert forms lying on the deck, and that if she did this she might be given honey. Several men woke yelling under her enormous weight, until Silvester chained her on too short a chain to reach any sleepers.

XIII

Mud Bank

IT WAS like the night the Huns had come. Silvester woke to shouting, to sweat on his clothes, to gray smoke filling the air. But the shouting was that of the men working the enormous sweeps, the sweat was dew, and the smoke was a heavy river mist, through which a few looming shapes moved. No wonder the Alan had marsh fever, Silvester thought.

Bubba lay beside him, fast asleep, silvered with innumerable drops at the end of each hair. He crept through the mist to visit Urrguk, who insisted on lying among the horses; he was asleep, too. Silvester crawled to the raft's edge to wash his face in the river and found it oily, the color of an old sword, and still breathing out fresh layers of mist.

"Knowing your way?" said the raft captain cheerfully.

"No," said Silvester as he stood up. "How can you tell it's time to use the sweeps?"

"Am smelling," said the raft captain, flaring vast nostrils with ginger hair inside them. "This river I know, like a man is knowing his wives. One, two, three times in year I am bringing raft down, fast, fast. Merchants are paying, because best captain on river. True. Sell trees, take horse, mother across saddle, riding, riding to my home, because new raft waiting. Then winter, all ice, so staying at home, eating, drinking, loving my wives. Rich."

"Couldn't you leave your mother at home?" said Silvester, thinking that the journey upriver must be even less fun for the old lady than the journey down.

"No good. Long ago my mother is young. She is fierce with my wives, so my wives cry 'Take her. Take her.' Now she is old. Perhaps is dying when I am on my river, so my wives are eating her. No good. Much money to pay to my priests so ghost of my mother is not haunting my wives who are eating her. My mother becoming very fierce ghost, yes?"

"I hope she is well this morning," said Silvester. This was no mere politeness; he didn't want Bubba haunted by fierce ghosts. But the raft captain had turned away into the mist to shout at the sweep men.

In fact she was much better. During the night her joints had loosened enough for her to hobble out from under the platform to curse her son, who picked her up and waltzed her round on his arm like an uncle playing with a tiny girl. He brought her to show to Silvester and Bubba, who had worked the cure, and she cursed them both in her hissing cackle, but the raft captain was laughing with delight.

This was just as well. Suddenly, in the space of a few seconds, all the smoky grayness turned pale gold, their circle of vision widened, and the raft drifted into sunlight. The flat banks were brilliant with morning and the sunlight dazzled along the river before them. And over toward the south bank, clear of the sun dazzle, a big rowing boat was coming heavily upstream. Sunlight winked off the soldiers' armor and gleamed dully from the pate of the fat man who posed in the bows, like a figurehead, holding the white wand.

"What is?" said the raft captain, laying his mother gently on the deck. "More taxing, no?"

Silvester looked with despair to the northern bank, almost a mile away. That promised land of freedom might have been so much mist.

"They are hunting for me," he croaked. "I am on the Lists."

"Ugh," said the raft captain, squinting at the boat. "Fetching your crazy friend."

Holy John was at his prayers, but not in trance. Though he was angry to be disturbed, he came at once. Another man now stood on the platform; Silvester recognized him as one of the crew who manned the sweeps, but now he stood with his legs well apart, balancing slightly forward onto his toes, while a big thong of leather hummed softly in his right hand; it was twice the size of the sling with which the shepherd boy had killed the hare.

"Stopping!" called the raft captain suddenly, when the rowboat was fifty yards away. Now that it had come into the main current to meet them it was actually going backwards down the river, despite its eight oars, but the raft was moving with the current, and the boat was making steady progress relative to that. The gap continued to close.

"Stopping!" shouted the raft captain again and pointed to his slingsman.

"I have the Emperor's commission," called the bald man. "I carry the white wand."

To Silvester's astonishment he spoke not with the deep

voice of authority but in the high, almost giggling tones of a eunuch. He held up the white wand to show it to the raft people.

The raft captain spoke three words—a question—to the slingsman, who nodded. The hum of the circling sling became a whistle and a snap, answered by a crack and a clang from the boat as the slingshot broke the white wand into two halves and ricocheted on to bounce off a soldier's helmet. The eunuch wrung his wrist and a soldier put a startled hand up to his head. The sling was loaded and humming again before the commotion in the boat had settled.

"Steering to there!" called the raft captain, pointing to a station between the raft and the south bank. The eunuch was going to argue, but someone else in the boat gave an order, the four starboard oars belayed, and the boat's course curved to take it to the place that the raft captain had pointed at. There the oarsmen rested and the current took boat and raft together, side by side, towards the Black Sea.

"Making talk," said the raft captain in a low voice to Holy John. "No long time."

Holy John raked a hand through his filthy beard, then raised it to bless the Emperor, the eunuch, the boat and all who sailed in her.

"That's all very well . . ." shrilled the eunuch.

"The raft captain has asked me to explain your reception," boomed Holy John. "By a coincidence his raft has already been attacked, higher upriver, by pirates disguised as a party bearing the Emperor's commission."

"But I will show it to you," cried the eunuch, drawing a roll of parchment, grubby with travel, from the folds of cloth at his chest.

"Alas," said Holy John, shaking his head at the wicked

ingenuity of robbers, "our other friend had a roll like that.
This is a dilemma, sir. If we let you close enough for you
to be able to prove that it is not forged, then supposing it
is forged you will be close enough to attack us. These im-
pudent pirates . . ."

He began to describe in meaningless detail a totally
imaginary attack, until the eunuch interrupted him.

"The boy! I only want the boy! He is on the Lists.
Throw him in and we will pick him up."

Silvester sensed a quiet movement among the raft people. He turned and saw that the audience was quietly
moving back to its own concerns. Even the merchant
they'd talked with the night before had his back to the
boat, as though he was interested in something on the
northern bank.

"Can you swim, boy?" snarled Holy John.

Silvester shook his head in misery. This was a hopeless
game.

"The boy cannot swim," said Holy John apologetically.
"If he drowned his death would be on the raft captain's
head, and he is a peculiarly superstitious man, much
troubled with ghosts. Do *you* want the boy drowned?"

"No! No! I need him alive—for a while. But . . ."

This could not last. In a minute or two the eunuch
would lose patience, take cover behind the thwarts, and
order his men to close while the soldiers protected themselves and the oarsmen behind their shields. Many as the
raft people were, they could not fight off eight well-armed
soldiers—besides, they had no cause. Except the Alans,
perhaps. They were said to be the meanest fighters in
Europe, and Bubba had walked on their friend. The
merchant still had his back to the boat, but Silvester could
see he was listening intently to the argument.

"Couldn't your men . . ." Silvester began hopelessly.

"Very sorry," muttered the merchant, giving the universal salesman's shrug. "I'd help you if I could, but I trade with the Empire, under license. I cannot risk my license. Same with everyone on the raft. Even the raft captain—but his honor's at stake. The river is free water, and he'd count it a great disgrace to let you be captured on it."

"I thought it was because Bubba walked on his mother."

"That too. I don't see how he can hold out much longer, though. He has some plan, still . . ."

At this moment the raft captain called out and pointed ahead. There on the bank, a mile down the river, was a dreary collection of wooden huts and warehouses, a village only, but walled and garrisoned, sited there because the current bore close in. This made the game even more hopeless—no pirates would dare to operate so close to a garrison. Indeed the eunuch was already beginning to argue this point when the raft captain spoke in a low voice to Holy John.

"Aha!" cried the saint. "The good Lord has sent us a solution. Our raft had not intended to halt here, but we will do so and carry the case to the magistrate. If all is as you say, you shall have the boy."

The eunuch, who far outranked any magistrate of a squalid provincial village, smiled haughtily and picked up the longer piece of his snapped wand before adopting his impressive pose in the bows of the boat. The raft captain ordered the sweeps out and frowned at the river, scratching his buttocks. Silvester stared across the bright sheet of water, narrowing all the time, that lay between him and prison and the torturer. What plan could the raft captain hope to have, in this emptiness—or was it something to do with the particular magistrate at this horrible village, something that would yet allow him to snatch the prey away from the taloned grip of punishment? But that

was hopeless too—you couldn't expect this barbarian to
know what a powerful official the eunuch was, the moment
he stepped onto the bank. The law might be a blind monster, but it never let go. The raft people flicked quick
glances of curiosity at Silvester. His name was on the Lists,
but in a week, a month (please Christ, no more!), it would
be crossed off, because the blind monster was satisfied.
With his blood, with his agony.

He turned his back on the glances of people who could
not afford to feel pity, and stared again at the water. There
was only one ripple in its smoothness, spoiling the clean
reflection of the dirty village—like a flaw in a mirror
which stretches out one part of your face and compresses
another. The ripple stayed quite still, despite the invisible
drive of the current. Silvester's mind, seizing on trivia to
dull the ache of terror, tried to imagine why.

He heard the raft captain shout, and the grunts of the
crew, and the creak of the sweeps against the thole-posts.

"Keep inshore!" shrilled the eunuch, like a worried
woman.

The raft captain answered in pidgin Greek, broken
beyond understanding, and pointed with commanding urgency at landmarks, distracting the eunuch's eyes from the
water. The boat reached the ripple.

Smoothness was smooth no more, but muddy foam and
lost oars and tumbling bodies. The boat had stopped so
suddenly—as suddenly as if a river demon had gripped its
keel—that the eunuch and two of the soldiers had fallen
overboard, and the other soldiers fell among the oarsmen.

The raft captain yelled. The raft lurched and began to
twirl. Silvester saw Holy John straining his old back at a
sweep handle. The huge poles were out, and prodding into
the water, and still the raft was twirling, away, downstream. The merchant was shrieking at his Alans to help

with the sweeps. The water between the big logs was sucking and guggling now that it was trying to move faster than the burden it carried, and a humped wave rose against whatever edge of the stickily twisting raft happened to be facing upstream. And then the raft was free, still twirling, but moving fast down the river while the town and the boat diminished into the distance.

"What happened?" said Silvester, shaking his head slowly from side to side. The raft captain was grinning with pride at his own cunning and knowledge of the river.

"Hi!" he shouted. "Running him into fat shoal. My raft only touching one corner, but boat all stuck. See, not rowing her off because stuck, not pushing her off because mud too soft. Hi!"

Silvester, sick with relief, sat down on a bale of furs and gulped and sobbed. He didn't notice Holy John standing beside him, nor hear the meditative discussion with the raft captain, while the rest of the raft people chattered like apes in the background.

"You must stir, boy," said Holy John at last. "The eunuch must have ridden all night, and commandeered soldiers in the village. They will have another boat out soon, though the raft captain says they will not have another so large. He thinks that the eunuch will ride again, to the next town."

Silvester looked up. He couldn't stop the slow movement of his head from side to side. It was like an ox trying to shake some entanglement out of its horns, only Silvester was trying to clear the fog of dread from his mind. He felt he could no longer live on this cliff-edge, being continually dangled over the drop and then snatched back. It would be better to jump, to ask the raft captain to put him ashore on the southern bank, to go to the magistrates and say "Here I am. My name is on the Lists. Take me."

"In a few miles the current crosses the river," said Holy John. "You must land with the bear on the north bank and journey overland. We can wait for you, for a fortnight, at Great Bend. We cannot wait longer. I must not lose this chance that God has given me, to carry news to the Khan of the Emperor's dealings with the Utrigurs."

"All right," said Silvester dully. Nothing mattered, except that somebody should tell him what to do, give him orders, treat him as what he was—a slave.

"There is a Slav on the raft, boy. He says that the Slavs are unlikely to hurt or rob a poor-looking traveler, and they will be amused by the bear. And the All-creator will give you courage, for you are part of His purpose. Come. This Slav must teach you a few necessary words, for food, and sleep and how to ask your way."

Silvester forced his lips to smile.

"And for honey," he said.

XIV

The Lake

SILVESTER sat cross-legged in the dust and played his flute.
The air reeked of cow dung. The fire in the center of the
circle was built with dried cow dung. The warriors of the
village kept their elaborately curled hair in place with cow
dung. Even the mud huts of the village looked like huge
cow pats. And beyond the thrilled ring of watchers the
cows themselves mooched and snorted and added to the es-
sential odor of the plains.

Bubba danced. She was puzzled by the silence of her audience until an old woman brought a flat drum out from one
of the huts and biffed away at it in rhythm with the tune.
Then the warriors began to stamp with each footfall.
Three younger women began a chant, not at all muffled by
their veils, a single phrase repeated and repeated like the
calling of wild birds. Luckily Bubba was not tired, as she
had only had to walk about eight miles from the river, and
she was in a good temper because, though the villagers had
no honey, they had produced a sweet, liquorice-tasting
black root which she thought excellent.

Silvester allowed the tune to slow and tried to sign to

the other performers that he was bringing the dance to an end. They understood at once, the trio altered their chant and the old women built up a fantastic rattle of drumbeats ending in a long roll in the middle of which Bubba sat down, bewildered. Then the whole village began laughing and cheering at once. A naked fat baby, black-haired and black-eyed, tottered into the cleared space near the fire and started to pat the fur of Bubba's hind leg. Bubba snatched her up. A woman shrieked and ran forward. Silvester jumped up and caught the woman by the arm, just in time to prevent her feeling the slashing arm-stroke of an irritated bear. He picked up the last of the little bundle of black roots and dangled them in front of Bubba's nose. She opened her mouth, expecting him to feed her, because obviously she couldn't fend for herself while she was hugging the baby. When he tossed the roots onto the ground a few feet in front of her she put the baby down and ambled over to get her prize. The woman snatched up the baby, which was laughing and still reaching out towards the bear. Bubba came back chomping the roots, but had already forgotten what she'd been doing before she'd been distracted, and so was content to be petted and told that she was beautiful and clever, besides being one of the world's great dancers. The talk which had stilled at the incident rose again.

Silvester didn't notice the sudden fresh hush because Bubba had chosen to interpret his caresses as an invitation to a wrestling match and he was lying on his back in the dungy dust trying to roll away from under her weight. She would soon be coming in heat and this made her very sentimental; wrestling was an excuse for hugging and being hugged; she also slobbered over Silvester when she had him pinned down, so he called her rude names and scrambled clear. Only then was he aware of the silence.

"Graeculus esne, puer?"

"Ita," said Silvester, turning towards the voice. "Atqui linguam Latinam cognovi."

He saw by the spurting reed-light an extraordinary figure; a Slav, square-headed, squat and hideous—uglier and older even than the village headman; his hair was grizzled and cut very short, and he was clean-shaven; otherwise he might have been just another elderly warrior peasant who had come to watch the dancing bear. But he was wearing, instead of the sacklike russet tunics of the villagers, a white toga, like the old Romans, like the Lord Celsus. The whiteness of it, in that dirty place, was astounding; it must have been the finest cloth on the market, fresh laundered. The old man smiled a cold, uninterpretable smile and continued to speak in Latin.

"Aha," he said "Good Ciceronian, and not these modern barbarisms."

"My master, the Lord Celsus, insisted . . ."

"A quite good family. My name is Antoninus."

Silvester blinked. He noticed the thin triple line of purple running along the edge of the toga. The last of the great emperors of old Rome had been the Antonini. He bowed very deeply.

The headman of the village approached, very deferential but not fawning, and pointed to Silvester and Bubba and said something in the hissing, clicking language of the Slavs. Antoninus replied easily in the same tongue. A woman approached carrying a big wooden goblet with a silver rim and offered it, kneeling, to Antoninus, who sipped and passed it with a little nod to Silvester.

"Drink a little and pass it to the headman," he said.

Silvester sipped. The liquid in the cup was the color of cream but thinner. It tasted very sweet and prickled slightly on the tongue.

"Bubba, my bear, would like that," he said.

"Fermented cow milk," said Antoninus, and spoke in Slav to the woman, who took the cup back from the headman and carried it over to Bubba.

"Tell her to be careful," said Silvester. "Just let Bubba put her paw in it. Otherwise she'll drink half of it and spill half."

"She'll be very drunk if she does," said Antoninus, and called again in Slav. The woman managed Bubba's greed very neatly, whisking the cup away before Bubba had finished licking her paw and had made up her mind whether she liked this new taste. She did, and followed the woman all round the circle, whimpering for another helping. The whole village sipped, even the tiny baby, and in the end Bubba was given the cup to lick clean.

Beyond the miserable lights of the village the night was very dark. Antoninus had brought with him two elderly house servants, who walked in front carrying lanterns on short poles, so that it was possible to walk without stumbling. The path, surprisingly, was paved with flat stones and seemed to curve round the base of the slight rise in the ground which had been Silvester's only landmark as he had come, dismal with sudden loneliness, across the plain.

Antoninus leaned heavily on Silvester's shoulder; his left foot dragged at each slow step, and his breath wheezed each time he drew it in between sentences.

"They sent a message up that a bear had come to the village; they think a bear a luck symbol. The killing of a bear is an occasion for a feast, and they would be hurt if I stood aloof from their simple gaieties. So I came, though it is far for my old legs. If you are wondering why I did not have myself carried down in a litter, the answer is that my Slavs are not like you Greeks. Barbarians though they are, they have the notion of liberty deep in their spirits. To carry another man, though he were a prince of his people, would be an injury to their honor. They are not slaves. I have, indeed, seen them carry a wounded comrade from the battlefield where a Greek would have let him lie, but that is another matter. I am not too old to walk. And I feel it my duty to foster this notion of liberty among them, for they have, like many of the barbarians, a core of virtue in them such as Rome had before luxury rotted her fibers. You Greeks . . ."

To Silvester the old man seemed to grow heavier with every slow step, and his grip fiercer. Beyond the tiny, creeping orb of light in which they moved lay the limitless plain, all smelling of the same lush growth. Bubba, padding beside him on a loose chain, whimpered with excitement at some of the smells.

Quite suddenly the dark had a shape in it, a wall of old masonry and a door as solid as the door of a fort. The bridge on which they crossed the dry ditch could be raised, too; the chains gleamed with oil. Inside the door was a large, dim hall, lit by a single resin torch flaring from a bracket inside the chimney-space. The silent servants lit good-quality candles at its flame and put them on a table whose surface was a cunning inlay of ivory and ebony. The candlesticks appeared to be gold. Antoninus at last let go of Silvester's shoulder and settled with a sigh onto a couch by the table. The servants brought him a wine bottle and a single glass, and on a nod from him departed. Bubba slumped with a grunt onto the floor, but Silvester stood by the table while Antoninus looked him over with a cold, shrewd gaze, like a horse dealer considering the purchase of a colt.

"You are a slave," he said suddenly. For the first time in his life Silvester felt that the word was not just a description of the truth—that was what he was—but a degradation. He nodded his head, though, in acknowledgment.

"Yes, you have the slave look," said Antoninus with some satisfaction. "And you spoke of this Celsus as your master. Never mind that. You may sleep in the room above mine. Climb the tower stairs for two stories—it is the only door. The bear . . ."

"Bubba can sleep with me, sir. She's very clean."

"Very well. But I do not like animals in the house. We must think of a better place for her tomorrow."

"But, sir, tomorrow . . ."

"No more of that. You may go to bed now. Take one of the candles."

There were no holy pictures on the walls of the bedroom, no mother of Christ, no Crucifixion. Only, on the floor, there was a chilly mosaic which showed a pagan sea goddess rising bare-breasted from green curling waves. Bubba, whom Silvester had had to kick awake downstairs, flopped on the marble with a grunt and went straight back to sleep. Silvester turned over the slightly musty furs on the bed, checked his bearings and blew out the candle. With a sigh of worry he went and leaned on the windowsill and stared out into the dark.

He was afraid of Antoninus, this Slav who pretended to be a Roman, who was clearly regarded as a great man by the villagers, who behaved despite all his talk of liberty as though what he desired was the only thing in all the world that mattered. What did he mean about finding a place for Bubba to sleep tomorrow? And why had Silvester, coming across the all-revealing flatness of the plain, not seen this tower? It clearly was a tower; Silvester's room had windows

on all four sides, with the curve of the staircase bulging out
of one corner; but the windows on two walls were narrow
slits, while the one he was at was wide enough for him to
poke his head and shoulders out.

His eyes became used to the dark, until he thought he
could make out some sort of high-walled garden below
him, and beyond that, water; and beyond that something
he thought too dark to be just starlit plain. And yet he had
seen none of this by honest daylight. He shivered. Was Antoninus some kind of pagan sorcerer, able to hide his tower
by magical enchantment, so that only he knew the words of
power which could lead you to it? And in all the stories en-
chanters of that sort used their towers as traps—if you
reached them you never escaped. Never.

Even when he lay down and wrapped himself in expensive furs it took him a long time to begin to feel warm.

"We Romans knew our business," explained Antoninus.
"Climb the tower and you can see for twenty miles all
round, but the hill hides it from the south and prevents it
showing above the skyline from the north. The outer walls
are strong, too. I have stood three attacks with the help of
my villagers—not that the savages who attacked us knew
anything of the art of siege—they were just ill-disciplined
raiders."

The place was in fact an old Roman garrison camp,
built to house a legion with all its pack animals and equip-
ment inside its gaunt square of wall. The tower had originally been a narrow wooden structure, built just high
enough for the watchman at the top to be able to see and
signal south across the low mound which Antoninus called
the hill. The Antonini had rebuilt, much more grandly, of
stone, making it a place suitable for a gentleman, with tall,

cool rooms decorated with mosaic and marble. The camp itself was now garden and orchard and vineyard; against the outer wall were built kitchens, stables, rooms for servants and so on. Close to the tower was a little marble temple, with fluted columns and a triangular pediment, in which a lamp burned with a thin blue flame on a plain stone altar. When he showed Silvester the place Antoninus took a pinch of powder from a jade bowl and sprinkled it on the flame. At once the air was fuzzy with the smell of incense.

"I shan't ask you to do that, little Greek," said Antoninus with his wheezing chuckle. "There will be no one to do it when I am dead, and the ghosts of the Antonines will go hungry."

Silvester became restless as the tour continued. Antoninus gripped him by the shoulder, leaning on him heavily, only occasionally letting go to pull Silvester's ear to make sure he had noticed a particularly fine turn of Latin, or some rare word he'd found in the books and parchments in his library. Silvester answered as best he could, blessing the Lord Celsus for his severity over the Latin lessons. It wasn't a language he enjoyed, being slow, heavy and inflexible, quite unsuited to the mercurial Byzantine mind, but he had learned it well. Since Antoninus was determined to show him the whole estate, there was no point in making his impatience to be gone too obvious. They came at last, in the far corner of the garden, when they seemed to have seen almost everything, to a well-built stone shed.

"I thought the bear might be comfortable in here." said Antoninus. Bubba was asleep in the sun at the foot of the tower.

"Sir," said Silvester, "I am very grateful for your hospitality, but I have an errand to perform. I must go today."

Antoninus stopped wheezing and looked at him, his

162

THE CAMP

square head cocked obstinately to one side. There was a
bleak look in his eyes.

"I would prefer you to stay."

"My lord . . ."

"No titles, boy. In Rome all men are equal. But not
slaves. Certainly not runaway slaves. They are flogged. Or
crucified."

"Sir . . ."

"No more of that."

"But if I were a runaway, north of the Danube, what
better haven could I come to than this? It is beyond
dreams, sir."

"Greeks have ready tongues." At least he sounded
pleased with the compliment to his house and lands.

"May I tell you my story, sir?"

"And Greeks are ready liars."

Silvester could only shake his head in distress, and think
of the packed raft drifting in to Great Bend, and Holy
John and the Hun settling down to wait for him for one
short fortnight.

"Well, boy," said Antoninus, "shall we inspect my boathouses?"

"If you wish, sir."

As they moved out of the garden square Silvester began
to feel that the grip on his shoulder was not simply for support. It was the grip of ownership. Just so a child clutches
all day long a new toy he has been given, tight, tight.

The two boathouses lay about a hundred yards beyond
the wall, on the bank of a sluggish, fly-swarming lake,
which stretched east and west out of sight, though its far
shore was less than half a mile away. The far shore was
wooded with a forest of stunted trees, many of which had
fallen into the water and lay there with dead gray branches
protruding from the slimy surface. One boathouse was

made of wood and held a number of small rowing boats; but the smaller one was stone, and in it was a cermonial barge, built to be rowed by twelve men aside, and carrying on its raised stern a bronze throne, all green with verdigris. Antoninus didn't explain its use or meaning, but led the way to a willow tree by the lake, where he sat carefully down on a low stone bench, then pointed to the ground by his feet. Silvester settled, cross-legged.

"Well," said Antoninus, "I am tired now. Perhaps it would rest me to hear a story, true or false."

Silvester, looking across the hazy water to the dark wood beyond, explained in a low even voice all that had happened to him since the visit to the fish quay. When he showed Antoninus the seal-brooch the old man took it from him and held it at arm's length, squinting at it with intense curiosity; but he wasn't remotely interested in the ruby.

The mottled pattern made by the sun shining between the willow leaves shifted gradually across the ancient paving. Sometimes, being wholly concerned with putting his facts in sequence, Silvester got into a tangle with his grammar; then Antoninus pulled him up sharply, made him correct himself, and perhaps suggested a more elegant choice or order of words. Silvester didn't look at him, but in his mind's eye as he spoke the square, smooth face seemed to become monstrous, ogrish, the very symbol of cruelty and prison. When he finished he sat motionless until a big insect bit his arm and his slap broke the spell.

"Yes," said Antoninus, "your story is true."

"Thank you, sir."

"Oh, it is not your voice or winning ways, boy. But I cannot believe that you would have put yourself on the Lists if you were inventing a tale to fuddle my old wits. I have heard of those Lists. You must have wished to leave

that element out—for it gives me a strong hold on you.
Did you think of that?"

"Yes, sir. But I thought too that if I left it out I might
make some mistake patching the hole over, and that might
make you believe the entire story was a lie."

"Of course."

There was another silence, seeming to reach into haze as
limitlessly as the plain and the lake. Silvester wondered
whether he might steal a boat one night and row across to
the forest with Bubba and escape. He was afraid of forests
and shivered at the notion. Still, if he had to . . .

"My old carcass is seven-eighths savage," said Antoninus
suddenly. "But my mind is all Roman, and I can recognize
virtue. My thought was that you had been sent me as a
reward for my piety to my ancestors. I am marooned here,
as Ovid was in the Chersonese, with no one to answer
when I speak the noblest of all languages. I can walk my
halls and mutter to my statues, but they are dumb. My eyes
are failing, so that I cannot even read my books. Then you
came, with your bear, like an omen the augurs would have
understood—a handsome boy, clear eyes, quick mind, who
has lived in cities and knows men and their manners, to
walk with me round my lands by day and to read to me in
the evenings—and when I die to build a great fire with my
barge at the top of it and my body sitting upright in my
chair, so that the last of the Romans might go fully ready
to Charon. But now I see this: if I keep you here I will
break your path of virtue, and in so doing I will cancel out
all my long service to the old gods, so that I might as well
have died like a wild Slav of the plains, who never knew
the meaning of Rome, or like some sniveling Christian."

The lake stirred with a vague breeze coming from
nowhere and with nowhere to go. Antoninus chuckled, a
sound sadder than any sighing.

"We will strike a bargain," he said. "I will let you go, you and your bear, in a week's time. I cannot let you go before because my silly villagers, though they are Christians, keep one of their old feasts at the day when true summer begins, in six days' time, and would be dismayed if I sent the lucky bear away before then. The bear must dance at their feast. Till then we will talk during the day, and perhaps fish, and you can read to me. On the day after the feast I will send you to Great Bend with an escort. It is an easy three days' travel, so you will have time to spare. That is my side of the bargain. Your side is this: if you do not find this girl you will come back to my tower and live with me, as long as I survive. Is that a contract?"

"It is very generous, sir," said Silvester gravely. "Before I go, while you are resting, I can copy out as much as possible of one of your books in large writing that you can still read. Horace, perhaps?"

"I do not need eyes for Horace," said Antoninus. He struck an actor's attitude and in his wheezing voice proclaimed verse after after verse of the old parasite's loves and scoldings and forebodings of death.

Seven mornings later they rowed down the lake, with Antoninus sitting on his green throne and quoting Virgil, Silvester sitting by his feet and sighing with relief, Bubba in the bows and peering suspiciously at the mean forest, and all the oarsmen and escort groaning with hangovers from the drunken feasting that had signaled the coming of summer. They rowed abominably.

XV

Wagon

FROM GREAT BEND it was six days' journey to the borders of the Khan's country—six rough days. The track was bad, water scarce, food nonexistent. Urrguk became weaker with the pain of travel. Holy John spoke all the while to himself or to his God in Hunnish. One night they stood off an attack by a small pack of wolves, with the help of a good fire and Bubba's snarls. It was hardly even an attack, more of a famished inspection by the mildew-colored creatures of the night, but it was very frightening. But all the while Silvester was cheered by the thought that they were getting near to their goal, that he had escaped from the magician's tower of Antoninus, and that they were away from the settlement at Great Bend.

This last had been a horrible place, the final trading camp before the Danube reached its reedy delta, where the amber trail came down from the north. It was a dirty and impermanent collection of hovels, built on silt, out of driftwood. Nothing *belonged* there. Even the plants in the thickets looked footloose and peregrine. Its inhabitants were human silt, washed there by the river's trade to bar-

166

gain and contrive. No one was anybody's neighbor, though their shacks leaned on each other for support. It was an obscene parody of the City.

But at least you could buy anything there—at a price— so Silvester had bought honey and fresh herbs and left gladly with his already impatient companions.

Now at last they stood on the western rim of a wide valley through which a sluggish river twisted. The country behind them had been broken and woody, so it was astounding to stand on the edge of an enormous sweep of grassland, already silvering toward brown as the stems dried and seeded, and to look east to the lion-colored hills twenty miles away.

Urrguk cried an order which made the horse circle until he cried again at the point where he could look forward along the track they still had to travel. He twisted carefully, squinted at distance and pointed. Silvester peered down the line of his arm and saw nothing that looked like a landmark except a few black spots by the river. Bubba padded ahead to try the slope, but it wasn't steep enough for rolling. Urrguk cried to the horse which circled again and moved on, shaking its head and stepping with a gayer pace, as though it smelled at last the air of its own country.

The black spots became blobs, just as meaningless. Only when they stood on the riverbank and looked across to the far side could Silvester see that the blobs were spreading, shaggy tents, each with a couple of skeleton wagons standing beside it. A horseman was coming up the far bank at a busy canter—no, a horse-girl, for she wore a veil though she rode like a man. She saw the travelers, reined harshly in, and called. Holy John boomed a question across the water, and waved when she pointed north. She waved back before riding on to chivvy a couple of stray cows back to the little herd she seemed to be minding.

"That Centurion could have learned from her," said Holy John, shading his eyes to watch the way she balanced into a curve.

"She'd be lost in the City," said Silvester sulkily.

"Of course," agreed Holy John. "All nations have their own arts and excellencies, as well as their own vices and stupidities. You come from a city of intricate beauties, and also of intricate evils. You come to a land of simple beauties and of simple evils. Only the All-creator is permitted to weigh your intricacies against their simplicities."

He was frowning, a face of judgment, when he took the bridle.

As they plodded north along the bank Silvester saw that Urrguk was gazing across the river all the time with a strange expression on his harsh and pain-etched features. Usually the Hun's face was hard to read, but there was no mistaking this huge happiness. Just to have got him this far, Silvester thought—that makes the awful effort all worthwhile, whatever else happens. He began to wonder, as he seldom allowed himself to do, about Addie.

Holy John had refused to say anything at all to Urrguk about Silvester's motive for the journey, allowing him to think that the boy was simply running away from some sort of legal trouble. He had explained to Silvester that the Huns would be more generous if he didn't try to strike any kind of bargain before they had got Urrguk home, and certainly he had made no attempt to start his mission by converting Urrguk; but Silvester suspected that Holy John's main motive was not to imperil his great mission by dragging in unimportant details about captive girls. So there had been no way of asking how her captors might have treated her—he could only wonder and guess. This time, perhaps because of the look on Urrguk's face, his guesses were more cheerful than usual.

Another horseman appeared on the far bank, quite definitely a man this time, cantering south. He reined in when he saw the travelers and shouted a question. Silvester heard Urrguk's name in the middle of Holy John's answer. The horseman echoed it, his astonishment carrying clearly across the water. Holy John repeated what he had said, and the horseman wrenched his horse round, struck his spurs into its sides and galloped north, leaving behind him a plume of dust like blown smoke.

Ten minutes later a larger dust-cloud appeared in front of them, on their own bank, and a thudding noise, deeper than drumming, began to fill the still summer evening. Two or three riders appeared in front of the cloud, leaning over their horses' manes and lashing their haunches with little quirts so that they came in a lather of furious speed, like fugitives from a battle. But just as they seemed destined to gallop past without even noticing the travelers they all hauled cruelly on their reins, forcing the horses to a rearing halt. Bubba bellowed at the beastly exhibition; the horses shied away from her but their riders controlled them with no apparent difficulty. The foremost man leaped down, ran across to the litter, spoke Urrguk's name, knelt, and placed Urrguk's hand to his forehead. Urrguk spoke but his voice was drowned, for now the thunderously drumming dust-cloud was upon them, and it was all horsemen. Bubba bolted.

A frightened bear can move surprisingly fast, certainly faster than a tired boy who is trying to call her name between laughing-bouts of hysterical relief. It was a mile before she stopped and lay panting. As Silvester dragged her back, calling her all the rude names he could think of,

he began to worry about how he was ever going to control
her in a country whose sole population seemed to be horsemen.

But Holy John had already imposed his will on the
Huns. The main body had taken all the horses north, and
left only an escort of eight warriors to accompany the litter
on foot. These men were not at all put out by Bubba's
rudeness, but laughed and shouted at her and tried to
explain to Silvester the significance of the word Kutt-ri to
the Kutrigurs. It was clearly a new notion to them that
there was anyone in the world who couldn't speak Hunnish.

Two miles farther on they reached a place where a far
larger collection of black blobs dotted the farther bank,
and about fifty wagons, with people moving among them.
Here a fenced raft floated on the river, and from its farther
side a dozen sets of leather thongs dipped into the water
and emerged again near the other bank, where they were
tied to the harness of a team of horses. All the horses on the
near bank had been gathered into a group some way off,
and their riders formed a sort of avenue through which the
travelers had to pass to reach the raft. These Huns too
were very excited by Bubba, laughing and pointing at her
with a kind of triumph, as though she were a beautiful
princess from southern lands who had been brought captive, like Helen of old, to their country. Bubba was used to
public acclaim and enjoyed it. She stood up on her hind
legs, grinned at the men, then dropped back on all fours,
tested the gangplank with one paw and followed the litter
confidently onto the raft.

Holy John let go of the bridle and returned to the edge
of the raft. There he made the sign of the Cross in the air,
and blessed the men in Hunnish. They looked at him
baffled, but when their leader saw that he had finished he

answered politely and shouted across to the far bank. An answering shout came back; whips cracked; the leather thongs tautened clear of the surface with water streaming down the curves to drip from each knot. Silvester could see the team of horses hauling away on the far bank, and looking back he saw another team of horses being led toward the river and the thongs on that side already trailing into the water. So the raft could be hauled back whenever it was needed. It was really not a bad way of crossing rivers, despite the current's tendency to drift the whole contraption downstream, and had one advantage over a bridge— you could drag it along the bank to whatever point you wanted it.

At last the raft grounded with a mild jar on the far bank. Holy John stalked ashore alone, halted, and blessed land and sky and the astonished watchers in a tone whose rapture shone like the sun breaking through clouds of meaningless Hunnish. Silvester led the horse onto the gangplank and splashed back to ease the litter ashore without jolting. Urrguk, wide-eyed like a dead man, gazed at the sky. Silvester could see that he was already very spent with the emotion of his homecoming.

A rich-robed young man strode to the litter, knelt and placed Urrguk's hand to his forehead; then he stood, still clasping the sick man's hand with both his own.

"Balzann," whispered Urrguk. The young man smiled and the other Huns began jostling into a ragged queue to perform the same homage. Silvester heard a whimper from the raft and turned to see that Bubba was poised by the gangplank, determined not to be left behind but just as determined that she didn't much care for Hun ways. By the time he had coaxed her ashore the Huns had finished their homages, so they came crowding round to look at her, throwing their arms round each other's shoulders and shouting with excitement. Bubba sat down looking smug; she had been starved of applause during the journey and was ready to take it from anybody, even a pack of smelly horsemen.

The tents reeked of the half-dressed hides from which they were made, and also of the crowd of veiled women who lived together under each fetid cover. The young chief, Balzann, welcomed the travelers to the largest tent, but Silvester soon decided that the rancid heat was bad for a sick man, so he had him carried out and laid on soft rugs in the shadow of a wagon. The dressing on the wound had slipped, and while he was easing it back into place he heard a metallic twittering and felt something clawing at his shoulder. He looked round to see a bent, veiled figure whose thin hand plucked at his tunic while she told him —quite clearly, though he didn't understand a word—that he was managing Urrguk's wound all wrong.

"This appears to be the local witch," said Holy John. "In her opinion the wound should be filled with horse dung over which she has said secret words."

"No!"

"I will reason with her."

But the old witch was reason-proof. More of the Huns gathered and seemed to be taking her side—after all, she had probably treated all their sicknesses for many a year, and those who survived knew quite well that the right treatment for a wound was to fill it with magic horse dung. Encouraged, she made a snatch at the bandages, and Silvester was only just in time to pull her hands away. She stood back and shrilled at him.

"Now she is calling up demons against you," said Holy John in an interested voice. "I can at least outcurse her."

He thundered at the witch and the crowd drew back a little, not wanting to be too close when the powers of heaven appeared to fight it out with the demons of under-earth; but all that happened was that Bubba pushed her way into the ring to see what Silvester was doing and why he was neglecting her. The witch chose this moment to start belaboring Silvester on neck and shoulders with weak but horny fists. Bubba had never approved of other people, especially women, paying much attention to Silvester, so she ambled across and cuffed the old woman away with a blow which sent her spinning into a heap in the middle of the ring. Silvester stopped his work and dragged Bubba away by the collar before she could sit on the witch, which was her favorite way of proving that she'd won a wrestling match. He tethered her to a tent peg, then went to help the old lady to her feet.

"I'm very sorry," he said. "I ask your pardon for the behavior of my bear."

Holy John translated, and immediately the witch started back in terror, knelt, seized Silvester's hand and put it to her forehead, shrilling all the while.

"The Holy Spirit has put the right words between your lips," said John. "To own a bear is the sign of a great magician among these innocent people. I will tell her that she is forgiven."

Urrguk, wide awake now, had twisted his head to watch the contest and was grinning like a well man. In a feeble voice he said a few words to the watchers, who cheered and dispersed, leaving only the old witch to watch bright-eyed everything that Silvester did.

They held a bear-dance that night. All the young warriors danced, in a ring, with Bubba and the young chief Balzann in the center. A dozen women played different-shaped drums, the big instruments thudding out the basic beat of the tune while the smaller ones rattled elaborate rhythms round it. The men leaped and spun, fantastic steps that sent their pleated kilts circling round them. The older warriors cried encouragement. Silvester could see that this wasn't a suddenly invented dance, improvised because a dancing bear had turned up, but an old dance, often performed. And yet they made Bubba part of it, using her as a moving maypole to which they were linked by invisible ribbons. Suddenly Silvester saw that behind all the ritualized leapings and whirlings lay a story; the dance was a sort of play in which the steps and movements were the words and the plot was about a brave hunter who went out to kill a bear. Probably they usually did it round a bearskin stuck on a pole, but now they had a live bear to perform with.

So the young chief posed and hurtled, the ring pranced, the drums beat, Silvester blew on his black flute, and Bubba did what she always did, because that was all she knew. And out beyond the tents the horses and the gathered herds of cattle shuffled and snorted in the dark, like a restless sea.

Bubba began to tire. Silvester tried to slow the tune on the flute but the drummers responded by quickening their beat and further complicating the pattern of taps while the ring of dancers whirled faster and faster and Balzann embarked on an incredible series of spinning leaps. Bubba lost the beat and sat down, panting for honey. Then for the first time she seemed to notice that there was anyone else dancing and peered at Balzann with dubious astonishment, as though she was hoping nobody was going to ask *her* to perform antics of that kind. Silvester rolled across the beaten earth the little pot of honey he'd prepared for her and she lost herself in an ecstasy of sweetness while Bal-

zann brought the dance to its climax, leaping several times
clean over her unseeing head as he asserted the triumph of
Man over brute nature.

"These people are ripe for Christ," muttered Holy John
below the drumbeats. "They have the instinct to worship,
but they know no worthy god. They are like a precious jar,
waiting to be filled with the spices it was made for."

"Will you preach to them?"

"The lust is in me," said Holy John, frowning. "But that
is vanity. The All-mover has not spoken in my heart. And
more, I must live among these people and learn their
hearts and minds as well as their language. But be sure,
boy, the moment will come. Christ will strike fire from me,
His steel from my flint. Nothing He does is vain, nor has
He linked this long chain together for idleness. You see
now how the bear is part of His purpose—how could we
have guessed that, back in the City?"

"I hope Addie's all right."

"The girl? Christ is merciful."

"They may have sent her back when the Emperor paid
the gold."

"As I have told you, no general can hold a beaten army
if he tries to separate his soldiers from their loot. No, she is
part of His purpose too. She will be there."

His mutter had risen to the big, bronze tones he used for
preaching and the Huns watching the end of the dance
shushed at him, but he didn't notice. He was staring out
beyond the noisy, lighted circle to the dark silences behind
the stars. Silvester was comforted—Holy John hadn't been
wrong so far, though his rightness had come true in
peculiar ways.

The dance ended. They drank milk, fermented and
flavored with wormwood and other bitter herbs, then
slept.

Next day there were four horses, chosen for their smooth paces, to carry Urrguk's litter. With great difficulty Silvester tricked Bubba into climbing up into one of the wagons, and tethered her fast. Holy John mounted a horse and once again they were on the road, this time with a fair-sized escort, including Balzann and his chief warriors. But before long the horsemen became impatient with the slowness of the wagon, though in fact it wallowed east at a faster pace than Silvester could have managed on foot. There was a shout, followed by several whooping calls, and they waved their spears and bows in the air and cantered ahead. In half an hour they were a smudge of dust moving up the farther hills toward the horizon.

The light wagon was so crudely put together that at each lurch all its joints groaned. Nor were the wheels very round, nor the axle smooth, so the groans were joined by squeaks and thuds while the whole contraption rocked across the plain like a boat in a choppy sea. Bubba, myste-riously, slept through it all. The two Hun wagoners talked and sang, and Silvester watched the river diminish behind him under the arch of hide which covered the wagon. By the time they reached the ridge of the hills and could look eastward across an endless rolling plateau of grass, he was very depressed.

The exhilaration of the first welcome of the Huns was gone like a good dream you forget on waking. The fear of facing the Khan was beginning to swell inside him, a shapeless mass of unease, like dough on the rise. In some ways it is easier to endure a long and wearying trial, such as the journey north, than to face a climax where you have just one chance and if you fail you fail. Forever. This feel-ing that he might fail was increased by the alienness of the people with whom he had to deal—their impossible lan-guage, their uneatable raw meat, their inhuman horse-

manship. He was like a ghost among solid men, unable
to make the Huns feel his touch at any point in their lives,
except in the brief, wild ritual of the bear dance. Ghosts
are lonely.

But there was something else. He stretched himself out
to rest on the rough, reverberant timbers and thought
deeper into his soul. Antoninus had done something to
him. Antoninus had changed him. He was not now the
same Silvester. "You have the slave look." Yes. In the City
he had been a slave but he had also been a person, part of
the humming hive, his role known and respected; but to
Antoninus he had been a toy, a convenience, a possession,
a *thing*. Oh, the old man had let him depart, had permitted him to go and be a person again; but he had gone
altered, infected. Once having been a thing, he would
always have dead matter in him. The demons of the
steppes groaned at him through the boards, saying that he
would never escape the magician's tower. Never. He had
the slave look.

They reached that night's camp by moonlight and did the
bear dance for a scarred old chief who ruled forty wives
and a vast tract of plateau and who, at the feast after the
dance, kept selecting specially good strips of raw meat from
the dish before him and passing them to his guests to chew.
He himself had so few teeth that one of his wives chewed
his meat for him.

XVI

The Khan

SILVESTER dreamed again and again a dream in which Nonna was leading him and Addie into a lemon orchard, and woke again knowing that Nonna was dead. He rose miserable in the early dawn and took Bubba down to a stream to drink. (Despite the torrid heat of the valleys, all the Hun encampments were by rivers during the summers, so that the cattle should have water.) When he came back to the camp he found Balzann supervising the construction of a big litter, double the size of the one Urrguk had traveled on. Eight horses, harnessed in pairs, were standing ready to carry the poles.

"Kutt-ri?" said Balzann, pointing to the rough platform in the middle of the litter.

"She won't like it," said Silvester to Holy John, "but I'll try. Can you tell them to take the horses away for the moment, and ask for some salt. I haven't got enough honey to spare if she's going to get her proper reward after all these bear dances."

Bubba was extremely suspicious of the platform, nosing round it as though she knew it was a trap, but she forgot about it when a Hun came back with a lump of rock salt, white and glistening cubic crystals, like a jewel. She knew about salt really, but always forgot she knew and had to make up her mind fresh each time whether she liked it or not. Silvester allowed her a lick, and she drew back, startled, then nosed in for another lick and got the same electric shock. Silvester put the salt in the middle of the platform, fastened the middle of her chain to her collar and one end to a corner of the platform, so that when she went to try and up her mind about the salt again he could fasten the other end to the far corner. A strong leather thong on the other diagonal fixed her firmly to the center of the square; Silvester made a few adjustments until he was quite sure that she was comfortable when she lay flat and could move enough to ease herself but not enough to fall off. Then the eight horses were led back.

Her whimpers of distress rose to bellows of outrage as twelve Huns took the poles and hoisted her into the air while the frightened horses were harnessed; she wrenched at her ropes like a tent in a gale, but they held. A Hun brought up a shaggy horse and motioned to Silvester to mount. He looked round for Holy John and saw him already mounted.

"I can't ride," Silvester called. "I've never tried!"

Holy John spoke in Hunnish. The Huns jeered like schoolboys. A man ran off and came back with a quite different sort of saddle, more like a long footstool with a pole rising at its forward end. Two Huns seized Silvester as soon as the new girth was fastened and flung him up onto the stool with both legs dangling down one side; he snatched at the pole to stop himself from overbalancing and discovered that that was what it was for. His reins were handed to a Hun on another horse, who took them sulkily, and then the old chief cried aloud and the whole party, including Balzann, thudded out of the camp.

At first he was busy clinging to the pole, but when he'd found that he wasn't going to fall off provided he sat reasonably still, he had time to look and see how Bubba was taking her ride. She was hating it, and lay absolutely terrified, slumped on the platform with pitiful eyes. Occasionally she would raise her head and see the horsemen all round her and duck back at once; luckily the pitching motion made her afraid to wrench at her ropes. Only, gradually, her peeps at the passing world became longer and more inquisitive, and her attitude of repose less abject. Silvester was wondering whether it had begun to seep into her slow brain that she was getting somewhere without having to walk when his attention was distracted by his reins being passed to a different Hun.

This happened about every half hour. The Huns made a lot of noise as they rode, rowdy back-chat and jeers; it was some time before Silvester saw that whoever was leading him came in for the noisiest jeers and answered most sulkily. When Holy John took over he asked him why.

"You are riding a bride's saddle. When a warrior of the Kutrigurs wishes to marry a wife he brings to her father a gift of horses and cattle and a saddle such as that. The father accepts the beasts but returns the saddle and one horse, and the warrior puts the bride on it and leads her away."

"Yes, but why . . . ."

"These Huns have virtue. Among them to be a lover of boys is a disgrace beyond disgraces."

"Then you'll have to let your bishops marry," said Silvester cheerfully. But out in this cruel, innocent air the old City jibe felt curiously ugly.

For four days they traveled in this fashion over the wide

and windy steppes, any part of which looked just the same
as all the other parts, though the escort of Huns seemed to
know where they were going. From the sun Silvester could
see that they were not journeying straight, but zigzagging
east, stopping overnight in a fresh village of tents and
doing the bear dance. Urrguk, visibly stronger each day,
took great delight in this, commenting critically on the
way it was done and comparing the merits of the main
dancers. Silvester squatted cross-legged beside his rugs and
kept the old tune moving, not understanding a word
Urrguk was saying but quite able to see that none of the
dancers—it was usually the son of the local chief, or some
close relation—was as remarkable a performer as Balzann
had been. Then next morning they would move on, taking
with them the local chief and another half-dozen warriors,
so that Urrguk should come to his Khan with a fitting escort.

By the third morning Bubba was convinced of the
merits of her new mode of travel, and on the fourth
Silvester found she had slipped her tether in the night and
was already sitting on the platform, ringed by shrilling
children.

On the fourth night they found a camp beside a moder-
ate river flowing east, and on the fifth day they followed its
valley, riding close beneath brown hills. The valley
ground was richer than the uplands had been, and the
herds of cattle larger; even when feeding they looked dangerous—long-horned, short-legged and shaggy. He noticed
that at one point the whole escort party made a long loop
into the hills to avoid crossing the path of a moving herd.
The herdsmen were children, no older than he was, the
girls distinguishable only by their veils. Silvester thought
it odd that women who had learned to ride as if they and
their horse were a single creature obeying the human will,

should in the end have to be fetched from their fathers'
tents on a saddle for incompetents, such as the one he rode.

Their valley widened and widened and became an enormous plain that ended in pale hills fifty miles east. A heavy
heat-haze lay over the lush midsummer flatness, but as far
as the eye could see the big groups of cattle grazed. The
faint remains of a marshy smell hung in the air.

"It's like the Danube," he said.

"We are coming to the big river," said Holy John. "The
Khan keeps his summer camp on its banks."

The river, in fact, was only about half the size of the
Danube, but still a mighty stream. They crossed it on ferry
rafts where two islands split its passage—it would not have
been possible to work the thongs over the full width from
bank to bank. The islands were too narrow for horses to be
able to haul effectively, so here the thongs were pulled by
slaves, who chanted a sad, slow chanty as they strained for
each fresh heave. They seemed to have come from twenty
nations, tall blond men and men yellower and squatter
even than the Huns and a black man from the far south
and gaunt Alans—and several Greeks who cried to
Silvester for news of their own world. They seemed
surprisingly cheerful, and while the raft was being hauled
back to bring over the second half of the escort Silvester sat
among them, enjoying the lively ripple of Greek talk
again.

"Not so bad," explained one of them. "They're stupid
barbarians, Huns, so of course they've got some crazy ideas
about life. Look at that gang over there, on the second
island—they're not slaves at all: they're poor Huns doing a
three-year stint on the rafts, and they don't expect to be
treated any different from what we are, but when they've
done the Khan will give each twenty cows and a couple of

horses, so they can go back to their clans and set up with a
wife. Me, I've another two years to do, and then the Khan
will give the twenty cows to the Hun who caught me, first
place—down on the Euxine, that was, after I got
shipwrecked—and he'll have to set me free. Then I can either go home, or stick it out another three years and set up
with twenty cows of my own."

"Sure," said another Greek. "It sounds fine, but if you
think you're going to live in a black tent with a couple of
obedient Hun women, they won't let you. They're too
keen on keeping the Hun stock pure."

"But they take foreign women captive," said Silvester.

"Course they do," said the second Greek. "And sometimes they marry them—if you can call it marrying. Thing
is, women don't count with them. They think all the child
comes from the father, and the woman's only, well, like a
sort of wine barrel he's put his wine in to let it mature."

"I might buy a couple of foreign wives, then," said the
first Greek. "I'd get them cheap, only a couple of cows
each. Huns like their own kind, a fat yellow girl with hair
like horsehair and a greasy skin. The smellier the better."

"Then why do they bother to take foreign captives?"
said Silvester.

"It's like this. They marry a new wife every two or three
years, and naturally the newest one is the one they're
keenest on. But the rule is the newest wife has to wait on
the older ones, and of course they're bitchy to her. So if
you want to keep your new wife sweet, you get hold of a
slave for her, to do the waiting, and Huns won't use other
Huns as slaves, not even women."

"It all makes sense," said a third Greek, "once you've
cottoned on to the twisty way the Hun looks at everything.
Men first, horses next, cows next and women last of all."

This should all have been comforting, but Silvester was

again depressed and nervous as they trotted north along
the far bank of the big river. The fact that there was a rea-
sonable chance that Addie was alive and unharmed only
gave him a greater chance to fail. And how would Urrguk,
with his Hun notions of honor, take to knowing that
Silvester had tended him and brought him home not for
his own sake but because of a despised foreign girl? He
began to think that he'd made a mistake in not trying to
learn Hunnish himself, because Holy John would certainly refuse to help by asking for Addie if he thought it
would in any way compromise his own mission. He was
biting his lip with nerves when they came, three miles upstream, to the place where the Khan had set up camp.

If the other camps had been villages, this was a town—a
walled town, for it was ringed with wagons; every so often
a gap had been left between the wagons—just like the
gates in the great Wall of Theodosius—and now from
these gaps troop after troop of horsemen came spurring out
to meet them, yelling one wild cry which Silvester suddenly realized was Urrguk's name. These troops circled
and joined the escort so that they rode into the camp of the
Khan like a small army. And inside the ring of wagons the
tents had not just been settled anyhow, as they had in the
villages, but with wide streets running between them,
worn bare of grass so that the horses moved almost in
silence over the powdery surface and everyone in the
procession, except those at the very front, became covered
with a bone-colored layer of choking dust. The people of
the camp gathered round this moving dust-cloud, cheering
Urrguk, crying in excitement at Bubba, jeering at Silvester
on his bride-saddle.

The camp was set at a point where the river ran out of
the west toward a broad mound and then curved away
south; the street they were on followed the river until it
met an even broader avenue which started at the apex of

the curve and ran up the mound. On either side of this avenue were tents larger than any Silvester had yet seen, and it ended at the top of the mound in a tent that was clearly a palace, high as a two-story house, guarded by armed warriors and topped with banners where the four huge tent-poles projected through the ridge. This avenue was wide enough to leave room between the flanking tents and the central route for a whole crowd of Huns, mostly sitting on the ground in a circle before each tent. As the cavalcade moved toward the majestic tent at the top it began to split up, chief after chief with his retinue trotting over to one of the circles of men, who leaped to their feet with glad cries, took the horses and led them away, and brought out of the tent behind a pitcher and a lot of drinking-horns. Each warrior took a horn and filled it, then raised it to the sky; the chief cried out, the warriors answered him, and they all drained their horns with one draught and threw them on the ground. That ritual over they sat down, the chief on a low stool with his back to the tent, the warriors in a circle before him in the dust, and exchanged news.

Silvester had seen the process repeated several times when something different happened: the circle of warriors outside the tent nearest the palace on the left broke from their formation and came running down the hill in the wide-legged waddle of men who would normally use a horse if they wanted to move faster than a walk. As they ran they cried Urrguk's name. They surrounded his litter, pressing his hand to their foreheads. They were weeping, all of them, through their laughter, and Silvester was astonished to see Urrguk's hard face also runneled with tears.

"This is common," said Holy John in a strange voice. "True warriors count it no dishonor to cry like children."

His own face also was working as though he were trying to master some emotion too strong to hold in. Silvester recognized the symptoms and slid from the bride-saddle just in time to catch Holy John as he flung out an arm as if to ward off a blow from heaven and then toppled, shuddering but rigid, from his saddle. Silvester eased his weight down into the dust and saw that his trance had locked his feet back under his buttocks but that the rest of his body lay straight. He was already in the position of prayer. With an effort Silvester heaved him onto his knees and balanced him there.

Urrguk must have noticed what was happening, for Silvester found himself surrounded by the grinning Huns from the tent, who as soon as he had finished with Holy John took turns at hugging Silvester to their stinking chests and slapping him with bruising goodwill between the shoulder blades. He thanked them politely in Greek and tried to persuade them by signs to pick Holy John up and carry him back to their tent. But they immediately became grave and shrank back from the weird figure in the dust, muttering to each other. Their high spirits returned when Silvester led them to lower Bubba's litter so that he could release her. Bubba stretched like a cat awaking from a doze, looked suspiciously up and down the vista of tents, noticed that a Hun was once more hugging Silvester, and cuffed him aside.

Jeering and cheering, the whole party straggled back up the slope, leaving Holy John on his knees, rapt, an object of strange awe. The crowds who continued to pour into the avenue gave him a wide berth, however thronged the rest of the space became.

A seemingly endless procession of chiefs came with their retinues to pay their respects to Urrguk. Silvester was quite unable to persuade the men of his retinue that these greetings might be too much for their master's strength. He saw that it was a matter of honor—they must show the world that they had their chief back alive even if it killed him. Honor, Holy John had often said, was the Devil's virtue; now Silvester saw what he meant.

The sun was slanting down the western sky, making the whole reach of the river gleam gold, when fresh warriors came to the entrance of the great tent and the previous sentries shambled off. An enormous horn, fully ten feet long and made of crudely carved wood, was brought out by a Hun who placed the farther end on the ground and the mouthpiece to his lips. He blew. The sound was a deep and windy groan, like a sick giant's sigh. Another Hun in a ridiculous tall turban stood beside the horn blower and chanted a short announcement. The horn groaned again. Everybody in the avenue leaped to his feet and started toward the great tent, in no particular order. Urrguk's retinue picked up the litter and dashed for the doorway, making signs to Silvester to bring Bubba along. But she was recalcitrant and wary. Perhaps she'd decided that the horn was some monster challenging her to battle—if so, she was not in the mood for battles. Silvester had both to coax and kick her before she would come draggingly towards the big crowd jostling round the entrance.

Silvester's first thought was that they would never all get in, least of all a foreign boy with a bear, but a couple of Urrguk's retinue were waiting for him on the fringe of the crowd and brutally jostled a way through. And then Silvester found that not all the Huns were actually trying to enter. A chief with his retinue would come swaggering up to the sentries, turn, and pass his weapons back; a couple of his warriors would do the same, and only those three would stalk weaponless into the tent, while the rest of the retinue struggled back out of the hurly-burly. Warriors with no retinue simply threw their weapons down in a pile beside the sentries.

Silvester's guide said something to the Hun in the double-decker turban and pointed at Bubba. This man shouted to one of the sentries, who threw down his weapons on the pile and motioned to Silvester to follow him into the tent. All the sentries wore the fringe of blue beads below their turbans.

Bubba jibbed again at the entrance, but after a couple of whispered curses from Silvester padded with a low growl through the opening.

It was like walking into hell, raging hot, reeking of sweat and leather, jostling with silent men, and after the glare of the evening sun almost pitch dark. A little light came through raised flaps in the far wall of the tent and from a few dormerlike openings in the roof, so after a couple of blinks Silvester was able to get his bearings and follow the sentry along a narrow aisle of silent men toward the top end of the tent. Here there was more light, coming from a dozen fat candles of low quality arranged round a sort of dais or altar. The candles smoked and guttered in the reeking air, and threw their erratic light on a gross and hideous idol that sat on a stool on the altar, and on the greater chiefs who stood in a ring before it. Silvester was led almost up to the altar, and there he found, in the space left by the ring of chiefs, Urrguk lying on his litter. Bubba padded up and sniffed at him, as though to make sure that here at least was someone she knew. Urrguk raised his hand and teased her ear and smiled, but said nothing. Silvester wished Holy John was there. He noticed an old man with a white face, not at all like a Hun, crouched on a throne by the idol's legs.

The jostling from the door gradually stilled, and the rest of the tent was quite silent. Silvester could never have imagined that a crowd of rowdy Huns could keep so quiet. Perhaps they were all in church. But they worshipped the sun. He looked again at the idol. Even by Byzantine standards it was quite realistic, except for being uglier and crueler and fatter than any imaginable Hun.

The silence was complete. Another man in a tall turban strode in front of the altar and cried aloud the name of the Khan Zabergan. Silvester looked about to see where he would enter.

Into the silence floated words. The idol spoke. It was no trick. Silvester saw its lips moving. He couldn't understand the words, but his vision shifted and he saw that that gross face was alive. The candle-shadows had made it hideous and inhuman, but now he could see what he should have seen all along—it was a man. It was the Khan Zabergan.

The crowd in the tent rustled at the words. Four chiefs picked up the litter and carried it shoulder-high to the throne, so that the Khan could reach out his hand to Urrguk without bending down. Urrguk took it and placed it to his forehead, speaking his homage in a strong voice. The Khan made a short speech to the warriors, in the middle of which his arms shot out to point at Silvester—he sounded angry and scornful about something. The litter was carried back.

"Greek boy?" said the old man at the Khan's feet, tilting his head inquiringly; the shift showed Silvester that he was blind, and not simply because his eyes had failed—they had been removed.

"I'm here," said Silvester, the words coming gulpingly through his fear-dried throat.

"Kneel at the Khan's feet. Place his right hand to your forehead. He has praised you before his warriors, saying that you have brought home his cousin whom they left on the battlefield, his favorite captain, the First of the Van, Son of the Bear, Slayer of Armies and a lot of other titles that will mean nothing to you. Say something polite and then come forward."

Silvester could think of nothing to say. Desperately he

adapted the formula which litigants were supposed to use to praise the impartiality of a Byzantine judge (whom they'd probably been bribing for weeks).

"It was my fortune to be able to help so great a Prince, and doubly my fortune that it means I have stood before the great Khan."

The blind Greek recognized the formula and translated smiling. Silvester knelt trembling on the step of the dais and raised the Khan's hand to his forehead; it was slimy with some kind of sweet-smelling precious oil, the odor of which followed him back to his place. The Khan spoke again to his warriors, apparently settling some other business of which Silvester knew nothing; a dozen warriors knelt at the dais, and were given various assignments, or confirmed in their new chieftainships, or whatever it might be. A dispute was settled by the Khan's word and confirmed by the acclamation of the warriors. Time dragged. Silvester longed to yawn in the stale heat. Suddenly he saw that the Khan was speaking to him.

"It is the Khan's desire," translated the Greek, "that we should celebrate the return of his cousin with a performance of the bear dance."

Silvester looked at Bubba, lying on the ground near his feet. During the previous half hour he had heard her emitting a series of curious low grumbles, not of fear or boredom but a kind of puzzled rage, as though she would be furious about something if only she could remember what it was. She was certainly in no mood to dance.

"I don't know whether she'll do it," he said. "She's not used to places like this."

"There is no other place like this," said the blind Greek, drily. "She has performed for lesser chiefs—it would be a conspicuous blow to the Khan's honor if she refused to do so for him, and before all his warriors. The bear is a power-

ful symbol among these people. I advise you to persuade
her. The Khan's favor is not quickly given, but it is
quickly withdrawn."

Twenty minutes later Silvester settled cross-legged
against one of the smaller tentpoles and put the black flute
to his lips. He was streaming with sweat and very nervous
about Bubba, who was still emitting fitful growls despite
having been appeased with half the remaining honey. The
tent was still reeking, still as crowded as ever, except the
space for the dance which had been cleared in front of the
dais. The Khan was visibly impatient, fidgeting on his
throne and sucking his blubber lips in and out.

With one last wish that Holy John would wake from his
trance and take command, Silvester blew the first notes of
the dance. One drum picked up the rhythm and the others
thudded in. The ring of chiefs who made the circle clapped
between the drumbeats and started to move sideways with
a curious loose-kneed step that allowed their bare feet to
scuff the bare earth with a pattering sound, adding another
noise to the repeated pattern of sound. Balzann spun into
the circle, stripped to the waist, glistening with oil and
sweat, twirling with outstretched kilt round the stolidly
shuffling bear who was the center of it all.

Only Bubba spoiled the effect. She would dance a few
steps, stop as though she'd remembered something more
important that she ought to be doing, cock her head on
one side, growl, then all of a sudden start dancing again—
but without any relish. Silvester was worried. She looked
wilder—much less like a trained bear—than usual.
Perhaps she was ill. Or perhaps it was the stale heat of the
tent. Balzann seemed to appreciate the difference, because
he danced with a greater frenzy then before, spinning and
stamping dangerously close to her in her present mood.

But she took no notice. At the end of the first cycle of the tune Silvester tossed her as usual a little cake all sticky with honey, but she dropped it, which he'd never seen happen since first he'd taught her to catch. She stopped dancing, lowered herself onto all fours and gobbled her prize absentmindedly. It was some time before she rose onto her hind legs and began dancing again.

The pattern of the dance changed. Balzann started his series of astounding leaps while the ring of chiefs, instead of circling, closed in on the center and then expanded again. The Khan Zabergan sat grinning on his throne—he at least was satisfied with the performance; and of course most of the others hadn't seen Bubba dance before and so did not know how much better she could do than this.

The drumbeats quickened. Soon, Silvester thought with relief, Bubba would lose the rhythm and sit down and her part in the rite would be safely over. Yes, she was stopping dancing ... But at that point she shook herself as though she'd suddenly remembered the important business she'd forgotten. The bristles on her back rose; she bellowed and made a lurching rush at the chiefs, broke through, leaving a couple of them sprawling, and disappeared into the crowd of warriors. The drumbeats wavered. Cries of warning rose from the darkness, and then a cry on a different note—a yell of agony.

Silvester snatched up her chain and dashed through the turmoil of the ruined dance. He found Bubba crouched growling in a little space in the second ring of warriors, where the spectators had barely been able to shrink away from her because of the crush. But she was paying no attention to them. She was growling at the man whose legs Silvester could see twisted beneath her.

He seized her collar, kicked her ribs, and hauled with all his strength while he whispered his curses at her. Even in her fury she must have recognized his voice, for she gave a final barking growl and came. He used her momentum to rush her to the main tentpole, to which he chained her on a short chain. She lay down, growling again now, deep in her throat. Silvester went back to see if he could do anything for the man.

It was a warrior of the Khan's tent, wearing the blue beads. The crowd were still straining clear of him, as though he were unlucky to touch. Bubba had killed him bear-fashion, knocking him down and biting his throat out.

In a daze of shock and astonishment Silvester looked round the tent. All he could see was the Khan Zabergan, motionless on his throne, still grinning.

XVII

The Law

"So the penalty is three times death," explained the blind Greek in his mild, tired voice. "First, you have brought a weapon—the bear—into the Khan's own tent, and for that the law of the Huns says death. Second, you have slain in the Khan's presence, without his command, and for that the law of the Huns says death. Third, you have slain a man of the Khan's own following, Azerbad, and for that the law of the Huns says death. But the Khan is merciful, acknowledging that you have touched his hand with your forehead, and so his protection is over you that you shall not die in the same manner as a foreigner would who had done these things. Instead you are given the rights of a Hun. That means that you may plead your case to the Khan, and if he discerns any justice in it you may then fight for your life against three warriors of the kinship of Azerbad, one for each death."

"I cannot fight," cried Silvester.

The Greek interpreted so that all the tent could hear. For the first time the Khan frowned. But before he could speak his anger there was a cry from the floor and a com-

motion in the front rank of chiefs. Turning, Silvester
thought at first that two of them were wrestling with each
other; then he saw that Urrguk had reached up an arm and
was hauling himself upright with the help of the chief
beside him. The chief on his other side put his arm round
his shoulders and steadied him into a standing position.
His face was gray with pain and streaked with sweat, but
he freed one arm and flung it out to the Khan. When he
spoke it was not in the thin voice of illness but with harsh
strength. The crowd became utterly still. Silvester saw the
blind Greek beckoning, and moved over so that he could
hear the whispered translation.

"How these Huns love a good harangue," said the old
man, smiling as though no boy's death was in the balance.
"The Prince is reciting his titles and his kinship with the
Khan. Now he is talking about the battle before Byzantium. He led the charge. He says that he alone of all the
Huns upheld the Khan's honor, and didn't run away but
fought until he was surrounded and pierced in the back
with a lance and left for dead on the battlefield. His horse
stayed by him, and when he came to his senses he pulled
himself into the saddle and started for home. But his
wound weakened him, and his wits left him, and he lost his
way and made camp by a stream and prepared to die far
from his tent and his wives and his longed-for country. But
you found him, with your bear and an old man, and
brought him home to the comrades who had deserted him.
You nursed him like a woman but endured dangers like a
warrior. You saved the Khan's honor, he says. If you have
taken a life, you have paid one back by bringing the
Khan's cousin home alive. So there are only two of the
kinship of Azerbad to be fought, and as you are no warrior
he will fight them himself. Today, if the Khan decrees. He
swears that the bear is a good bear, and gentle, and healed

him with its magic, and fought against wolves in the forest. If she has now killed Azerbad he believes it must be for some magical cause—that she knows of some secret wrong he has done, or, since the Khan's house is under the protection of the bear, she saw into Azerbad's heart and knew he was plotting a wickedness against the Khan. He says, finally, that his life is yours, and swears that for the Khan's honor it is better that he should die and you should live. What now? What now?"

"He has fainted," said Silvester, and ran weeping to ease Urrguk back onto the rich furs his followers had spread for him. That this hard, fierce, half-wild soldier should so fight for him! He stood slowly up, unseeing, only vaguely aware of the low mutter of the warriors gnawing the speech over.

"Come back, Greek boy," said the interpreter. "The Khan speaks."

Silvester sidled across to hear the meaning of the ugly, chanted rant from the throne.

"That is all Hunnish boasting," whispered the blind man. "Very typical. He has been put at a disadvantage, so he boasts about his glory while he thinks of a solution. He's reminding his warriors how much gold the Emperor paid him, and saying that they have all had their share. Ha! Now he is talking to you. He has picked up the notion that Azerbad was plotting against his life; he wishes to know if you are a magician; also, what reward you expected for bringing his cousin home. Urrguk has set him a problem, bringing the Khan's honor into the argument, so he will try to save you if he can. But these barbarians are mighty sticklers for the law, so he must find good reason to cancel three death penalties. One moment, boy. My advice is that you tell the truth. Forty years ago I came to the Huns to trade. I was a free man then, and I had eyes, but I thought this people were simple barbarians and easily deceived, so now I am a slave and blind. You understand?"

Silvester found himself floating on a curious tide of calm. Nothing mattered except the truth, and that he now knew with a simple and perfect clarity, as though God had slid a finger of sunlight into this fetid dark and shown him.

"May someone look at the dead man's left arm?" he said. "Between the wrist and elbow there should be the scars from a bite, about a month old."

It depended on the toughness of Hun skin. But he had tasted blood. He thought he could taste it now. The blind man put the request into Hunnish.

Silvester stood silent during the scuffling interval while a torch was brought and the body examined. Several voices called out, all together, the note of surprise and assent unmistakable. His toothmarks were there. He let the noise die and settled to telling his story, much as he had told it to Antoninus, but concentrating more on the sack of the Lord Celsus's house and less on his journey. Someone cried out in agreement when he came to the loot and burning, and when he told the story of the dying slave merchant there was a curious anxious whispering. He made no bones about his reasons for helping Urrguk. He took the big ruby from his pocket and unwrapped it, holding it up to one of the candles so that all the tent could see its brilliant, pulsing glow. Sometimes, when he paused for the interpreter to translate, he caught the deep growl of Bubba still remembering her enemy.

"So," he finished, "I think that my bear, who had never in her life been hurt or punished, must have remembered the smell of the warrior who struck her. She was troubled all the time she was in the Khan's tent. It is the same man —my toothmarks are on his arm. I am no magician. I do not believe that my bear has magical powers. That is all. If

you want witnesses for the truth of what I've said, there's
an old man in a trance before the Khan's tent, and a girl in
the tent of Azerbad—at least I hope she's there."
    The Greek interpreted. The Khan gave an order, which
was followed by a bustle round the entrance. The Khan
spoke again, one short question.
    "You say you are a slave?" translated the Greek.
    "Yes."
    Frowning, the Khan rose from his throne and began to
yell at the warriors. He was so squat that he seemed barely
taller standing than he had sitting, but he cowed his men
with the power of his rage. Now he truly was the figure
from Byzantine nightmares.
    "He is rebuking his warriors," whispered the Greek.
"He says there are only two real men in the tent; one is a
cripple and the other a boy who rode into the camp on a
bride's saddle. The rest of them are not men but pigeons.
(The pigeon is always the coward in Hun fables.) He says
it makes his heart boil in his belly (they have strange notions of anatomy) to think that a slave and a Greek should
have made this journey for the honor of the house he
served. It makes him think that if he'd commanded an
army of Greek slaves, instead of pigeon-livered Huns, he
would have taken Byzantium and now rule all the world.
Does he sit? Yes? Good. Now he says he will pronounce on
your crimes. He says that Urrguk's argument is good—that
though you have slain one of his so-called warriors in the
Khan's presence, you have brought a real warrior back to
the Khan's presence. So is the first death paid for. He says
that the ruby is the color of blood, and will count for the
blood you would have shed for bringing a weapon into the
Khan's tent. So is the second death paid for. What
happens? What happens?"
    Silvester shook himself out of the shock of learning that

the Lady Ariadne's ransom was gone—gone to pay for his own trivial life—and craned from the first step of the dais over the heads of the warriors and chiefs.

"They're carrying in my friend, Holy John," he said.

It was impressive entrance. The men who had fetched the saint had been too superstitious to disturb him more than they must, so they had lifted him bodily onto a shield and were carrying him in on their shoulders, while one man steadied him in his kneeling position. His gaunt shape stood for a moment sharp against the daylight, weird. A whisper of awe rippled across the tent. Silvester explained to the blind man.

"Epileptic, is he?" answered the Greek. "These savages think that the spirits of the dead speak through the mouths of epileptics."

When the bearers lowered Holy John to the ground before the Khan, he certainly looked like a man in touch with other worlds, locked in his insensate ecstasy, blind as a statue.

The Khan grunted, like a spectator at a play who is pleased with some new twist in the plot. The Greek spoke briefly with him. There was a pause. The next commotion at the entrance seemed to be only a few more warriors crowding in and pushing towards the front—but no, Addie was with them.

Veiled, her head covered, her body hidden by a muffling robe, she was still unmistakable from the way she moved, gawky with fright, the same doll that she had been at her betrothal feast. When the Khan spoke to her and pointed at Silvester she turned and stared as though she too were in a trance. She took a stiff-jointed pace towards him, half raised a pleading hand, then turned awkwardly back to the Khan.

"Who is the boy, child?" said the blind man impatiently.

"S-s-silvester he was c-called. He was a s-s-lave of my f-father's."

She spoke as if he were a ghost, sucked from the dead by Hunnish witchcraft. She didn't look at him again.

"Tell the Khan how you came to the tent of Azerbad."

Stammering badly, she told the story of the sack in a bloodless whisper. The Greek questioned her about the fight in the cage and translated her answers to the Khan. Then the Khan sat frowning, and the warriors started to fidget with impatience, as though they were losing interest. Suddenly the Khan lifted his hand and at once the jostling stilled. The Khan's harsh voice boomed through the reeking tent.

"Let the bear be brought to the Khan's feet," said the Greek.

Silvester walked to the tentpole and found that Bubba, though still very disturbed, was in a changed mood. She knew that she had done something to earn Silvester's displeasure, but had now forgotten what; but he had punished her by leaving her chained on a short chain in this dark place full of smelly men. When he knelt to undo her chain she fawned like a dog against his side.

"You're a silly old cow," he said crossly. "I'm facing the death penalty because of you."

The tone of his voice must have told her she wasn't going to be punished anymore, because she started sneezing with released tension as she followed him back to the throne while the warriors flinched out of range of her. The Khan held up his hand again and spoke in ponderous tones, like a lawgiver declaring new laws to his people. He paused long enough between sentences for the Greek to translate.

"To whom does the boy belong? He was the slave of the

girl's father, who is dead with no other child. The boy belongs to the girl. Is it so?"

The warriors answered with one deep, baying shout.

"It is so," they thundered.

"To whom does the bear belong? It will obey none but the boy. The bear belongs to the boy. Is it so?"

"It is so."

"To whom does the girl belong? She was the plunder of Azerbad, who was slain in fair fight by the bear. The girl belongs to the bear."

"It is so."

This time the warriors' shout ended on a different note as they began to laugh and stamp their feet and slap each other on the backs because of the cleverness of their Khan. They kept repeating the joke to each other as they pointed at the two Greek children and the Greek bear.

"It is a fair jest," said the interpreter. "But the Khan has some further purpose. My advice is that you make a charade of obedience, each to the other, in front of the Khan."

Silvester nodded. This was what the Lord Celsus would have done, arranging the entertainments for a feast—after strong emotion, give your audience something frivolous. He walked across to where Addie stood, knelt, and raised her trembling hand to his forehead. As he stood again he whispered, "Do that to Bubba." He flicked the chain so that Bubba reared onto her hind legs; still with her puppetlike movements Addie knelt, took Bubba's paw and raised it to her forehead. Silvester could see that Bubba thought she was going to have her armpits tickled for her, and was bewildered when something different happened. Silvester gave another tug on the chain to make her drop on all fours, then held out his hand to touch her forehead.

The Huns yelled with pleasure to see the triangle of sub-
servience completed, but Bubba, again bewildered, backed
off to see why Silvester had missed her mouth with whatever sweet he was offering her. All he could think of was to
rub the back of his hand across his forehead in the hope
that some of the Khan's scented grease remained there, and
offer her that to lick. The gesture must have meant something to the Huns, some passing on of authority, for they
all cheered and shouted again while Bubba took a couple
of discontented licks at Silvester's skin.

The Khan raised his hand, stilling the uproar as though
he had closed a door on it. Silvester moved back to stand
near the blind Greek.

"There is still one life to be repaid," said the Khan. "Is
it so?"

"It is so," cried the warriors as Silvester's hopes seeped
away.

"The law of our people is that the master must pay for
the crime of his servant. Is it so?"

"It is so."

"And these three are of our people. I have taken the boy
under my shield for his services to Urrguk. The girl is of
the tent of Azerbad. And we are the people of the bear, so
how should the bear not be of our people? Is it so?"

"It is so."

"Then which of them shall pay the life, as each is master
of the other? It must not be more than one, or there will
be fresh deaths to be paid for. Who speaks otherwise?"

Not a whimper of disagreement rose.

"Now the law is also this: when an injury is done under
a man's tent and the doer of that injury cannot pay the
price, or cannot be captured, then the master of that tent
must pay. Is it so?"

"It is so."

"Therefore for the last life of Azerbad, I the Khan must pay."
"Great and merciful is the Khan."
"I cannot, by the laws of our people, pay with my life, for I am the Khan. But the brothers of Azerbad shall have the full blood-price, in soft gold. My shield shall be over the wives and children of Azerbad. And since bear and boy and girl each owes me the third part of a life, they shall join my household and be my servants, according to the customs of our people. Thus is justice done."
"Thus is justice done," bellowed the warriors. While their cheers rang the blind Greek whispered to Silvester, smiling with the malicious amusement of the old and bored.
"What a lawyer he'd have made in Byzantium, eh? He's wasted in this wilderness. I wonder what he's after in the tent of Azerbad—one of the wives, perhaps."
"Azerbad took two racehorses from my master's stables."
"That would be it. Now they belong to the bear, and so to him. You won't have a bad time in his tent, boy—you'll have your eyes, and you're already accustomed to being a slave . . ."
"But the Lady Ariadne! She must go home. Her cousins are cheating . . ."
"Impossible. The Khan has declared the law before the chiefs and warriors, and they have approved it by their shouts. It cannot now be broken or changed. That is the custom of the Huns."
"But . . ."
"He saved your life, boy. Quiet. He is about to speak."
But it was a different voice that rang through the silence.
"Khan Zabergan!" it cried.
Silvester swung, gaping, and saw Holy John upright in

front of the line of chiefs. Before the gasp of astonishment
from the warriors at this brusque outburst could change to
anger, he began to speak. His voice filled the tent. On his
tongue the ugly language took on depths and resonances
that Silvester had never heard in any of its natural speak-
ers. The Khan made one impatient gesture, but stilled it.
The warriors listened in silence. Silvester could sense the
leash of attention tightening on every savage mind. Only
the blind Greek was unimpressed—or rather was
impressed by the quality of the performance and not by
the message in the words.

"He has them," he whispered. "He ran a risk. Tongues
have been pulled out for speaking so to the Khan. But now
he has them."

"What's he saying?"

"Ha! He rides the language like a horseman riding an
unbroken stallion. What? Oh, he is talking of war—he has
learned something about the dealings of the Empire with
the Utrigurs. The Khan, since he returned, has been
trying to renew the old alliance with his cousin Huns to
the east, against the attacks of savages called Avars who
have been troubling our eastern borders. He must make
up his mind whether to wait for the Utrigurs or muster
again and ride east without them. So your friend has made
a cunning start: all Huns will listen to news affecting war.
... But now he is shifting his ground ... yes, he says that
the bear slaying a man before the face of the Khan is a sign
from heaven, not to be disregarded at the outset of a war.
It is a sign that the old Gods are withdrawing their protection . . ."

The old man stopped translating and cocked his head
on one side to listen, sucking his gray lips in and out.
Silvester shifted his glance to the warriors, all frowning
with attention, and then he noticed the Lady Ariadne still

standing stiffly before the Khan like part of the previous
game which someone had forgotten to tidy away. He stole
across and took her by the elbow and motioned her to
kneel beside Bubba, who lay now with her jaw between
her paws, flat on the ground. The Lady Ariadne's hand
moved unthinkingly over the glossy hide; she started to
relax, bowing her spine into a soft curve; she became a
person and not a doll.

Holy John boomed on. He made the warriors laugh a
couple of times. But then he pointed at Silvester, Addie
and bear in turn, speaking all the while with careful urgency. Could he be demanding that they should be sent
home? No, the warriors' faces suggested some more
puzzling notion. The blind man suddenly grinned widely
enough to show the three remaining teeth in his lower jaw.

"What's he saying?" whispered Silvester.

"He has nerve! He has wit! He has used you three, and
the way in which the Khan's word now binds you, to illus-
trate the doctrine of the Trinity. Once you put a notion
like that into their noddles you'll never get it out. Now
they'll believe the Holy Spirit is a bear."

The old fraud, thought Silvester angrily. He must have
been out of his trance ages before he spoke if he picked up
a point like that. Probably he came to when he was carried
in, and had spent the time since then shamming, listening,
waiting his moment. Well, at least he'd taken his chance.
You could hear now from his tone that he was working
toward an end. Silvester recalled two of the images he had
used for himself—the flint from which God struck the
spark, the flute through which the breath of God blew.
The pictures mixed in Silvester's mind and became a fur-
nace with the wind of heaven roaring through the bellows
and forcing the charcoal to whiter and yet whiter heat
until it could melt the stodgy metal of the souls in the tent

into a golden liquid, and then they could be poured into whatever mold God willed.

But Holy John spoke the last few sentences hushed, allowing the little syllables to ripple liquid into the dark. He bowed his head.

The Khan made a slow movement, like a man waking from a daze. The murmur of the warriors swelled. Bubba sat up and sneezed.

"It is finished," said the Greek. "Give me your shoulder, boy, and I will lead you to the private tents of the Khan."

XVIII

Thongs

SILVESTER became a thing again, an object, one of the Khan's innumerable unnoticed possessions, important only because he kept the much more important bear content. Things have no feeling—they are numb. So he settled into thingness numbly and without complaint. What saved him from total numbness was not a residuary feeling of having been free—he had never been that—but the knowledge that if he was a possession he did not really belong to the Khan but to the Lady Ariadne, and through her to the household to the Lord Celsus. That was his proper place, his home. He did not think about this much, but the certainty lay deep inside him. Despite the torrid and implacable heat of that valley he was like a frozen river, lifeless and rigid on the surface but down below the eternal current flowing toward the sea. That sea would be reached when he got the Lady Ariadne back to her heritage. So, at odd intervals, he thought about her escape. He started to steal the kinds of food that would not rot, and to hide them.

Addie herself seemed perfectly happy as she was, happier than he had ever seen her. He could not see that she had experienced a change exactly opposite to his. In the City *she* had been a thing—the inadequate channel through which a great estate was to be passed from one owner to the next—but here in the camp she was a person. She made friends with the blind Greek (who turned out to be a colossal old snob and greatly impressed with her family connections) and coaxed him into arranging that she should help to herd the Khan's cattle, veiled and anonymous, reveling in her horsemanship.

Silvester, though, had few duties. Provided that Bubba was fit to perform in the bear dance which was held every full moon, no one questioned where he went or what he did. Here there was no medical tuition from the learned Solomon, and no clerking. Urrguk's wound healed slowly —poor Urrguk: when he realized that he would never again walk, nor ride a horse except on a bride-saddle, he spent his days and nights drinking or drunk. Holy John hauled him out of that pit and you will find him in *The Life and Miracles* under the name of Urgucius, a Hunnish nobleman, crippled but restored to health by the Saint's intercessions. The author of that book was a fool. It was just as much of a miracle how Urrguk learned to make light of his illness, to endure it with calm, and remain admired and loved by the savage tribesmen. He started to compose weird hymns to Holy John's new God, which the warriors bellowed after the bear dance.

Silvester, though, idled the summer days away, mostly in the steep dry gully where he hid his escape supplies. It was between the camp and the ferry and near where Addie did her herding. He could tether Bubba at its river end to fish, and its walls provided the only shade he could find away from the stinking tents. He was down there one August morning when he heard the drum of a coming horse above

him, so he lowered a flat stone back over his hiding place
and moved away. Addie reined in at the gully's edge, black
against the harsh sky.

"Where's Bubba?" she said.

"Down by the river."

"Tied up?"

"Yes. She still can't think why I do it."

(The trouble was that Bubba had shown a fascinated curiosity about the big herds of cattle, and kept trying to
stalk them. Perhaps some ancient instinct told her that a
young calf makes good eating; certainly the cattle regarded
her as just another dangerous carnivore, and twice she had
only been rescued from a lethal charge by the cracking
whips of the herdboys. So now Silvester tied her up.)

"What were you up to?" said Addie, dismounting. "You
looked like a thief when I came."

"I am a thief," he said. "Come and see."

She picked her way down the steep clay bank and he
lifted the stone again and showed her his larder—three of
the dark Hun loaves, shaped like bricks and almost as
heavy. Strips of dried meat. An empty water-skin. Six gold
coins.

"What's that for?" she said.

"If we don't leave soon we'll be caught by winter."

"Leave! You mean run away? But they've got hundreds
of miles to ride us down in—besides, you can't ride. And
the Khan . . . Oh, Sillo, I heard a foreign slave dying who'd
displeased him. It took ages."

"Yes, I know. I'm not going to try if we don't get a good
chance. But if it happens we've got to have food."

"Yes, I suppose so."

She was frightened, of course, but so was he. Then he
noticed that there had been a different undertone in her
voice, a simple reluctance. He had never, either in nightmares or daytime schemings, thought of that.

"We could just stay here," he said slowly. "If you prefer."

After all it was for her to give the orders.

"I quite like it here," she answered after a pause. "I didn't till you came, but, well, Azerbad had a wife who . . . oh, I like herding, and sitting by the river, and being with you, and not mattering. That's what I like best—being a scrawny foreign girl, the bear's slave and nothing else . . . but I suppose, yes, if a safe chance came, we ought to try. Except it won't. Oh, how I hate *ought!*"

"In five days the Khan is going to take his warriors east, mustering as he goes."

"Against the Utrigurs?"

"No—it's these Avars. The interpreter told me this morning. They've suddenly started flooding out of the east, not all in one army but separate raiding parties. Anyway the Khan wants to take Bubba with him for luck in battle."

"No! That means you, too."

"I'm going to dose Bubba. She'll be too ill to go."

"But that'll be a terrible omen! He'll be furious with you!"

And that was true.

Silvester could still feel the bruises of his beating a week later. He was not resentful. Slaves are beaten, sometimes as savagely as he had been. It had hurt beyond screaming point, but somehow he had managed not to scream, and then it was over. The blind Greek told him that the Khan (who had watched the beating, smiling all the time) was pleased with him again. That didn't matter either.

Now he was crouched in the gully in one of the shrunk shadows of noon and showing Addie how to play knucklebones with ten small pebbles. It was an old slave game, played in dusty courtyards during those endless

waits which all slaves know. Addie was absurdly eager to
learn it, but very clumsy. There was no shade at the riverbank so Bubba lay tethered in another patch of shade with
her long tongue slopped out for coolness. She had
recovered from her dosing—in fact it had probably done
her good, a purge she needed now that she was taking less
exercise—but no bear could really enjoy such dry, persist-
ent, battering heat. Silvester cocked his head on one side
and let the pebbles fall.

"What's that noise?" he said.

It was a shouting from the south, down by the ferry.
Hooves thudded on dry earth. Silvester scrambled up the
gully wall and poked his head into the blazing glare. Out
of the heat-haze came a single horseman, bent low over the
neck of his galloping horse and whipping cruelly at its
quarters. He dipped through the gully where it had been
half filled, nearer the river, and raced toward the camp.
The noise from the ferry continued.

"Do you think the Khan's come home?" said Addie.

"Not from that side of the river. And that's the wrong
noise—that's not cheering. That's a fight. . . . It's over."

Drums rattled in the camp. The big horns belched their
deep note. Above them rose a steady shrilling, not a noise
Silvester had heard before.

"What's that?" he said.

"Women. They all shriek together when anything goes
wrong. They go on and on. They did it when we got here
from Byzantium, the wives of the men who hadn't come
home. Perhaps the Khan's been killed. What shall we do?"

"Wait here. Untether your horse and send him home.
There's nowhere else to hide in all this emptiness."

They waited. The yells from the ferry had stopped, but
the shrieks from the camp continued. Bubba was whimpering with restlessness and tugging at her rope. Silvester
ignored her, shifting his position sideways along the bank

until he was partly hidden by a straggling juniper bush
which had somehow clawed a roothold there. To the south
the heat-haze held a thicker patch, no, a dust-cloud,
moving nearer. He craned round. The few warriors left by
the Khan were forming up before the camp, also screened
by the haze and dust. The herdsmen were all gone from
the large herd of cattle which mooched unheeding away to
his left, between the gully and the camp but farther from
the river. The horns groaned again from the camp, and the
warriors started to canter down the riverbank. The dust-
cloud to the south was now so near that Silvester could see
the warriors in its van, naked except for their armor, their
shields oval, wearing not turbans but clumsy iron helmets.
They were coming at a full gallop, despite the heat. Their
lances were longer than the Huns'. They used proper
stirrups, and now he could see that the flesh of their bodies
was painted with bands of orange and black, and that a
couple of round white objects joggled at each waistline—
skulls.

"Get under this bush," he hissed. "Keep down!"

"What *are* they, Sillo? They look horrible. Worse than
animals."

"I don't know. Avars, perhaps. They must have crossed
the river somewhere else, and come back at the ferry. It's
all right, they'll miss us, and the guard's coming down
from the camp."

"But there's practically no one in the guard. They've all
gone with the Khan."

"There's not many of this lot, or they'd have taken
longer to cross. They're . . . Where's Bubba?"

The shrub to which she'd been tied was broken, and the
gully empty.

"No! Sillo! Don't look for her now! They're too close!"

Clenching and unclenching his fists, Silvester wriggled
farther under the stiff, flat-needled branches and watched

the oncoming savages. There were more of them than he'd thought the ferries could hold—perhaps they'd swum their horses, in which case the animals would be exhausted, but they didn't ride like that. They yelled like wolves as they came, an erratic, quavering howl. They certainly outnumbered the warriors in the camp. He watched their charge dip thundering through the shallower part of the gully, reform, and hurtle on. He twisted and craned until he could see the warriors from the camp charging down to meet them.

"Two to one!" he said.

"But fresh horses. Oh!"

The two sides met with a wild cry and the clash of metal, and then the cloud of summer dust hid them all. For a while this cloud stayed in one place, sometimes full of shouts and clashes and sometimes falling into lulls through which the monotonous shrieking from the camp pierced. Then, slowly, the mass of men was moving back toward the camp, leaving on the ground the bodies of a few warriors and horses. From the far side of the cloud the first Huns broke in flight. At that moment Silvester's terrified attention was broken by a deeper noise. He looked to his right.

The idiot bear had been stalking cattle again, had got too close, and now there were no herders to turn the charge. She was racing across the plain with the whole herd after her, bellowing and implacable. Silvester would never have believed that she could move so fast, stretched into a gallop like a fat dog, ears laid back. For the moment she kept her distance, about twenty yards in front of the herd, but she must tire soon. Without thinking he scrabbled to the top of the bank and called "Bubba! Bubba!" and waved his arms. It was impossible that she should hear his voice through the double uproar from the fight and the cattle.

But she did.

She had been racing in her panic straight toward the river; now she skittered round at a right angle and headed toward him. Only the few cattle on the near wing of the herd could follow her round—the rest were already committed to the line of their charge by the press and momentum of the animals around and behind them, none of whom could see their target. Even so she had to race clear of their ragged front.

She cleared the horns of the nearest bulls, hurtling under their noses. As they tried to follow her the bulls behind them crashed into them in a bellowing tangle. None of the other cattle could see her at all in the dust, so they thundered straight on. She tumbled like a falling rock into the gully and lay there, panting, but Silvester had no time to look at her. He was watching the end of the fight.

Just as the main body of Huns—what was left of them—broke free, the hurling dust-cloud of the cattle drove into the stationary dust-cloud of the horsemen, hesitated for a moment in a storm of bellows and yells, and swept on, unstoppable, to the river. Silvester stood watching. The cattle milled and bellowed. The dust-cloud thickened. But still no more warriors from either side emerged from its pale obliterating swirls. And the Khan was gone with his army, so there was no one now to bother about the disappearance of a slave boy and girl; not many people would notice for a day or two, even, that the totemic bear was missing. He slithered back down the steep wall of the gully.

"Shall we go now?" he said.

"All right. B-but if they catch us . . ."

"We can say we were cut off from the camp. They'd expect us to be running away from these raiders."

"But it might be them."

"Stay close to Bubba. Smile. Talk Greek. Take your veil off and you won't look so like a Hun."

No guards watched the ferry. A few ferry horses lounged, bewildered, in the shade of the single spreading ilex that grew on the near bank, molested by nothing but the appalling flies of the plain. Silvester approached the tree alone, plodding out of the heat-haze. He had made a widish circuit so as to avoid the busy route up and down the bank, and now came draggingly towards the tree, licking his dry lips. For a while he stood in the humming shadow, peering at the islands. A few bodies sprawled here and there—by their dress he could see that they had been the ferry slaves. That Greek would never earn his cattle now, nor set up with his wives. Silvester walked back a little into the glare and called; he was wondering whether he dared risk a louder call when two shapes shimmered in the haze and solidified into a bear and a girl.

Now all that was left was to board the near raft, tether Bubba to its rails, unmoor it and pole it into the current. Only Silvester couldn't move it. The attackers had hauled it too fiercely into the bank. Dizzy with useless effort, he sank onto the rough logs, his ears ringing and the world black about him.

"Sillo?"

"Uh?"

"I could swim some of the horses out to the island—I think I could manage three—and if we fasten their traces to the other side of the raft they could pull it off."

"Are you sure?"

"No, but there's not much current here. I can always swim back."

By Hun standards the horses were fairly docile. Addie caught them one by one and Silvester held them while she unraveled the tangled thongs. Saddles were piled against the tree trunk and harness hung from the branches, so she had reins and bit to manage the beast she mounted. It balked for a moment at the water, then skittered in, splashing and tossing its head. Silvester led the other two down and handed her their halters; they too made a token refusal and plunged in.

Addie headed her mount for the near island, keeping its head reined harshly back with the cruel Hun bit, so that that was the only land it could see. Silvester paid out the traces, thinking how well she handled these three half-savage animals, compared with the difficulty she found in all ordinary life—or at least what he believed to be ordinary life, the buzz of the City and the intricate interlockings of caste and kin. Here, among the wild plains, she had been happy, or at least half happy. Back in the City (if she got there—and Silvester would never know, because he could not follow her), in the City she would again become a hawk on the wrist, hooded in shyness. He sighed. There seemed to be no right end for her now—or for him, but that didn't matter. They were leftovers from the purpose of God, who had moved on to work with other tools. He sighed again as he watched the horses scramble streaming from the water among the bodies of dead men.

She used the brief stillness of the animals while they got used to their weight in air to tether them to one of the many hitching posts on the island, so that she could fasten their traces as taut as she could pull them. Silvester picked up his pole; her shout floated across the water and a whip cracked. He bent his back and heaved. Nothing happened. The thongs rose almost level across the surface. Panting, he wondered whether Addie could use the horses to haul him and Bubba from island to island. It was strange that he didn't even know if Bubba could swim.

Then the pole was sliding away from him and he could walk with small, straining steps from log to log, and the sluggish current was gurgling under his feet. Soon he could

pole no more—and of course there was no one on the bank
to manage the after traces and stop the raft from drifting
downstream. It began to edge sideways. Addie kept her
team pulling and plunging until they were out of sight
behind the low round of the island. He shouted. The raft
was moving faster now. He saw the thongs slacken and
tauten again. Slowly the raft swung out into the stream
until he could see between the islands—she had fastened
the thongs to another post and was already forcing her
horse into the current. Knowing its master now it plunged
straight in and headed for where the raft hovered motionless with the water churning round it.

He pulled her up onto the logs and cut the thongs. As
the raft slid away, the horse tried to follow her up, but
couldn't, so after swimming beside them for a few minutes
turned away and headed for the bank. Addie, dripping but
already beginning to steam under the furious sun, watched
it land while she slowly loosened her hair from its Hunnish pigtail and let it fall over her shoulders, then
unhooked her veil. It was a gesture of farewell to a life she
had liked; from behind her it looked sad, but when she
turned she was laughing, with happy eyes.

"What is it?" he said.

"Now I have done something for you, instead of you
always doing everything for me."

He shook his head at the unnatural notion. A slave
serves. That is what he is bred and trained for. But it was
lovely to see her laughing, steaming and content. He too
laughed.

"What is it?" she mimicked.

"The top half of your face is brown and the bottom half
white."

She ran to the side of the ferry to try and look at her
reflection in the rumpled water, while Silvester gazed

down the broad but winding river and wondered how soon they would ground. He was the raft-master now, but he had no control over its movements, no control at all.

PART IV · THE TOWER

XIX

Wild Bear

"N-NO. I won't g-go if you c-c-can't."

She hadn't stammered for two months, though she had
babbled and sung as the twisting river slid them south,
and then, as she lay in the dark little hut in the fishing
village waiting for her foot to mend (Bubba had rolled a
rock on it their first day ashore) she had told Silvester all
she could remember, every day, every hour, since she had
been snatched out of the smoke-filled bear's cage. She had
left out nothing, not even the absent minded brutalities of
the Hun flight north, but she hadn't stammered. She had
even chatted happily with the three fishermen who for a
gold piece had sailed them across the shallow and treacher-
ous Euxine to the uppermost mouth of the Danube.

But now, as they stood quarreling in the steady wind
that blew across the iron-gray river toward the Empire, she
stumbled over almost every syllable. The wind was on
their backs, making her hair stream out before her face,
ruffling the fur along Bubba's spine so that it looked as
though her hackles were raised in anger. The wind came
from the north and smelled of winter.

"Your father, the Lord Celsus . . ." began Silvester again.

"Is d-dead. N-no one can tell me what I m-must do—n-not even you. I'm the only p-person who kn-knows that."

"But your lands! Your houses!"

"B-Brutus can have them. S-somebody was going to h-have them anyway, as soon as I m-m-married him. I've been f-free, Sillo. Free. Why should I ch-chain myself to all that? M-mother was a s-s-slave—m-more than you were."

"But my lady . . ."

"N-no. B-be quiet."

Silvester looked despairingly over his shoulder. The settlement at Great Bend was dying for the winter, the shacks being allowed to fall apart as the traders went south with their profits to look for a kindlier sun. The Lady Ariadne could travel with one of them, while Silvester stayed on the north bank, safe from the grip of the law. Among the broken huts a few losers and outcasts scavenged for kit and provisions to keep them alive through the snows. Silvester was an outcast, too. The Lady Ariadne took him by the shoulders and turned him to face her.

"What were you g-g-going to do, after you'd sh-shipped me south and g-got rid of me? What about y-you?"

"*Rid* of you?"

She wasn't smiling. It was no kind of a joke.

"Wh-what about you?" she hissed.

"Oh, I suppose—well, Antoninus said I could go back to his tower."

"We'll g-go there, then. I c-can read Latin, too."

He had never told her what Antoninus was like—only what he had said and done, softening even some of that. He shook his head. Once in the gully in the plain, and once again as they struggled to free the ferry, he had been troubled by the concept that she wanted something else than the inheritance that she had been born to. But he had shut his mind to it, half-hoping that as the possibility of return became more real, more near, she would accept it. She *must* accept it. It was her proper fate, as being a slave was his. The Celsus family was old and rich. Men die, but estates continue. If the true heir can be cheated out of them, as Brutus wished to cheat, then the proper and continuing City would be cheated. Silvester had been moved by many motives during his travels: fear at the beginning, and a passion to foil the Lord Brutus; honor for his dead master; love of the Lady Ariadne, and a longing to see her rich and happy; and an unreasoning belief that somehow, if the Lord Celsus's true heir could own and command the old house up towards the Charisius Gate, then all that vivid community would come alive again, changed but still singing. But deep under all these motives lay his sense of the City, a sense like that a bee must have of its hive, without knowing it has it.

"If B-Bubba hadn't been there when F-Father d-d-dropped me, someone like B-Brutus would have had it anyway."

"Yes, but then he'd have had a *right* to it. Now . . ."

"I'd like to see this t-tower."

"But . . ."

"N-no. It's an o-order, S-Silvester."

She had never called him that before, even in the presence of her father. She looked at him, biting her lip. He could not see that she was as distressed as he was.

When they left the camp he walked a little behind her shoulder, as a slave should. She took his arm and talked gaily, without a stammer. He answered numbly, walked the flat miles numbly. He was the doll now.

"The Dictator Sulla died of passion, watching a slave being strangled," wheezed Antoninus. It was a sign that he was tired, and perhaps a little drunk, for then he always led the talk round to slaves and slavery, and usually ended by referring to the death of Sulla. The subject obviously obsessed some deep part of his mind, but the business of the day overlaid it and kept it in check. Only in the evenings he started to pick at it again, like a scab.

Bubba hibernated. Winter owned the land. The north wind, blowing out of dark Scythia, ironed the great plain to a single whiteness, starched with cold. The Slavs from the village took sledges across the frozen lake to the forest and cut timber, hauling it back to warm their smoky little huts and crackle on Antoninus's marble hearths. In front of such a fire the three of them would sit on dark days and winter evenings, Silvester and Ariadne reading aloud in turn to Antoninus until he took it into his head to expound the greatness of Rome and the reasons for its fall. He had nothing but scorn for Byzantium.

"It is a hermit crab," he said, "living in the shell the Romans left. It is soft, a city of slaves. If it lasts for a thousand years it will still be a city of slaves, just as your Christianity is the religion of slaves—your reward is in heaven, so on earth you know your place and grovel like slaves to your Emperor."

"It's not like that," said the Lady Ariadne.

"I have seen it," said Antoninus with a sneering chuckle. "I have several times traveled to Byzantium on embassies from my cousin the Slav King. Do you know how they try to impress savages like me? I was conducted from hall to hall by soft eunuchs and shown at last into a big room smelling of incense, where all the courtiers stood in rows, as if they were afraid to move. I was shown the exact place where I must stand, so I stood and waited. And at last a throne rose from the floor, surrounded by brass lions

which roared, and tritons from whose mouths squirted
rosewater, while a jeweled dove descended overhead. And
on this throne was an old, tired man with big black eyes.
He needed a shave. Just a man coming out of the ground
on a large toy. And they thought I was impressed. I am a
Roman, so I did not laugh in their faces."

"Laugh?" cried Silvester, who had thought the description very impressive.

"Well, it was certainly very ridiculous," snapped Antoninus.

"My father loved toys. He had some s-singing crystals."
The Lady Ariadne always stammered slightly with him,
for though he was polite to her he was as cold as the Slav
winter.

"How curious," he now said, without interest. "On one
of my embassies the Emperor sent me back with such a
gift, saying that they were the only ones in the world. I had
of course taken him some barbarian offering from my
cousin. I have never opened the parcel—you will find it in
the chest at the back of the small room where the candles
are stored."

Silvester stood up, but the Lady Ariadne was first to the
door.

"Let the girl go," sneered Antoninus. "They are a toy to
please children and idle women. We were talking about
cities."

"But no one was really free in Rome either," said
Silvester. "Look how the Dictators and Emperors could
just have citizens killed and their estates taken. Look how
Cicero died, and Seneca."

"That was not the true Rome. Rome is a state of mind.
While I live Rome's last outpost has not fallen, but endures in me—just as your city of slaves endures in you."

He continued to expound the virtues of his ideal city until the Lady Ariadne came back with what he'd called "the parcel." In fact it was a wrapping of finest linen, sealed with the lesser Palace Seal. Inside that was a wrapping of silk from the Emperor's looms; and then an ebony box holding, in nests of more silk, the crystals still unbroken. When they were placed on the hearth and warmed they each gave out a pure, strange note, and another as they were moved back into coolness. Even Antoninus stopped talking to listen. Silvester remembered standing beside Addie when they were both so small that the windowseat in the study was shoulder-high, and watching the Lord Celsus moving his crystals from sun to shadow, making them play a slow, unearthly tune.

All that was dead. Those crystals were smashed. There were only these other ones, the lying gift of the Emperor to a Roman barbarian who despised them, up here in the drear flats beyond the Empire, still singing.

Antoninus broke the spell with a wheezing yawn.

"What a small thing," he said, "to hold us three so tranced. You can judge a man by what absorbs him. Now, the Dictator Sulla died of passion, watching a slave being strangled."

Bubba must have smelled the winter coming. She had eaten enormously and grown gross and somnolent, and with the first snows had retired into her stable and burrowed deep into her straw. Silvester had heard of the hibernation of bears, but she had never done this in the City, so he piled fresh straw on her, checked each day that her water was unfrozen, and otherwise left her. She didn't sleep solidly all winter; when the first heavy snowfall had settled and the sun glittered out, though with a wind that seared the nostrils and stung the eyes, she padded sleepily out, snuffed around, drank, growled at her enemy the billy goat and went back to her world of dark dreams.

The Lady Ariadne loved the snow. She dressed in the clothes of a young Slav warrior and took Silvester out on the communal deer hunts, organized by old custom among thirty villages so that each hunter should be at his station before dawn broke; then a twenty-mile noose of whooping warriors, mostly on foot, would begin to close on a common center. At the start of the hunt your nearest neighbor might be two hundred yards away across the flat whiteness, but the air had had all the mistiness frozen out of it so that you could count thirty or forty hunters diminishing in a long sweep to right and left. But even in that sharp air the deer seemed to rush out of nowhere, racing for one of the gaps, with the hunters on foot running to turn them, yelling like wolves, and the horsemen spurring in, lance lowered, for the honor of an early kill. Some broke through, but there were usually a good few left when the noose closed for the last slaughter, with the hunters shoulder to shoulder and the big stags at bay. It was dangerous then, but Silvester had trouble keeping the Lady Ariadne out of the bloody turmoil, for she rode with a spear like a warrior and her eyes glistened and the blood was in her cheeks and the nostrils of her fine nose were wide with the lust of the hunt.

It was there Silvester learned to ride, competently and understanding his animal, perhaps as well as a Slav but never with the grace of the Lady Ariadne or the man-and-beast union of the Hun horsemen.

They both learned Slav, Silvester simply as breathing but Addie with toil and tantrums, though it was her idea. The village witch taught them some of her art, which Silvester thought mad and odd, though it had pockets of sense in it—not only about the uses of local herbs but about such things as the prevalent marsh fever, which she swore was sent by a demon who lived under the marshes and used the mosquitoes as his messengers. The books said this fever was caused by breathing marsh air, but Silvester instinctively felt that it was a sickness of the blood, and mosquitoes did drink blood. The Lady Ariadne took her lessons in witchcraft more seriously, though she was always careful to discuss with Silvester whether any new step would imperil her immortal soul on Judgment Day. She was very popular with the Slavs, though they did not think her at all beautiful; but the heroine of one of their old legends was a demon huntress who led lost warriors home, and they often spoke as though Addie were that demon. So with both her and the fortunate bear living at the tower they felt that their community was blessed with good influences.

In February Antoninus almost died. The cold got into his lungs, filling his chest with agonies, which he endured grimly but uncomplaining. He could hardly breathe, and a high fever followed which lasted two days. Silvester stayed in the sickroom night and day, sleeping in snatches on rugs on the floor. The third night the fever dropped with alarming speed, but Antoninus's mind seemed to clear. Just before midnight he beckoned Silvester to his side. "Friend," he said in a croaking whisper, "I go. I have lied. In the gray book." And then he was unconscious.

Silvester took fresh bricks which he kept heated by the constant fire, wrapped them in cloths and slid them under the rugs to lie against the gross body. He took Antoninus's hands and rubbed them for an hour, keeping the tired blood warm and moving. Just moving.

Next day came a sudden warm spell. The crystals sang

on their shelf without being moved. Antoninus slowly—
and Silvester thought reluctantly—heaved his soul back
from the pit of death.

The true thaw did not come till April. Then the whole
plain squelched, the shortest journey outside meant returning home with mud up to your thighs, and a careless
rider out in the pastures could lose his horse in a mudhole.
They endured three weeks of that, and then a dry wind
came out of the east, turning the mud to crumbling earth.
At once all other work was forsaken to get the wheat seed
into the ground so that its roots could achieve depth
before the earth became dust for the wind to sweep away.
And hardly was that work done when a raid erupted across
the plain. From the tower you could see villages ablaze to
the north, thirty miles away. For the moment the long lake
protected them, but even so every man and beast from Antoninus's villages crowded into the garden square and it
became a fort again.

Antoninus never allowed the stocks in his storehouses to
fall below a month's supply for everybody. Now he took
Silvester round, explaining just how and where scouts
must be posted, and checking all the devices of defense,
many of which he had copied from old Roman textbooks.
It was an elaborate system, with each family of Slavs
responsible for different work but all so feckless that they
needed constant nagging to think about tomorrow's possible disasters. Silvester carried with him Antoninus's
careful lists of duties, which included such matters as
which machines needed frequent inspection and repair in
time of peace. Where a man had died during the year, or a
boy grown old enough to be useful, Silvester adjusted the
list.

"If this had not happened," wheezed Antoninus, "I

would have staged a practice siege later in the year. There are always new contrivances to be thought of, new problems to face. The Huns—insofar as they are capable of learning anything, have learned to leave us alone. But perhaps this lot are the Avars you have seen. Now, the next row of latrines . . ."

In the middle of the hubbub Bubba woke, lean, molting and surly. The villagers were encouraged by the sight of their talisman bear, and cheered her till she shambled back into her stable to escape the din. The raid faded away northwest. They spent a morning flinging stones from the catapults at practice targets, and punished a group of families who had got drunk during the siege by making their menfolk ride into the booby traps on the road. Then they went back to work.

Summer baked the plain, mitigated by a few merciful thunderstorms. Bubba became very restless, and Antoninus kept Silvester too busy to pay proper attention to her. One evening Silvester went to fetch her from where he had tied her to fish by the lake, and found that she had chewed her rope through and was gone. He called and called. In the morning a Slav came to the tower, dressed in his best robes, to say that his son had been herding further along the lake the previous evening and had seen bears.

"Bears?"

"Two big bears, lord, playing like cubs. Ah, I know my son for a liar, so I beat him, but he still says he saw two bears."

Silvester thanked the man and gave him a rope of beads for his son, then took two horses and rode to the village to find the old tracker. Together they rode the twenty miles round the lake to the forest, usually by the tracker picking out undiscernible scufflings in the dust but once or twice coming to the broad impressions of pads on the banks of streams.

"That is your bear, Lord," said the tracker. "And this is the other. He is heavier than she, and limps with his left forefoot."

They followed the tracks some way into the forest. Suddenly the tracker stopped and sniffed.

"No further, Lord. Mating bears, very dangerous."

"Are they near?"

"Perhaps, perhaps."

Silvester called to the silent trees for twenty minutes and got no answer but deeper silence. Then they rode back.

Ten nights later he was awakened by a yammering at the tower door, below the slit window of his room. He went down to the hall and found one of Antoninus's servants listening to the racket with nervous astonishment. Silvester opened the door cautiously. Bubba was sitting there under a big moon, extremely disconsolate and resentful at being locked out, when she'd only gone off for a few minutes to visit a friend. She came surging into the hall as though she were afraid of the dark, snuffled at Silvester for his scent, padded straight up the stairs to his room and flopped on the floor with a sigh.

An hour later, when he was once more deep in dreams, he was awakened by her growl, and opened his eyes to see her lying in the patch of moonlight that came through the large inner window; but it was at the slit in the outer wall she was staring. He crossed the chill mosaic to look out and at first could see nothing special, only the mottled levels of the plain, all gray with dust and moonlight. Then a shadow detached itself from the shadows under a birch copse and ambled into the open, where it stopped and reared on its hind legs—a big, lean bear, taller than Bubba, missing its left ear. It emitted a strange sound, a mournful, pleading bark, on a higher note than the bear's normal bellow of rage or fear. Bubba simply growled in the dark behind him, announcing that she didn't want to have any truck with disreputable wild bears. She was civilized, she was.

Silvester watched the shambling brute with a curious sympathy. He felt like bullying Bubba back to her lover's embraces, only he was sleepy and didn't want to have to intervene in a bear fight under his window. For a long time after he lay down he heard the animal moving about below, close under the tower wall, occasionally singing his tragic serenade. Bubba only growled at the sound, and after a while came over to Silvester's bed, nuzzled the rug aside and laid her head on his naked chest, drooling saliva. When she started to snore he eased her back to the floor and went to sleep.

Harvest came with choking dust and chaff. A prickle of winter crept into the evenings. Antoninus summoned the village head men, and with them for witnesses in the little temple adopted Silvester as his son, using the thousand-year-old ceremony of the Romans.

He had given Silvester no warning before the ceremony, and treated him no less demandingly after it. He still talked a lot about slaves when he was tired. He seemed to think of the arrangement as just a convenient way of seeing that somebody would give him a proper Roman funeral.

"I do not expect you to burn incense for me," he said. "Perhaps you could train the bear to do it. She has no soul, your silly priests say. My villagers know better."

The villagers seemed quite happy with the new arrangement. It meant that after Antoninus was dead both the bear and the demon huntress would stay and protect them, and Silvester would occasionally save them the trouble of thinking about tomorrow.

"I have written to my cousin the King," said Antoninus.

"He cannot make you chief here, or accept your oath of fealty, because you are not of the blood of the kings. But I've told him that if he disturbs you my ghost will haunt him. He is afraid of me, and busy with these new savages from the east. Provided you pay your tribute he will leave you alone."

"I cannot speak my thanks," said Silvester formally. "And I pray that it will be many years before it happens."

"None of that, boy. You are half a doctor. What chance have I of living through this winer? Without you I would have died in the last one. . . . Come on, boy. I wish you to bet. What odds will you lay that I shall see the icicles drop from my trees next spring?"

"Well, it's difficult . . ."

"None of that," said Antoninus in his hissing wheeze, always worse when he was moved by one of his strong, tight-reined passions. "The truth. What odds do you lay?"

"Evens," said Silvester reluctantly. He thought it was worse than that. He was right.

XX

The Gray Book

IN THE COLDEST PART of a winter colder than memory
Silvester took the Slavs across the lake to cut wood. In the
villages the women shrilled on and on. It took the men two
whole days to build the pyre in the middle of the lake, and
another to hoist the clumsy barge on top of it and settle it
firm. The men enjoyed the work, and the shouting arguments about the best way of doing things, and the
drinking bouts between-whiles.

The fourth day was windless and cloudless, as though
the air itself was beginning to freeze solid. The warriors
marched to the tower where the servants of Antoninus,
with their heads and shoulders sprinkled with ashes in the
Roman fashion, carried his body out and put it on a sledge
which the warriors dragged down to the lake. The business
of hoisting the body up onto the throne was less dignified
than Silvester would have wished—it was heavy, and the
ladders awkward, and the pile of logs a poor foothold for
lugging and shoving, but in the end it was done. The old-
est head man took a torch and Silvester another to light opposite sides of the pile. The wood was slow to catch. The

women, veiled and muffled in furs, wailed on the bank a
shivering, icy farewell. Several small logs burst into flame
together, making a small heart of heat. Silvester stood back
and watched the columns of smoke from either side of the
fire moving straight up, widening and becoming one. He
took from a servant the jar of incense which Antoninus
had kept in the temple and walked round the pyre, casting
its contents by handfuls into the flames. The color of the
smoke changed to blue-white and the cold air became pungent with expensive Eastern spices. The heat of the flames
forced him back. The warriors formed a line, linked arms,
and moved with a slow step in a clockwise circle round the
pyre, while the village chanter sang a long wail called
"The Journey of the Hero Han to the Land of the Dead."
He would chant a part of the story while the warriors
moved; when he stopped they stopped also and stamping
their right feet on the ice between each line sang the
refrain:

> *Han rode between dry reeds.*
> *White bone was his horse.*
> *His wives wailed, his tribe wept.*
> *He did not look behind him.*

And all the while the body of Antoninus, now wholly
veiled in smoke, stared south in the direction which
Silvester and Ariadne had decided must be roughly the direction of Rome.

Silvester and the head men had arranged the ceremony
between them, a combination of Roman funerals and old
Slav rituals. It satisfied everybody except a rather aggressive young Christian priest in one of the farther villages.
Silvester had hoped that when the bonfire was at its hottest
and the body all burnt the ice would melt through and the

whole flaming pile slide hissing into black water. But it burned till dusk, and by the time the stars came out Antoninus and the barge were gone and only a mound of embers glowed through a cloud of steam, round which a shallow pool of melted ice was already beginning to freeze again at the edges.

Bubba had eaten herself almost into a sphere that autumn and hardly emerged at all during the winter. Twice Silvester had seen her, on sunny days, sitting in the sheltered nook by her stable and sleepily licking her belly and crotch, and occasionally looking about her with a baffled expression as though she were still half in a winter dream. But after Christmas she disappeared for weeks on end. Her cub must have been born in this time, a naked blob no bigger than a man's clenched fist, which she suckled in her sleep while it grew its pelt and became a bear. Silvester didn't see it till April when he was tying in the earliest growths of the vines and she came up behind him and butted him in the buttocks so that he tumbled face first into the mud. Then, after sitting on him to make sure he was properly muddy, she went back to her den and cuffed her cub into the open. She wouldn't let him near it, however, snarling like a wild bear when he came within ten paces of it. It cowered under the huge sky, terrified of so much world. Its pelt was a much lighter shade than hers.

"I expect it takes after the father," said Silvester.

"I bet Bubba thinks *you're* the father," said the Lady Ariadne.

"What shall we call it? Something that would please Antoninus—Virgil?"

"It doesn't look like an epic bear. What about Terence?"

Yes, that would please Atoninus—all the best characters in the old Roman comedies were slaves.

Antoninus, after his earlier bout of illness, had never mentioned the gray book again, and he had died in his sleep without speaking. Silvester had long ago decided that the words were part of some dream or delirium. He found the book by accident.

The slogging heat of summer, which seemed to tan the fast-growing wheat strips under their eyes, drove everyone into the shade for the middle of each day. The marbled floors of the tower seemed to retain a little of the chill of winter, and gave a merciful release from the torrid air. The Lady Ariadne was happy to doze and dream or patch clothes (which she was slow and clumsy at) or move the singing crystals in and out of shadow for hour after hour. But Silvester was no good at doing nothing.

He was oppressed by the amount of work and care that the tower of the Antonines needed, even in this dead interval when the hay was in and the plain waited for the wheat harvest. The tower was Rome, it was Byzantium, adrift on the river of time, and Silvester was its Emperor and its Count of the Outfields and its day-long slave. But it was too hot now to water the vines or bully the improvident Slavs into sending a corvée up to deepen the well, and the leather was still tanning that would provide fresh thongs for the catapults. He had sent his taxes to the King in the name of Antoninus, as though he were still alive. There was nothing that he *must* do. So he spent the heat of the day looking through the books of the library to see whether any of them were being eaten by worms, or cracking with drought, or needed other repairs. It was boring and dusty work.

"Hello!" he said. "Here's a Greek Bible!"

"He knew a lot about Christianity," said the Lady Ariadne lazily. "I used to wish we had Holy John here to argue him down."

But when Silvester opened the Bible he found that the centers of all the pages had been cut away, leaving a hollow in which nestled a smaller book, bound in gray linen. It had no title or title page, but started straight off: "In the 854th year from the Foundation of the City the Emperor Trajan invaded Dacia for the following reasons." The language was elegant, but the accounts of wars against forgotten tribes were all as dry as the dust on the bookshelves. Silvester read on for a bit, curious that Antoninus should have troubled to write all this down and then hidden it, but after a while he gave up and went back to his worm hunt.

He had made a sort of tent of muslin on top of the tower so that they could sit up there in the evenings and not be bothered by the fierce mosquitoes from the lake. The villagers kept their cow-dung fires going all through the summer nights for this purpose, and certainly if you sat in the bitter drifting smoke you didn't get bitten, but Addie and Silvester preferred their gauzy tent because it meant that they could enjoy the breeze that sidled up from the river at dusk, smelling of the south. It was almost too dark to see the letters when he finished reading the gray book.

"He was a slave himself," he said.

"Who?"

"Antoninus."

"But he's the King's cousin."

"Yes. All that's true. But he wasn't Roman at all. It started with a slave—his family I mean—a man called Hercules who killed his master and escaped across the Danube just when the Romans were being driven out. He was very strong, and he set up as a river pirate, and then he found this fort empty and came to live here. He made himself into a sort of robber chief and married a Goth princess. He called himself Antoninus to impress the barbarians, because they still remembered Trajan, but he was really a Greek slave. And his family carried on like that, keeping up the lie and marrying women from whatever tribes happened to be in possession. Chiefs' daughters. The lake protected them, and they were useful because they understood the Empire, so they managed to hang on whenever a fresh lot of barbarians came out of the east. And I suppose the lie was useful too, because it meant that they always felt they owed their real loyalty to Rome and so they could choose here whatever side looked like winning. The book says there are other areas in Dacia where Romans, real Romans, still live. But Antoninus was a slave. That's why he was always talking about slaves. That's why he chose me."

"It doesn't matter."

"Yes it does. It makes one different. The first time he saw me he said I had the slave look."

"It doesn't mean anything at all. We're both free p-people. F-freer than we would be anywhere else in the w-world."

"We belong in the City. If I weren't on the Lists we could go back there, and everyone would know I was your slave. We're here because you ordered me to come here and I obeyed because I am your slave."

"B-but here you are the m-master. He g-gave it to you. The v-villagers call you 'L-l-lord'."

"They are barbarians. A slave can own no property. I am managing the estate for Antoninus, because that was part of the bargain, but it is not mine. Perhaps that's another reason why he chose me—he knew it would all still be his."

Silvester spoke quietly, without any feeling. This numbness was correct; it enabled him to be used, as an object, by a dead man; and so it enabled them both to live here in safety and such happiness as exiles can achieve. He had ransomed the Lady Ariadne not with her father's gift, the ruby, but with himself. That was proper.

She seized his arm and shook it with fury, stammering so badly that she couldn't get a word out. So she let go of him and slithered out under the muslin. He followed her out, but let her run alone down the twisting stair while he leaned his elbows on the parapet and stared at the dark distances towards the Empire. That was where he belonged, far south beyond plain and hill-range, in the live City where the quick Greeks schemed and throve and the streets rattled with argument, but he did not dare go. The terror of the Lists was still enough to make his palms and cheeks break out in sweat, even here, on this cool evening. Still in his imagination he could see the eunuch with the white wand roaming from town to town on the south bank of the Danube, asking for news of a boy with a bear. And now dead Antoninus had bound him to this tower.

Antoninus had longed for Rome, but he had never seen it. His Rome had been a dream, but Silvester's City was real. Yet Antoninus had lived his lie until it became true. "Rome endures in me, just as your city of slaves endures in you."

Silvester didn't think he could do that. Anyway, it wasn't for him to choose. That was for the Lady Ariadne.

She came back with a lantern and a bundle of oddments. Silvester helped her into the muslin tent. A few moths followed the light in, flapping unhappily against the glass. She hooked the lantern onto the tentpole and spread on the lead below it the things she had brought—a writing board, two pieces of the best parchment, spills, quills, ink, and a stick of black wax.

"Write me a m-manumission. It's an o-order . . . Sillo."

He settled onto his stomach and ran his fingertips over the top sheet of parchment, until he found a flaw near one edge. The second sheet was perfect. He chose the best quill, dipped it, and wrote.

I, Ariadne Celsus, of the House of Celsus, by this parchment and my seal hereto appended, free from my bondage and service forever the slave called Silvester Antoninus, late of that House and now of the Tower of the Antonines. Henceforth let no man, either official or private, seek to deny that the said Silvester is a free citizen, under the full protection of the law.

The ink dried quickly in the dry night air. Ariadne took the parchment and read it carefully.

"N-nice writing," she said. "I am losing a g-g-good clerk."

She lifted the lantern off its hook and opened the glass. A couple of the moths that had followed it down rushed into the flame, burned white for an instant, and made the air prickle with the dusty smoke of their deaths. She lit a spill at the flame and withdrew it. More moths danced in to die. Silvester took the spill and held it steady under the point of the wax, turning the stick until it glistened with melting and joined its dark smoke to the flame. The bubbling drops fell into a shining black pool below the writing.

"Quick," he said.

She pulled at the silver chain round her neck and drew out from her shift the red sard-stone seal with her little crucifix tinkling against it. Her small red tongue licked at

the stone. Firmly she forced the seal down into the soft
wax. Silvester put his hand over hers to hold it there,
counting until he was sure the wax was quite hard. He let
her move her hand then, and carefully eased the stone
away. Every detail of its imprint snowed clear on the shiny
black. He hooked the lantern back onto the pole with a
sigh.

"I feel no different," he said.

"I t-told you it makes no d-difference. You are f-free,
B-but that's because you are you. It's not because of anything I d-d-do."

"Free. Like a Hun. They are free people, the slave
merchant said."

"Y-yes. You told me. They t-take what they want."

He slid his arm round her shoulders but did not have to
pull her to him because she was already moving. Her
hands roved gently across his shoulder blades, and her lips
that he had often seen so tense with stammering were very
soft and did not tremble at all.

Among good Byzantine families (and Silvester, having
decided to live the lie, was now of a very good family
indeed) the custom was for betrothals to last at least three
years. So he and Addie considered themselves very un-
ceremonious in deciding that a year would be enough.
Addie wore a veil now when she went out. Bubba
disgraced herself at the betrothal feast because Silvester
didn't notice some of the younger warriors deliberately
making her drunk. She had a hideous hangover next day.

They were married next year in the cow-pat-shaped hut
which was the church in the village nearest the tower. The
ceremony was Christian, and quite recognizable, but some
of customs which the Slavs considered proper accompa-
niment for a marriage were very strange indeed.

One night, not long after that. Silvester dreamed about
the eunuch with the white wand. It began as a nightmare

pursuit through marshes; he came at last to a vast river
where a miniature raft was moored, small as a bed, and on
it he found a bearskin which he rolled into a roughly
human shape lying on the logs. It was night. He hid
among the reeds. The eunuch, wheezing like Antoninus,
stepped onto the raft and Silvester pushed with his pole
and the raft slid out into the river, drifting away toward
the sea, with the eunuch waving helplessly. Even when he
was out of his dream, lying in the soft dark in their bedroom in the tower, he somehow knew that he would never
see the eunuch again.

Far off a cow lowed, emphasizing the vast quietness of
the plain. He shut his eyes and tried as usual to imagine
the nighttime stirrings of the City, the rattle of a late cart
in the Mese, the hooting cry of the watch, the ceaseless
faint pother of a million people living in one place. They
could go back there now, now that the eunuch was no
longer a danger. Addie could . . . No, never. There was no
question of her claiming back the old house on the Mese,
and all her wealth, not if she was married to a penniless
stranger. The whole Celsus clan would fight that, and find
out who he was, and then the Lists would claim him.

The reason why he would never see the eunuch again
was that he would never again cross the Danube. He
sighed in the dark.

"What's the matter?" said Addie. "You woke me
shouting in your sleep, too."

"It's all right," he said. "I'm sorry. It's an old nightmare
I used to have when I was sleeping out with Bubba on my
journey."

"I'm not a bear," she said, and growled at him to show it
was true.

He laughed in the dark. Yes, all that, all their love, was
true. Even the lifelong infection of the lie could not touch
any of that.

Epilogue

THE FOOL who wrote *The Life and Miracles of Holy John* records that the Saint lived to a mighty age, converted the Kutrigurs, advised the Khan on his wars and rode with his army in the charge. Some of this is true. Holy John reverted fairly soon to living on a pillar, and when the tribe moved he rode with it on Bubba's litter. The Kutrigurs became a very peculiar form of Christian, but fervent, largely because they believed that the Saint brought them victory in battle. In fact he was killed in a fight against the Avars (in the year that Ariadne bore her first daughter) but the Kutrigurs preserved his body by drying it and continued to ride into battle with then Saint among them, leading the charge, invulnerable. The effect was so terrifying that the Kutrigurs, despite their defeat by the Avars, became a dominant force again in the chaotic movements of barbarians sweeping west out of Asia.

As for Silvester and Ariadne (and Bubba and Terence) the rest of the story is lost. Dacia is now called Romania, which as well as its name retains many Roman words in its language and Roman-sounding towns and rivers on its maps. So some scholars believe that the Roman influence never quite died out there, despite countless raids and invasions and conquests, but was kept alive by pockets of Roman settlers who somehow survived through all these upheavals. If this is so, Silvester and Ariadne, living the lie of the Antonines, may have had something to do with it.

And certainly, if all travelers' tales are true, the behavior of modern Romanian bears can be very, very peculiar.